Andrew has a PhD in environmental and marine science, Grad. Cert. in strategic studies and a Grad. Dip. Ed. He has published in peer-reviewed science journals and co-founded the New Zealand Aquaculture Magazine. Andrew has served as a watch keeping officer in the navy. He has lectured and taught statistics, marine and maritime studies at a technical institute. During this period, he consulted to the fisheries and aquaculture industry. Subsequently, Andrew contracted to the offshore oil and gas industry in environmental management. He then taught secondary school science and mathematics and is a future schools STEM industry focus advocate.

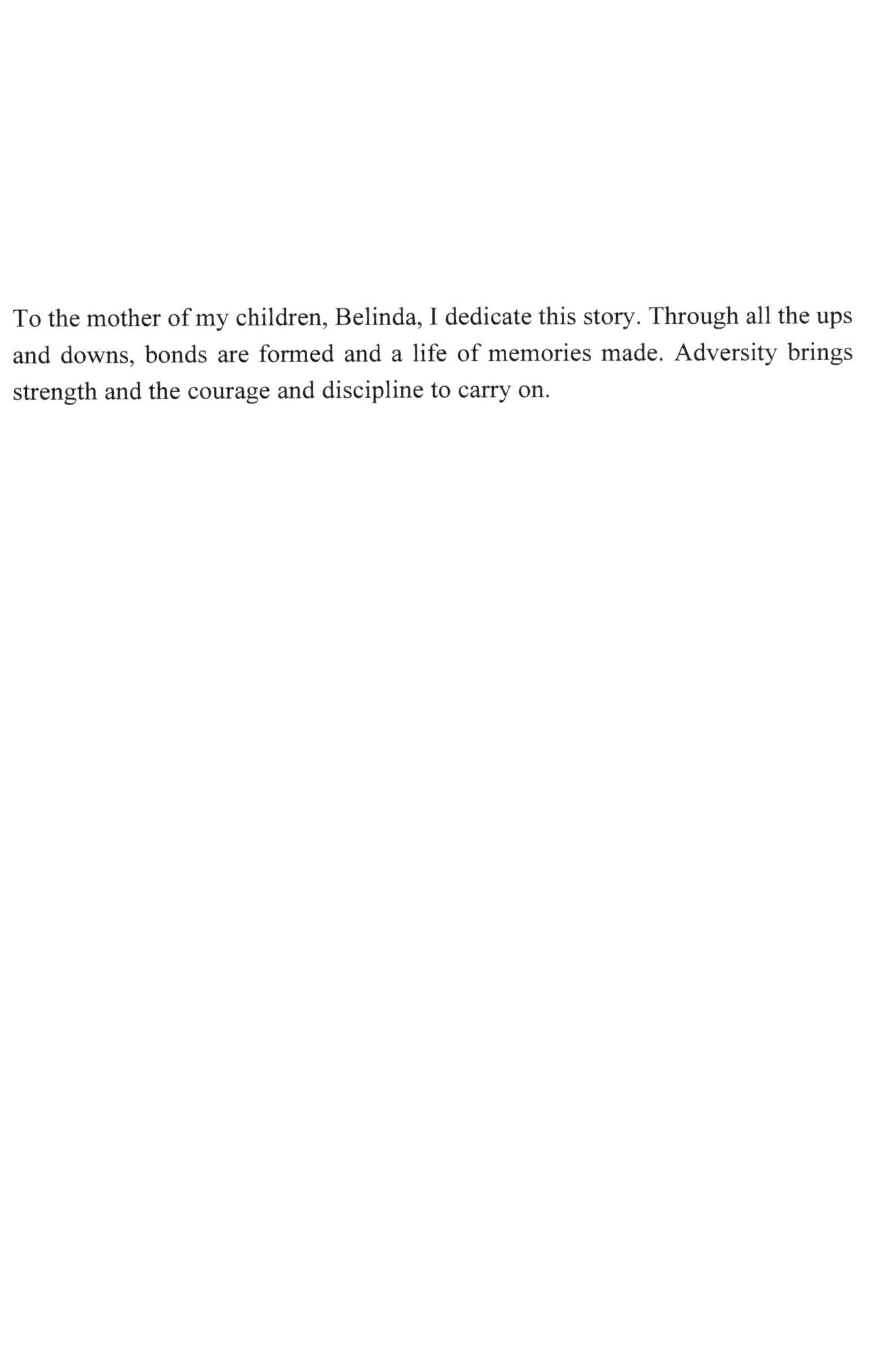

To the mother of my children, Belinda, I dedicate this story. Through all the ups and downs, bonds are formed and a life of memories made. Adversity brings strength and the courage and discipline to carry on.

A.D. Morgan

SKIMMER – MINE

AUSTIN MACAULEY PUBLISHERS™

LONDON * CAMBRIDGE * NEW YORK * SHARJAH

A CIP catalogue record for this title is available from the British Library.

ISBN 9781398472716 (Paperback)
ISBN 9781398472723 (ePub e-book)

www.austinmacauley.co.uk

First Published 2024
Austin Macauley Publishers Ltd®
1 Canada Square
Canary Wharf
London
E14 5AA

No people, in particular, have contributed to the telling of this story. However, I would like to acknowledge life's circumstances and all those that have passed through my life. In doing so, the experiences and insight gained over many years have brought this story into existence.

Hook

Amidst a raging supercell, a sub-surface mining skiff or Skimmer becomes the target of a rogue group intent on securing the technology. Meanwhile, the youthful crew onboard becomes aware of the broader plan for the Skimmers and must find a way to evade capture. Isolated and with help too far away to reach them in time, the crew must act to save themselves, their Skimmer, and the technology.

Mini Synopsis

Skimmer – Mine is the third book in a series set in 2040, about youth and their ability to adapt and cope with the situations they must face while working in the deep-sea mining industry. Ngarra's crew have left the Chinese owned GlobeCorpMining mineral Harvester in their Skimmer and continued their mining run. The plan is to run final tests on Connor's Xtract mining drone technology using the red queen sequence he has developed. However, concern is growing over piracy in the area. Tactics have changed and there are rumours that Skimmers are being rammed to board them. Ngarra's crew are informed by the Xed Ocean Academy crew monitoring that the pirates may have been infiltrated by another rogue group. It appears this rogue group may be using the pirates as a cover to try and access Connor's technology. The concern is growing over whether something has changed on the Harvester as well. Connor is convinced that someone is trying to gain access to the technology and use it in the mimic drone program Chang's sister has developed on the Harvester for GlobeCorpMining. At the Xed Ocean Academy, Rick makes the Sea Hunters aware of the evolving situation while also convincing Jonah of the need to push ahead with the overdrive trials for the Skimmers. Meanwhile, unbeknown to Ngarra's crew, a super-cell is developing in 'the Area' that inadvertently creates the opportunity the rogue group that has infiltrated the pirates have been waiting for. Isolated and alone, Ngarra's crew must find a way to overcome the standoff and avoid capture.

Chapter 1

The Xtract rose from the depths of the ocean with a load of manganese nodules. Ngarra watched from the SAI console. The outer hull shields were retracted. Above, the blue-green void stretched to the surface. Below, the black depths beyond the photic zone consumed everything.

His mind was wandering. He was thinking of his ancestors and the dreamtime stories passed on to him by the elders. Much of his life seemed to have led him to this moment. For some reason, lately, he had thought a lot about the origin stories and the sky people. *What did it all mean?* he thought to himself, *and why did it seem to have a connection with these Skimmers?*

Ngarra's thoughts shifted rapidly. A short attention span due to his condition meant he was always up to something. He snapped out of his contemplation, paced around, and watched as the Xtract stopped level with the nodule trays. It hovered briefly then moved across the Skimmer wing and unloaded its bin of nodules. It was a sight that always fascinated him.

Perhaps not much different from mining off-planet, he thought to himself. He paused and watched the Xtract dock onto its clamp to charge. The crew had been on and off their monthly mining rotation several times. It had been some months since the incident on the Harvester.

Every time they arrived, at the Harvester moon pools and offloaded their load of nodules comments were made about an increasingly uncomfortable feeling on the Harvester. Some crew choose to stay on their Skimmer rather than use the accommodation facilities.

'The crew seems to think something has changed at the Harvester,' he said to himself out loud as he paced around the SAI console. 'Connor is always nervous while we are there. Hell, even Chang says something isn't right and his sister is one of the ones in charge of that thing.'

Ngarra carried on pacing around and thinking about what might be going on. He paused and watched as another Xtract rose out of the depths. Another had finished charging. It launched from its docking clamp and moved across the Skimmer wing, stopped briefly and then started its descent. It followed the communication streamer back down to the seabed some four thousand metres below.

Looking down at either side of the Skimmer, the usual variety of marine life had gathered. Suspended about one hundred metres below sea level in the photic zone, after a few days, various forms of marine life gathered. At times, Yellowfin tuna even circled. He looked down at each side of the Skimmer again to see if any of them were there.

'Not today,' he said out loud wondering where they were.

'What's not today?' asked Jesse as she walked into the SAI console.

'No Yellowfin tuna swimming around the Skimmer,' he said.

She looks like something out of that old movie the Matrix, he thought to himself as he looked at Jesse. The crew had got used to it now. Jesse walked over and stood beside him. They looked out and back along each side of the Skimmer. They watched another Xtract as it unloaded.

'We leave for the Harvester in the morning,' said Jesse.

'Yes,' said Ngarra. 'The crew seems increasingly nervous about leaving the safety of the moon pools when we are there. On our last rotation out here, Connor and Chang thought something wasn't right on that Harvester. The Harvester security personnel seemed particularly nervous.'

'I'm sure it's because of everything that has happened previously,' said Jesse. 'After all, our crew has been through a lot. Other Skimmer crew weren't involved and just got on with mining. But now, like us, they are all tied up with these Skimmer overdrive trials. Busy times ahead.'

'You're probably right,' said Ngarra walking over to the SAI console. 'Still, maybe there is something in it. The Harvester, I mean. Let's see what Chang's sister has to say when we arrive to offload nodules.'

Jesse nodded in agreement.

'So, what's everyone up to?' asked Ngarra.

'Well,' said Jesse as she continued to look outside, 'Connor is working with his ocean bubble hologram and the red queen sequence, or Gilgamesh as he calls it now.' She smiled at herself. *How appropriate* she thought to herself. 'Stella and Chang are in the Xtract bay overseeing a repair drone working on an Xtract. As for Jonny, I think he is in his favourite place.'

'Where's that?' asked Ngarra smiling and knowing full well where he was.

'The rec area with a plate of food,' she said with a smirk on her face and raised eyebrows.

Ngarra laughed.

'Well, let's join him then,' said Ngarra as he pushed his stomach out and rubbed it, imitating Jonny and his antics.

The mood lightened.

They headed off to the rec area.

Walking to the rear of the SAI console, they exited through the watertight bulkhead and descended the stairs to the rec area below. At the bottom of the stairs on either side of them, the narrow esplanade stretched forward. It skirted each side of the enclosed overdrive; the inertial mass reduction propulsion system to the viewing area forward.

The overdrive had a variety of names. *The crew were still not sure what to call it,* Jesse thought to herself. Eventually, it will get a nickname. Bets were on across all the crew about what it might be.

'Jonny,' said Ngarra as they walked over, 'fancy seeing you here.'

'A Skimmer runs on its stomach,' he said with a mouth full of food.

'That it does,' said Ngarra smiling. He walked over and patted the sealed walls of the overdrive beside the stairs. 'But not your stomach.'

Trials with the overdrive were going well, Ngarra thought to himself. Rick was pleased with the progress of all the Skimmers. Some issues with the overspeed of the powertrain supplying the rim driven propulsion still occurred. But that was because the crew did not cross-check their alignment when the overdrive was initialised. The surge in energy discharge disrupted it. It had to be recalibrated after making a jump.

Amateurs, he thought to himself smiling, confident that both he and his crew had it all in hand.

Over the last few months, the crew had often sat and discussed how the overdrive worked and what the next phase was, after all the tests and trials were completed. *Not today,* he thought. They had to get ready to leave their current mining location.

'How's the load schedule looking?' asked Jonny as he looked up with a mouth full of food. 'Are we out of here in the morning?'

Ngarra could barely understand him as he chewed away.

'Looks like it,' said Ngarra with a chuckle.

Jesse and Ngarra walked over and sat down with him.

'What?' asked Jonny, as he shrugged his shoulders and raised his hands.

'The last of the Xtracts will finish overnight,' said Jesse ignoring him. 'SAI will secure the Skimmer first thing in the morning and we will transit to the Harvester.'

'Great,' said Jonny. 'As a Skimmer pilot, these stopovers to mine nodules really do my head in.'

'If you had it your way, Jonny, we would be running to the moon, Mars or even asteroids and back mining,' said Jesse.

They all laughed.

'I wouldn't laugh,' said Jonny as he finished his plate of food and pointed a utensil at them all. 'Where do you think this is all heading? With the Skimmers I mean.'

'One step at a time,' said Jesse. 'As far as I am aware there is no such intention.'

As the security and communications officer, she didn't want her crew getting distracted by rumours about, *the program or project Cygnus* as they called it or speculation about any broader objectives behind the Skimmers. Rick was adamant that in her role she kept the crew focussed on mining operations and completing the overdrive trials. Especially given the politics of it all. He had reiterated that quite clearly to all security and communications officers.

Stella and Chang came up the stairs from the Xtract bay below. They were going to head up the stairs to the SAI console and along to the information hub to see Connor. They had finished monitoring the repair drone working on the Xtract in the maintenance bay.

'You off to see Connor?' asked Ngarra as they entered the rec area.

'That we are,' replied Chang as he was about to climb the stairs.

'Yep,' said Stella. 'On second thought,' she said, seeing the others sitting at the table. It was an opportunity to hassle Jonny. 'Is this a counselling session for Jonny?' Stella walked over and sat down. Chang followed.

Stella and Jonny were always hassling each other. It kept the crew amused and entertained. Big Jonny, the Skimmer pilot of Tongan, Maori descent and Stella, a system engineer and a vibrant, outgoing Australian. They loved winding each other up.

'Actually, we were discussing having a group intervention with you,' said Jonny smirking. 'You've had a wardrobe malfunction and it's affecting the crew's wellbeing.'

Everyone laughed. Even Chang, or grumpy Chang as everyone referred to him, managed a smile.

'Careful, Chang mate,' said Jonny. 'You'll hurt yourself stretching those cheeks of yours.'

Everyone laughed again.

'Funny guy,' said Chang, frowning at him.

'Speaking of our wellbeing,' said Jesse. 'How are we all going, given everything that has happened? I mean several months ago, we were being shot at by Sue. Not to mention all the other stuff that has gone on. I don't know about you guys, but we've had a tough time.'

'Ying Yue was lucky that she was wearing a bulletproof vest,' said Jonny.

'She obviously had a fair idea about what was going on to put one on,' said Stella.

'Or maybe she orchestrated the whole thing,' said Jonny.

'My sister should get off that Harvester,' said Chang as his mood darkened and he glared at Jonny. 'My damn father. He has caused our family a world of trouble.'

'He is the Chief Operations Officer of GlobeCorpMining,' said Stella. 'I'm sure he isn't to blame.'

'You don't know our history,' said Chang. 'My mother, my sister and I, now have roles that have all stemmed from his involvement. It's like we are his puppets!'

Chang was angry now. Jonny's comment had set him off. He still had considerable animosity towards his father over what happened to their mother at the research lab some time ago. With his sister being caught up in things now as well, it seemed like history was repeating itself.

'Whatever is going on with that Harvester,' said Jesse. 'Lee and Ying Yue are now running the show. That mimic drone program everyone keeps going on about doesn't sound good though. Maybe that's why everyone onboard the Harvester seems so uneasy?'

'Depends on what the intention is regarding its use,' said Ngarra. 'It's meant to be part of automating mining operations. But with no direct human oversight, well, that sounds reckless.'

'Yeah, but Sue is in the PLA Navy,' said Stella. 'She seems to have other intentions. Chang's father took her with him after the shooting. Something is up and the crew on the Harvester seems nervous about it all.'

'Enough, let's stay focussed,' said Jesse. 'It's not our concern.'

'My sister is there,' said Chang angrily. His emotions got the better of him. 'It is my concern!'

'Point taken,' said Jesse as she tried to calm him down, 'but let's get our load of nodules offloaded first and back on a mining run. Besides, no matter what happens, no one wants to compromise their ability to operate in "the Area" under "the Authority" and the mining regulations or international maritime law for that matter.'

'But who do we trust?' asked Chang as he threw his arms in the air.

'Even the Sea Hunters seem to have an agenda. Look at how they pursued us!'

'Let's just focus on the Ocean Academy crew program,' said Jesse as she continued to calm the situation before it boiled over with Chang. 'These are contractor Skimmers. An agreement exists for their crewing and installation of the inertial mass reduction overdrive for the completion of tests and trials. There is much more to all this than any of us realise. Don't get distracted by it all, guys.'

'Zero-mass, gravity drive, inertial mass reduction drive, fun drive!' said Chang yelling and with a good hint of sarcasm.

'People don't even know what to call it.'

'Ha, good one, Chang,' said Jonny. 'Fun drive, now that's a nickname.'

The others laughed as well.

Chang managed a smile. He liked being the centre of attention. He calmed down a little.

'But it works doesn't it?' asked Jonny, giving him a wink.

'Then there's all Connor's work,' said Ngarra, interrupting them. 'It's important we get those final tests and trials done with the Xtracts as well. Removing the need for SAI to control each Xtract separately through the communication streamer is the key. SAI would then just monitor them. Connor has come a long way with the project. The mesh is largely independent of SAI now.'

'You mean Gilgamesh and his red queen,' said Stella smiling.

Everyone else started talking about the name.

'That whole red queen thing is just confusing,' said Jonny, talking over everyone. 'Learning group behaviour, I mean. Hacking code from script libraries on such things in nature and building algorithms that represent it. How on earth did he come up with all that?'

'Who knows,' said Jesse. 'Natural language processing means SAI has been able to do a lot of it. Amazing what data and information you can get from the animal kingdom and with SAI's help hack the code and make a stack of algorithms. It means all Skimmers will now have this sphere of his installed. Gilgamesh, as he so affectionately calls it. Red queen means it's now like a stubborn child that needs to be taught. Nodules are its lifeline and the Xtracts deliver them. The Xtracts compete for energy delivering the nodules. Thus, the analogy to the red queen effect in nature. At least, I think that is how it goes. The problem we have now is that everyone else seems to want what he has come up with. And for good reason.'

'Now that's an easy way to put it and understand it,' said Jonny. 'I mean for a simple mind like we have here,' he said looking and gesturing at Stella.

'Always the comedian,' said Stella. 'Speaking of children, do you need a bib?'

'What do you mean?' asked Jonny.

Everyone laughed as he looked down and realised he had a run of dried sauce on his top.

'Bugger,' he said, trying to wipe the dried sauce he had spilt off his top.

'On our next run, Connor will carry out final tests and trials with this sphere of Gilgamesh,' said Jesse. 'Xed Academy wants to know sooner rather than later. The plan is to replicate and install the sphere and its source code in all Skimmers.'

'What will Connor have to say about that,' said Stella. 'It's his baby and he seemed very attached to it.'

'True,' said Jesse, 'being on the spectrum for autism, we all know he can be overly obsessed. But I think his obsession is to our advantage. Jonah could give him oversight of a Skimmer-wide installation program for his pet project, Gilgamesh. Someone could accompany and guide him. At least, that is what I will suggest to Jonah and Rick.'

'Okay, boys and girls,' said Stella standing up, 'enough chit chat. Forget about Connor. We're off back to the Xtract bay to check on these drone repairs and the status of the Xtracts,' she said motioning Chang to come.

'Really?' asked Chang.

'I noticed a power discrepancy when some of the Xtracts docks recharged between runs to the bottom,' said Stella.

'I'll go down either side and check the docking displays,' said Chang as they left.

As Stella walked off, she handed Jonny something to get the sauce off his top and pretended to tie it on like a bib.

'Go away, woman,' he said, pushing her off as they left.

The others laughed.

'Make yourself useful, boy,' she said, glancing back as they went down the stairs to the maintenance bay.

They walked into the Xtract console monitoring bay. Forward of them and directly below the SAI console was the bulkhead that sealed in the overdrive propulsion system. Standing at the console they looked to the rear through the viewing area at the Xtract maintenance bay. Further back was the airlock and then the moon pool.

Chang walked to one side of the monitoring bay console and through a watertight bulkhead entrance. He walked down the passageway along the inside of the recess where the Xtracts were docked.

While he was doing this, Stella checked on the status of the drone being repaired. She walked through another watertight bulkhead entrance and into the maintenance bay.

'Found it,' said Chang to Stella over an internal comms link. 'The power banks for two Xtracts were offline. Must have been tripped by a surge.'

Issues still existed with initialising the overdrive and aligning rim driven propulsion systems. On a previous run, the rim driven propulsion powertrain surge from using the overdrive had also tripped out a few of the Xtract docking stations.

'Eventually, that drive will be on all the time,' said Stella, 'then it won't be an issue at all, and given its power source we will have all the energy we ever need indefinitely. You know those rim driven blades can retract leaving a metallic ring. The powertrain can then link directly with the overdrive when initialised. There are other plans afoot for these Skimmers. Even how the Xtracts are powered. There's talk of installing micro-reactors on them.'

'That is the brief from Xed, isn't it?' asked Chang as he listened to Stella over the comms link.

'Coming back now. I will check the other side.'

He passed through the monitoring bay and waved through the viewing screen at Stella to attract her attention, giving her the thumbs up. He could see her checking the repairs on the Xtract in the maintenance bay.

By the time they had checked everything and headed back up to the rec area, it was late in the evening. The others had gone off to the SAI console to make sure everything was ready so they could leave in the morning.

***

The next morning, everyone was up early getting ready to leave. Jesse and Ngarra were at the SAI console with Jonny. Stella and Chang were in the Xtract bay and Connor was in the information hub. No one had seen him since the day before.

'Did you guys see Connor last night?' asked Jonny, as he put his interface lenses on for departure.

'I assume he got some sleep,' said Ngarra. 'Last I saw him, he was in the information hub. I poked my head in and said good night while checking the rim driven propulsion system. He was so absorbed in his work I don't think he even saw or heard me.'

'I talked to him briefly,' said Jesse, 'and told him to get some sleep. He was excited. Apart from needing its own power supply installed, Gilgamesh is independent of SAI now. Not sure if he actually got much sleep.'

'Communication streamer almost recovered,' said Stella over comms from the Xtract monitoring console below.

'Last of the drones are docking,' said Chang.

'Roger that,' said Ngarra from the SAI console above.

They looked out.

The last few Xtracts were moving slowly across the Skimmer wings. They had released their load of nodules into the bins. They disappeared into the recess along each side and docked.

'SAI, confirm Skimmer is watertight,' said Ngarra.

'Confirmed,' said SAI. 'Skimmer is watertight.'

'Communication streamer secured,' said Stella. 'Samples recovered for processing and storage.'

The streamer had recovered seabed and water column samples. They were stored in the information hub as per the requirements for operating in 'the Area.' The Sea Hunters would collect them as part of their inspection regime.

'All Xtracts docked,' said Chang over comms.

'SAI, confirm life support and propulsion systems are nominal. Depart for Skimmer,' said Ngarra.

'Confirmed,' said SAI. 'Systems nominal, departing for Skimmer.'

The rim driven propulsion system powered up and the Skimmer started to move off. As the Skimmer accelerated, the marine life that had gathered fell away.

The outer hull shields were not closed.

Ngarra and Jesse watched as the Skimmer did a wide flat turn, gained speed, and straightened up, heading for the Harvester.

Jonny used his interface lenses to monitor navigation systems. He moved his hands and created an expanded view of their course, which appeared in a hologram in the middle of the SAI console.

'Here we go again, boys and girls,' said Jonny.

'What I really want right now is sun, surf and sand,' said Stella over open comms.

'I'm with you on that one,' said Jonny over open comms.

'Nothing like a day on that beach back at the academy,' replied Stella.

'Would you two focus?' asked Ngarra over open comms.

'In this self-driving beast,' said Jonny sarcastically.

'An automated tin can,' said Chang as he listened to the banter between Jonny and Stella.

'A very expensive one,' said Ngarra.

'Would you kids cut the chatter?' asked Jesse over open comms.

'Let's check everything off as per procedures. Then we can get out of here and relax.'

Jesse was like a mother hen to them all. She watched over them. That was her role. She was not sure whether that was a burden or something to embrace wholeheartedly. At times, she thought they really were like a bunch of belligerent children.

Chapter 2

It was early morning at the Ocean Academy. Students were entering the sim centre for training. Across the Xed campus, students were coming and going from various learning centres. The drone port at the top of the main admin building was busy. It was a clear and calm day.

Rick was in the crew monitoring and communication centre. He had got a morning briefing from the duty officer in charge on the operational status of the crew on Skimmers. With everything in order, he grabbed a coffee and walked up the wide stairway to the mezzanine and the conference room. He needed to catch up with the Sea Hunters about the increase in piracy activity across 'the Area.' Given there was no need now to hide in 'the room' and use and encrypted link to a node he could communicate more openly with them.

Placing his coffee down on the table he opened a message board on the virtual display.

'SAI, send a communication request to speak with the Sea Hunter Unit in "the Area".'

'Confirmed,' said SAI. 'Communication request sent to the Sea Hunter Unit.'

A pause followed and then Max appeared on the screen.

'Good morning, Max,' he said.

'Rick, how are you,' said Max. 'I was expecting to hear from you given the increase in piracy activity out here. Skimmer contractors and tenure holders in "the Area" want something more done about it.'

'As do we,' said Rick, 'for the sake of our crew.'

'To which "we" are you referring to,' said Max, grinning, 'Xed Academy or "your people" as you call them.'

'Both actually,' said Rick, smiling. 'The safety of our Skimmer crew is paramount. If these pirates get bold and start to intentionally damage Skimmers during these nodule heists, it could jeopardise the whole operation.'

'So, what do you think has changed?' asked Max.

'These pirates depend on the Skimmers being tethered to the communication streamer when on location. Why would they damage a Skimmer and compromise their black-market nodule supply chain into the future?'

'Rumour has it lately that these pirates are not just pirates,' said Rick. 'We think that amongst them is another group with another agenda. My people are not sure who they are or what it is yet. Their agenda I mean.'

'Your people again?' questioned Max with a smile.

'These Skimmers have their Acoustic Remote Cavitation or ARC weapons do they not?' questioned Max.

'Yes,' said Rick, ignoring his remark about 'your people', 'but it's just for defence. I don't want our Skimmer crew program turned into some sort of military operation against the pirates. These kids are barely out of their teens and it's not what they signed up for at all.'

'There is only so much we can do under our mandate as the security and compliance contractor in "the Area",' said Max, 'that includes ensuring the Harvester operations are not compromised and tenure holders like GlobeCorpMining continue to have uninterrupted access to their leases under "the Authority" for mining in "the Area".'

'But under international maritime law, Max, you have every right to step it up and hunt down all those involved in this piracy operation out there,' said Rick, 'that includes this other group my people think have got mixed up with these pirates. It may even be some of the pirates themselves that have bought into someone else's agenda.'

'Interesting,' said Max as he stopped, stretched, and took a moment to think.

Rick waited and watched him closely. Max was a hard man to figure out. Always outwardly causal, he was a very calculated person and constantly thinking about scenarios, possibilities, and outcomes.

'What about the testing program for the overdrive your people installed in these contractor Skimmers?' asked Max

'What do you mean?' asked Rick.

'Bring it online permanently,' said Max. 'It's capable of extreme speed. The zero-mass and no inertia you have mentioned previously. Directed energy weapons can still be used without compromising the energy field. When underway, pirates wouldn't have a chance. Your only vulnerability would be when stationary and tethered to the communication streamer during mining.'

'We still get overspeed along the powertrain for the rim driven propulsion system if it's not aligned when initialised,' said Rick, 'and a Skimmer has to orientate itself to the arrival coordinates for a location or destination using the overdrive. The crew still haven't got it quite right.'

'It's just an issue of calibration of frequency and resonance when discharging into the energy field, the plasma vortex isn't it?' questioned Max.

'Sort out the powertrain issues, increase the number of trials and bring the program forward.'

'True,' said Rick, 'and good point. You seem to know a bit about it.' Max seems to know about all this. *He knows more than he is letting on,* Rick thought to himself.

'We have acquired some kit out here onboard that we are trialling,' said Max, 'for surveillance that is and with some rather unique propulsion technology in it as well.'

'I will talk with my people about it some more,' said Rick. 'We know the overdrive propulsion system works. Even if we haven't quite figured out this overspeed issue along the powertrain to the rim drive.'

Rick thought briefly about how much he should say. But his people had given the nod when it came to the Sea Hunters. Maybe his people were also involved in this tech Max mentioned they had onboard.

'The overdrive works by generating this powerful energy field,' said Rick as he carried on. 'It combines electric induction and torsion in a vortex. Think of it like this. The Skimmer still has mass, but not relative to the space around it. And sound or resonant frequency carries mass. The high frequency discharge of energy into the plasma vortex cancels out mass and inertia and the Skimmer makes the jump. The mercury plasma vortex core in the overdrive has proven very effective at that. It's the ideal chemical element for such technology. Containment, control of the magnitude of the effect and its discharge making the jump to the arrival coordinates work well now.'

'But how does the drive actually work?' asked Max.

'The mechanics of it, I mean to generate the containment field and make a jump without squashing your crew at those extreme speeds.'

'Not for me to go into that,' said Rick. 'Come and join us here at the Xed Academy and maybe I'll tell you more,' he said smiling.

His people may have given the nod when it came to the Sea Hunters, but he was still cautious. *Besides,* he thought to himself, *Max was always prying for information on the overdrives*. He knew Max wanted to find out how much he knew about the propulsion technology being rolled out on the Skimmers. It was the deal of the century between his people, the Skimmer owners and the mining contractors.

'On another note,' said Max, not wanting to push the issue.

He was still thinking about whether such a propellantless propulsion system might operate with similar underlying principles to the 'dragonfly drone' surveillance program they were trialling for a contractor.

'That technology we were pursuing for you,' he said carrying on, 'the Xtract mining drone technology. Where is that at? Between your zero-mass drive or inertial mass reduction as you call it and this Xtract tech onboard that Skimmer there must be a lot of interest in what you have done.'

'That's the issue we have right now,' said Rick. 'They were originally constructed to specifications with assistance from GlobeCorpMining. Once the Chinese handed them over to owners and contractors, we installed the technology my people had been holding onto. It's a proprietary property with a patent, so contractors or anyone else for that matter can't just copy it. We have an arrangement. Contractors and owners benefit significantly and have a fair bit of control over things now. That doesn't mean the Chinese don't have some skin in the game, of course. They have the maintenance contract for the Skimmers. Who knows what they are doing out there on that Harvester? The point being that we know that as well as their growing interest in modifying Skimmer control and propulsion systems themselves they have also become interested in this tech for learning autonomous group behaviour in Xtracts that one of our crew members has developed.'

'So, the Xtract tech this Connor person has developed is well advanced then?' asked Max.

'Correct,' said Rick, 'his crew are running some final tests and trials. We intend to roll it out across all Skimmers.'

Max kept a straight face. Rick wondered what he was thinking.

'Maybe these pirates have realised there is something more lucrative here to pursue,' said Max, 'that being the actual Skimmers themselves. I mean hijacking one and taking it. Once in their possession, it wouldn't take them long. With a bit of help, they could figure it all out.'

'Could be, but who's help?' asked Rick.

'Either way, our crew are getting nervous out there. There is a big difference between monitoring mining operations and having nodules stolen while tethered compared to defending themselves against boardings and being hijacked by pirates.'

'It changes our approach as well,' said Max. 'You can be assured of that. Right then, we will look at increasing our surveillance and interdiction capacity out here as per regulations for security and compliance operations in "the Area".'

'Good,' said Rick, 'I will speak with my people about wanting to push forward with these overdrive trials and advancing the program. However, at present, our crew are still vulnerable to all this while the Skimmers are tethered. We need you to be on top of this.'

'Who's we?' asked Max again smiling.

Rick didn't react to Max's baiting. The 'we' behind the Skimmers was not something to discuss in too much detail.

'Will do,' said Max carrying on. 'Got to go. Let's talk again in a few days.'

'Let us know what you come up with,' said Rick.

'I must get going,' he said out loud as he looked at the time. 'I have that meeting with Jonah and then the Council meeting.'

Max nodded his head. His image disappeared and the message board closed.

For a moment, Rick was lost in thought. He walked over to the large glass pane and looked out over the crew monitoring stations to the main screen on the opposite wall. Ultimately, for his people, this was all about project Cygnus. For Jonah, it was about ensuring the viability of the Xed and the Academy into the future. Somewhere in the middle was common ground between them all. Between both the Xed Council and his people there was much enthusiasm to see it all come together. However, the relationship with GlobeCorpMining complicated things. Family ties made it even worse. But there must be a way to make it all work without compromising working in 'the Area' under 'the Authority' regulations.

Sometimes, it seemed that all he did was attend meetings, he thought to himself. He exited the crew monitoring complex and walked through the sim centre, then the training area or learning hub as they liked to call it and out of the main entrance into the sunlight and the day ahead.

Walking across campus, he greeted students coming and going from wherever they were meant to be. The grounds were well kept, and he enjoyed the walk. Despite modern technology and students using various means to get around campus, he enjoyed walking.

He entered the recreation complex. He was meeting Jonah there in the staff restaurant over a coffee and food. Jonah had expressed her concern about the increase in piracy activity in 'the Area' as well. She was worried about how her crew would cope given how bold these pirates were getting.

Spotting Jonah, they walked toward each other and met at the buffet to get some food.

'Good morning,' said Rick as he came up to her.

'Hi,' said Jonah, 'let's get some food and find a seat.'

Everything was automated. They selected what they wanted, and a dispenser delivered their meals.

'How is the crew monitoring?' asked Jonah as they got what they wanted to eat and went and sat down.

'Actually, there is nothing to report right now,' said Rick. 'It seems "the Area" is quiet.'

'The calm before the storm,' said Jonah as they sat down with their meals.

'You may well be right about that,' said Rick. 'I had a conference call with the Sea Hunters this morning over growing concerns.'

'We are in the final stages of testing and trials of Connor's tech,' said Jonah. 'It's something we own that will take us forward with all this automation. I have our legal people putting together all the documentation.'

'I want to push forward with the overdrive trials as well,' said Rick. 'We need to bring the schedule forward.'

'Should we rush that?' questioned Jonah.

'Our crew still have trouble with overspeed on the powertrain for the rim driven propulsion when that thing is bought online.'

'It's just training and practice to calibrate it to align the rim-drive powertrain properly,' said Rick. 'Orientation to the arrival coordinates to make the jump can't be that hard. I mean, in relation to the magnitude of discharge into the plasma vortex and the resonant frequency produced. Besides, mass and inertia are always cancelled relative to their surroundings, regardless. They will get it.'

'Why the rush?' asked Jonah cautiously.

She still couldn't get her head around how the overdrive worked. It was a language she was learning to understand. A language everyone was learning it seemed.

Besides, Rick was always up to something, she thought to herself. She knew he had an ulterior motive. She wasn't quite sure how that would fit into the future of Xed and the Academy. Still, her trust was in the fact that they both wanted the same thing even if their motives and approaches were different. But she was adamant that the Academy Skimmer crewing program should not be split out from Xed.

'If these pirates have become bolder,' said Rick, 'then maybe running stolen nodules is not enough for them anymore. It seems there might be a group of them up to something else. I am concerned. Some of them may be aware of just how much kit these Skimmers carry. I mean, between the overdrive and the tech we have developed for the Xtracts. It's a miner's dream, isn't it? Anyone could take one of these Skimmers anywhere and I mean, anywhere and carry out a self-contained mining operation. They just need some sort of large freighter or transport to deliver their loads to and get paid.'

'Yes, both on and off the planet,' she said, smiling at Rick. 'I get that, you're swanning around about it all I mean.'

Jonah was smart. She could see the huge potential of it all, but a game was being played. People were holding their cards close.

Rick didn't take the bait of course; about project Cygnus and the comment about swanning around.

Jonah sat quietly.

For a while, there was silence.

She thought about what Rick had said then continued the conversation.

'Our crew are still vulnerable when tethered to the communication streamer on location,' said Jonah. 'With Connor's tech rolled out, SAI would just monitor Xtract operations. No need would exist to control each one individually via the streamer like it does now. Technically speaking, there would be no need for that streamer anymore. The problem is, if the Xtract goes offline, we are totally reliant on the other ones to get it back to the Skimmer themselves.'

'That is the aim of Connor's tech,' said Rick. 'Truly autonomous operations. In the short term, we can't afford to get rid of the communication streamer, though.'

'That I agree with,' said Jonah. 'So, moving around "the Area" using the overdrive would ensure pirates never got anywhere near them except when on location,' said Jonah. 'At present though, we are still reliant on the Sea Hunters when they are tethered to the streamer for mining.'

'It would appear so,' said Rick, 'at least for now.'

They both sat quietly for a while and finished their meals.

The day was getting on and Jonah had a busy day ahead.

There was still a Council meeting to attend and she had to talk with Ngarra and Jesse about Connor's work and she had to contact Chang's father.

'I have to get going,' she said, looking at Rick and finishing her coffee.

'Let's catch up again at the Council meeting later today then,' said Rick. 'I will head over to talk with the Sea Hunter liaison officer.'

They both got up and went to put their plates through the collector. Exiting the restaurant, Jonah watched as Rick headed off. She contemplated where it was all heading and what the outcome might be.

Jonah then walked back to the admin building and made her way up to her office. On the way, she thought about what was going on.

It was a balancing act. Keeping Xed going while spending much of her time also ensuring the Academy Skimmer crew training program remained viable. The tech Connor had developed was now a key part of that. As was the finding provided by GlobeCorpMining. Perhaps Rick was right, once the overdrive and this Xtract tech were proven they could be largely self-funded through licensing agreements and partnerships for use of all this gear on the contractor Skimmers. Could they separate out the crewing monitoring program, though? She really didn't want to. What would Chang's father think of it all?

Was what, he thought, *even important?*

Somehow, she thought it was.

'Hi, Jonah,' said her secretary as she walked into the office.

Jonah jumped.

She had been deep in thought.

'Oh, geez! I was so engrossed in my own thoughts you scared me,' said Jonah.

They both laughed.

'Can you get hold of Skimmer crew monitoring and put me through to Ngarra's Skimmer please?' asked Jonah as she went into her office and opened the message board and waited.

Her secretary sent the request to Skimmer crew monitoring. Jonah waited to see if there was a nominal signal for a live feed.

'Hi, Jonah,' said Ngarra and Jesse as their images appeared on the screen.

'We are on our way to the Harvester to offload,' said Jesse.

'It must be nice for your crew to be back in some sort of routine again,' said Jonah. 'I wanted to give you a head up. Reports on the increased aggression of pirates indicate that they are more likely to attack and board. It could go beyond just taking nodules out of Skimmer trays when tethered. You need to be careful. A brief is being sent to all Skimmers to bring forward the overdrive trials. Overdrive protocols are to be used in transits whenever there is the potential to encounter pirates.'

'We got a brief earlier about the risk and the trials,' said Jesse. 'I have informed the crew. Besides, with more practice, we will overcome this overspeed issue on the powertrain to the rim drive when the overdrive is used.'

'You will still be vulnerable when tethered,' said Jonah. 'As I said, it seems some of these pirates may be after more than just nodules now. Information about both the overdrive and Connor's tech may have got out. You need to be careful. The Sea Hunters can't be everywhere at once.'

'What about not using the communication streamer?' asked Ngarra.

'Not yet,' said Jonah. 'Connor's tech still isn't fully proven. Besides, we have the Sea Hunters.'

'I still don't trust the Sea Hunters,' said Ngarra.

'You don't like them regardless,' said Jonah. 'Anyway, Rick seems to be on top of the Sea Hunters. They have something to do with all this. He assures me they are acting in our best interests. Still, I would be cautious when it comes to them as well over all this.'

'We will also watch ourselves when at the Harvester and get back out to mining as quickly as possible,' said Ngarra.

'Good,' said Jonah. 'I have to contact Chang's father and will be in touch later.'

With that, she swiped the message board clear and got her secretary to send a message to GlobeCorpMining requesting to talk with Chang's father. He was usually available and would stop what he was doing to talk. Unless, of course, he was in a CCP sub-committee meeting. That was pretty much the only time he would not stop and talk to her, or so he said.

After a short time, his image appeared on the message board.

'Jonah, what can I do for you?' he asked.

'We have a Council meeting today.' She replied. 'They will be asking about the increase in piracy activity in "the Area". Since when have pirates wanted to damage Skimmers?'

It was a leading question to see if he would shed any further light on the situation.

'Yes, my people on the Harvester have informed me,' he said. 'We have stepped up perimeter security.'

'That doesn't help my crews though,' said Jonah. 'The Sea Hunters can't be everywhere.'

'They want more minerals maybe,' he said, 'or perhaps they have come to see a Skimmer as more valuable. To take and do it themselves, I mean.'

'They would have to have someone to offload and sell them to,' said Jonah. 'I think it's more than that.'

'What do you mean?' he asked.

'Technology,' she said. 'The Skimmers have some pretty advanced tech in them now.'

'True,' he said, 'but as you said, it's no good to them without someone to sell to. It's all patented and licensed. Contractors have a vested interest in it. Your crew just monitor mining operations.'

'It can't just be pirates then,' said Jonah. 'Someone else would have to be behind it all. I mean, the pirates damaging Skimmers. Maybe they are looking for a weakness, a way to try to board them.'

'Maybe you are right,' he said cautiously. 'If this is the case, we can't help you. Our focus is the Harvester. Only the Sea Hunters, under their mandate and "the Authority", can do something about it. I suggest you tighten security on your Skimmers. They have their ARC defensive system.'

'They have always been vulnerable when tethered to the communication streamer though,' said Jonah. 'Anyway, I have to go and will let you know what we come up with. Above all, I don't want the supply of nodules compromised.'

'Neither do we,' he said. 'Talk again soon then.'

With that, his image disappeared. She wondered whether the conversation had achieved anything. Anyway, time was getting on and Rick would be here shortly for the Council meeting.

Jonah grabbed a coffee and looked over her notes.

'You seem worried,' said her secretary.

'I am,' said Jonah. 'A lot is at stake here. It's a crucial time for us. If we get it wrong, we will lose out on the opportunities before us.'

'You seem concerned about more than that,' said her secretary.

'True,' said Jonah, 'we are talking about people's lives. Young ones at that. Someone could get hurt or even killed in all this.'

'Surely no one wants that,' she replied.

'I wouldn't be so sure,' said Jonah. 'We need to be careful.'

Her secretary decided to stop pursuing Jonah about why exactly she was so concerned. Jonah sipped her coffee and they both waited for the Council meeting to start.

Chapter 3

Later that day, onboard the Skimmer, Ngarra's crew were carrying out routine monitoring of their transit to the Harvester. Nothing unusual attracted their attention. SAI had everything in hand. No need existed to use the overdrive and they were not due to run any more tests on it yet.

Chang was on watch and had gone to check on Skimmer systems at the SAI console.

Connor was in the information hub.

Stella had gone to the Xtract bay console to check on a drone that had been repaired and had been bought into the maintenance bay.

Jonny was in his cabin getting some rest.

Ngarra and Jesse were in the rec area sitting at the table discussing the success Connor was having with the Xtract tech he had developed.

It wouldn't be much longer before it was rolled out across the other Skimmers.

'I still think it's dangerous,' said Ngarra. 'Connor's tech means these Xtracts become independent of any human intervention or oversight. Even SAI will not have direct control anymore.'

'You may be right,' said Jesse, 'but he has modelled the tech on the animal kingdom, on nature at its best. Red queen, its source code and algorithm stack I mean. It ties them to Gilgamesh and maintaining Gilgamesh is tied to human oversight.'

'What if Gilgamesh determines that human oversight limits its own evolution,' said Ngarra. 'What if we become a threat to its development?'

'This sphere or Gilgamesh as Connor calls it has an interface that ensures human oversight is never compromised,' said Jesse. 'It's impossible to sever that connection. Connor made it that way. It would be the same for any sphere now installed on a Skimmer.'

'Okay,' said Ngarra, still unsure that such a connection could not be overcome, 'but, for example, what if we no longer had oversight of Skimmers and their SAI?'

'What are you getting at?' asked Jesse.

'What if humans no longer controlled the supply chain of nodules,' said Ngarra. 'Red queen is about optimising the mining of minerals, but to what end? What if Gilgamesh decided it wanted to make some improvements in mining operations itself and interfaced and overrode the Skimmer SAI? What if an AI decided what all these minerals were used for? For its own benefit, I mean.'

The conversation was interrupted.

'Incoming communication request from the Sea Hunters,' said SAI. 'Grid buoy and eel drone proximity nominal, live feed available.'

'Let's go up to the SAI console,' said Jesse. 'I wonder what they want.'

They got up and walked up the stairs through the watertight bulkhead and into the SAI console.

Chang had opened the message board for them. An image of Alex appeared; a familiar face given their previous encounters with the Sea Hunters.

'Jesse, Ngarra,' said Alex, 'I am sending another communication to all Skimmers but thought I would contact you personally. There is a further increase in piracy activity in "the Area". There have been instances where Skimmers have been damaged.'

'Yes, we know it's increased,' said Jesse. 'Xed Academy briefed us.'

'Just to confirm,' said Alex. 'Pirates have been identified on location. They recently tried to disable a Skimmer while it was tethered to its communication streamer. It seems they are testing for any vulnerability. We are concerned it will lead to an attempt to board.'

'We heard that might be the case,' said Ngarra. 'What on earth for though? They just want the nodules.'

He didn't like the Sea Hunters at the best of times but lately, their role in the Area was of growing importance.

'Something has changed,' said Alex, 'concern is growing they may want the Skimmers themselves and all the tech that goes with them.'

'That would have to be coming from someone else,' said Jesse.

'We have our suspicions,' said Alex, 'but need more time to confirm.'

'We have been ordered to be in the proximity of Skimmer mining operations as much as possible and not just for boardings and inspections. For now, a brief is going out that mining operations are to be grouped by region in "the Area" so Skimmers are closer together. It makes it easier for us to intervene.'

'Okay,' said Ngarra, 'but it also puts a bigger target on our backs. Being spread out actually made us harder to find.'

Reluctantly, *he didn't have much choice,* Ngarra thought to himself. They had to comply with emergency orders issued by 'the Authority' which the Sea Hunters carried out. Boardings or no boardings, the last thing he needed was to be disabled by pirates.

'We are in transit to the Harvester,' said Ngarra, carrying on. 'I am presuming then that our next mining location will be as a group in a specific region in "the Area" then. So, all the crew and their Skimmers will be nearer to each other.'

'Pretty much,' said Alex. 'The Skimmer contractors don't like it, but it's the way it has to be for now.'

'If Connor's tech has anything to do with it,' said Ngarra. 'We won't need the tethers soon and won't be so vulnerable. We could use our ARC weapons during mining operations then or the overdrive to get away, for that matter.'

'Yes, but we aren't at that stage yet,' said Jesse. 'We are still vulnerable.'

'Either way,' said Alex, 'we still may not get to you in time if there is an attack. You need a plan in case they want more than your nodules.'

'There is something that may work as a deterrent from attempting a boarding while tethered,' said Jesse. 'I will ask Connor about it.'

'Good,' said Alex. 'Make sure the other crews are aware of it. Sounds like you need to roll out that tech of Connor's for the other Skimmers sooner rather than later.'

'You're right about that one,' said Ngarra.

'I have to go,' said Alex. 'The change in circumstances out here has given us a whole lot of work to do.'

With that, his image disappeared.

Ngarra and Jesse looked at each other and then turned and looked out into the void beyond. The outer hull shields were still retracted. They watched as the black depths below and the blue-green void of the photic zone above passed them by.

Chang had been quietly watching. He listened to everything that was said. He wondered why a bunch of pirates would become so interested in the Skimmers themselves.

If that was what was really going on, he thought to himself.

'Why would a bunch of pirates want a Skimmer?' asked Chang.

'Maybe it's not the pirates that want one,' said Ngarra.

'Mining in "the Area" is becoming bad for my health,' said Chang with a grimace and a hint of sarcasm. 'Too many people with a vested interest in all this tech literally floating around out here.'

'You're right about that,' said Ngarra. 'Let's get the others together and discuss all this. I'm sure the other Skimmer crew will be doing the same thing after getting the briefs from Academy Crew Monitoring and from the Sea Hunters.'

Ngarra got SAI to request everyone meet in the rec area straight away. They left the SAI console and went down to the rec area. Jesse went and got Connor.

Ngarra and Chang walked down the stairs and across to the table. They sat down and waited for the others.

A short time later, Stella came bounding up from the Xtract bay below. She nearly bowled Connor and Jesse over as they came down from the SAI console, meeting at the foot of the stairs between levels.

'Whoa!' she exclaimed, grabbing them both.

Connor jumped back in surprise. He was sensitive to being touched.

'Close call,' said Jesse. 'Sorry Connor,' she said casually.

Connor nodded and walking across to the table and sat down with them.

'What's all the fuss?' asked Stella as she sat down.

'Everyone here,' said Ngarra. 'Where's Jonny?'

'I guess he didn't hear the call,' said Stella. 'I'll get him,' she said, jumping up.

'Stella, no!' said Ngarra as she grabbed a cup of water from the dispenser and raced towards accommodation.

The others laughed, knowing what was about to happen.

A brief silence followed then yelling and rapid footsteps.

Jonny came racing out in cotton boxer shorts. Stella was trying to get away. Jonny had wet hair and skin from a cup of water poured over him.

'You are one dead girl!' said Jonny, as he chased her around the table.

Everyone else couldn't help but laugh.

Jonny climbed across the table between everyone and tried to grab her. He just about sent everyone else flying in the process.

Stella avoided him.

However, Jonny was a big boy.

Leaping off the table he managed to grab her. Grasping her ankles, he lifted her upside down into the air.

'Okay, okay, I'm sorry,' she pleaded and laughed. 'Put me down!'

Jonny lowered her to the floor.

'Seriously you two,' said Ngarra laughing. 'I think you've been at sea too long.'

The others managed to stop laughing and everyone calmed down.

Breathing heavily, Jonny and Stella both sat down.

'It's a small Skimmer,' said Jonny smiling. 'Better watch yourself, girl.'

He was still in his boxers and tightening his muscles making a warrior face at her.

'I'll set my Xtracts on you,' she said laughing at him.

'Speaking of that,' said Jesse. 'Listen up, this is important.'

Everyone finally settled down.

Jonny looked down at his wet shorts and grimaced at Stella.

Connor was indifferent but his interest was piqued when he heard Stella talk about letting the Xtracts loose on Jonny.

He tended to take things literally.

'As you all know an increase in piracy is occurring in "the Area",' said Jesse. 'A Skimmer has been damaged. Future mining locations are going to be grouped more closely so the Sea Hunters can keep an eye on things.'

'Contractors won't like that so much,' said Jonny.

'The Sea Hunters think these pirates may be testing how vulnerable Skimmers are so they can be boarded and hijacked,' said Ngarra.

'Who's behind it then?' asked Stella.

'Doesn't sound like pirates.'

'Exactly,' said Jesse. 'Whoever it is, we need to think of a way to stop attempts to damage our Skimmer and board us while tethered. Which brings me to your comment, Stella.'

Connor turned towards Jesse listening intently.

'We are close to rolling out Gilgamesh across all Skimmers,' she said. 'Connor's trials, red queen and the sphere are almost complete. It works. Well, it works well enough to use.'

'What does that have to do with setting the Xtracts on Jonny?' asked Connor.

The others smiled at his remark.

'More than you think actually,' said Jesse. 'Remember your squid simulation from some time ago?'

'Yes,' said Connor, 'but it fell apart until I got the red queen working for Gilgamesh.'

'Well,' said Jesse, 'if anything were to compromise those Xtracts during mining would it not be a threat to Gilgamesh? So, what I am getting at is how then would the Xtracts respond to the Skimmer being damaged during mining?'

'I see what you mean,' said Connor. 'In the red queen, the reward for nodule loads is power, like food for Xtracts. The Skimmer feeds the Xtracts and in return, its nodule trays are filled. Red queen also means the Xtracts compete amongst themselves to continuously optimise the opportunity to feed or re-power and gain the upper hand.'

'Exactly,' said Jesse. 'So, if that process is interrupted externally, wouldn't it be perceived as a threat? Shouldn't the Xtracts then respond by removing the threat to that relationship? Shouldn't they learn from that experience and then adapt? That's what you developed the source code for in the red queen algorithm stack for Gilgamesh, isn't it? Independent learning of group behaviour responses to external stimulus?'

'Yes, but it's in its infancy,' said Connor. 'It's like teaching a child. That's why there is always a human interface with Gilgamesh. Without it, it would be like a child throwing a tantrum. Dangerous, if you ask me.'

'Still, it can be used, can it not?' asked Ngarra.

'Yes,' said Connor, 'but we might not be able to stop them. Like a shark feeding frenzy, until the threat is eliminated.'

'I don't think we have a choice,' said Ngarra. 'Let's make sure Gilgamesh is online permanently from now on Connor.'

'Sure,' said Connor, 'I will.'

'Next thing,' said Jesse, 'the overdrive. The trials have been brought forward. Any threat of piracy and we are to use the overdrive to escape. Overspeed on the powertrain for the rim driven propulsion will just have to be sorted out through trial and error. It could mean more downtime between mining runs through.'

'Point and go,' said Jonny. 'I know the mechanics of it all. It's set at 30-degree intervals, the capacitor or energy discharge ring that is.'

'Yes,' said Jesse, 'it's at the base of the mercury plasma vortex column. The plasma is spun using the magnetic semiconductor at its base. But we still haven't quite got the resonant frequency right and we still have overspeed along the powertrain to the rim drive when it's used.'

'Always wanted to know more about how it all works,' said Chang. 'We should enter the space down there and have a look sometime.'

'Don't we all,' said Jonny.

'Not now,' said Jesse, 'another time. It's a restricted area anyway.'

'Even without making a jump,' said Ngarra, 'the inertia cancelling means we can accelerate and reach pretty significant speeds.'

'At speeds less than making a jump, we should be fine. I think the overspeed on the powertrain for the rim drive is from making an actual jump,' said Stella. 'The opposing capacitor is apparently set at a much higher frequency. Maybe the resonant frequency causes a surge or vibration along the powertrain that also trips out the rim driven propulsion system. That's why it has to be recalibrated.'

'Maybe it's the actual base plate, the magnetic semiconductor that spins the mercury in the vortex,' said Stella. 'The spin and frequency produced from the energy field generated is not aligned with the resonant frequency from the discharge ring into it.'

'Could be,' said Jesse. 'If indeed that is how it operates. If the vibration or resonant frequency is slightly off, then interference from the energy field that is generated might disrupt the powertrain to the rim drive.'

'So,' said Stella. 'Have I got this right? If we discharge into the vortex and make the jump, at present it disrupts the powertrain for the rim drive when we go to use it. It is offline, and we must recalibrate it. We can deal with that in the short term. Whether we make the jump or just travel at an extreme speed, in terms of cancelling inertia and mass both have their pros and cons. Either way, we still get away from any potential threat these pirates pose to us.'

'You're confusing me now,' said Jonny, as he tried to get his head around how the overdrive worked. 'I have a basic understanding folks. All this technical talk and new language. My head's spinning.'

'It's a bit of a mind-bender,' said Stella.

'For all of us,' said Jesse, smiling.

She knew more about it than she let on. That was part of her role on a Skimmer. She had to know, and the overdrive area was restricted access. For now. Rick had said that to all the crew.

'Let's talk about this more later,' said Jesse. 'With the overdrive trials being brought forward, for now, it's a matter of learning how to cope with the overspeed and to work around it.'

The conversation turned to mining operations and how they were going to meet their schedule given the heightened risk of interruptions from piracy. It had been some time since group mining was carried out in 'the Area'.

Once contractor Skimmers were tried and tested, they spread out across the area, mining for the owners of mining tenements and the monopoly GlobeCorpMining had over 'the Area'. Contractors didn't like being forced together into regions. Nor did the owners of mining tenements that might miss out for the time being.

Chapter 4

The day was getting on. Alex and Max were in the Sea Hunter vessel drone bay. They were looking over the surveillance drone they had discussed previously. It had been undergoing trials and a couple of technicians were examining it.

Commonly called, a *dragonfly drone*, it used a form of advanced propulsion. The principles were like the Skimmer overdrive, but the mechanism was somewhat different. It also had the bonus of not being able to be seen due to the energy field it generated.

'Can the energy field be interrupted?' asked Alex to a technician.

'Possibly,' she said. 'If atmospheric conditions interrupt polarisation of the energy field.'

'So, a huge electrostatic force is generated by the implosion ring then discharging into it,' said Alex. 'The vertical rods act like a semiconductor and polarise the energy field.'

'Exactly,' said the technician. 'It's like having a halo over it. This creates lift, negative at the top, and positive at the bottom. The ionisation of the surrounding air just means you can't see it. Light is bent around it.'

'And horizontal movement?' questioned Max.

'Perpendicular to the direction of polarisation when discharged into,' she said. 'Our operations team then monitors and tracks it from here. At enormous speeds, it can go pretty much anywhere on the planet and back again very quickly.'

'Interesting isn't it,' said Max. 'Let's get this thing in the air. I want these trials pushed forward as much as possible. Then we can use it for the little project we've been asked to do.'

'Sure,' said the technician as they got back to work preparing the dragonfly drone for another trial.

A contractor had an arrangement with the Sea Hunters to trial it. The technology was cutting edge. The source of the propulsion technology was closely guarded, and the system was patented. The fact that the energy field for propulsion also cloaked it was a bonus. Using self-actuated software they could encode the dragonfly drone just by using the touchpad of symbols and thinking about what it needed to do. By looking at a navigation chart, it could be given a flight polygon and instructions for pausing and carrying out surveillance using thought alone.

While the technicians were looking over the dragonfly drone, Max and Alex walked out of the drone bay and onto the drone deck. It was a clear day and unusually calm.

Almost too calm, thought Alex as they looked to the horizon. He had an ominous feeling, the calm before the storm. Supercells were a real threat out here.

Off to each side of them were the two drone vessels, moving silently through the water, in formation and waiting for further instruction.

'This whole zero-mass propulsion thing, or inertial mass reduction has changed publicly acceptable science,' said Max.

'High-frequency electrical discharge into a counter-rotating polarised electromagnetic field has revolutionised propulsion tech,' said Alex.

'Vibration and resonance,' said Max. 'That's what it's all about I'm sure.'

'It's being able to control the magnitude of effect both vertically and horizontally to arrive at a set of coordinates that has made it workable,' said Alex. 'A scalar plot relying on relative position and nothing else.'

'We can go right back to old Viktor Schauberger and thank him for that,' said Max.

'Interesting story around that man,' said Alex.

'Mimicking nature, naturally occurring vortices and development of electrostatic implosion drives you mean,' said Max.

'Then there was Otis Carr's work,' said Alex. 'He also worked on electrogravitic drives as well. That work all got confiscated.'

'Indeed,' said Max, 'and here we are with some of that tech that has been acquired and developed. Speaking of drones. We need to do some more digging around that research program on the Harvester. These mimic drones I keep hearing about, I mean.'

In the distance, they could hear a humming sound. On the horizon, a patrol drone came into view. It was returning from the daily grind of regular searches for pirate submarine activity in 'the Area.'

Alex and Max walked back into the drone bay. An announcement was made over comms to clear the drone deck and prepare to receive the patrol drone. As they walked to the rear of the drone bay an alarm activated.

'Skimmer requests for assistance,' announced SAI. 'Pirate incident underway.'

'Stay here Alex and oversee drone operations,' said Max. 'I'll deal with this.'

'Right you are,' said Alex.

Max walked off to the SAI console on the bridge and left Alex to deal with the drones. He quickly went up the stairs, through the operations centre and forward to the SAI console.

The duty officer had already pulled up information on the incident and altered course towards the location.

'Sir,' he said as Max walked in. 'It's some distance from us. We may not get there in time to disable the pirate sub and apprehend them.'

'Any details on the incident?' asked Max.

'Apparently, they have been rammed,' he said, 'the Skimmer I mean. Unusual for pirates that just want the nodules. There is some damage to the Skimmer. Propulsion is offline and their communication streamer coupling is damaged.'

'Okay,' said Max. 'Send our drone vessels ahead and set a perimeter polygon. Get a patrol drone in the air when we are five miles out. Prepare an interceptor drone and a breaching pod to deploy and board and assist as required. Get a fast recovery boat ready to launch in case they surface. Alert the medic to prepare for injuries as well. Arm our ARC defensive array.'

'Yes, sir,' he said as Max spouted off a string of commands.

The duty officer quickly organised the response with operations and together they got everything in place.

The outer shields were retracted. Max looked out as the drone vessels on either side picked up speed and deployed their hydrofoils. They took off into the distance.

'Contact operations to coordinate all this. I want those drone vessels to engage the target on arrival,' he said to the duty officer. 'Disable the pirate sub and its drones.'

'Yes, sir,' replied the duty officer as he contacted operations to bring defensive weapons systems online.

'Patrol drone recovered,' announced SAI. 'Dragonfly drone deployed.'

Good, Max thought to himself. Alex is onto it down there. He'll be working with Cam to get that interceptor drone ready and the sea boat as well.

'ARC defensive array armed,' announced SAI.

'I'm going to operations,' said Max. 'Inform me when we are five miles out.'

'Yes, sir,' said the duty officer.

Max had a quick look at the SAI console and the navigation hologram of their position and the assets deployed. He left the SAI console and walked back through to operations. The timing was everything when it came to pirates. Too early and the pirates would likely spot them and get away. Too late and they would miss the pirates altogether. Catching them in the act was key. It was hit and miss in 'the Area'. But ramming a Skimmer was a change in tactics. It also meant the chances of intercepting one was higher given it represented an intent to board.

***

The situation onboard the rammed Skimmer was tense. A drone from the pirate sub had rammed one of the propulsion drive rims. It was offline. The impact had also caused the communication streamer to shear, which was now jammed. They were still watertight.

'Get some slack in that streamer!' yelled the Skimmer operator over comms to the Xtract bay.

'It's sheared and going to rip the coupling and cylinder spool off the superstructure.'

'We're trying,' came the response over comms from the Xtract bay.

'SAI, deploy a repair drone to secure the streamer and extend the cable.'

'Confirmed,' said SAI. 'Deploy repair drone to secure and extend streamer cable.'

The outer hull shields were closed, and the camera system activated.

Outside, the scene was chaotic. Between the pirate sub, its two drones and their Xtract drones it was hard to tell what was going on.

'SAI, position Xtract drones to block pirate drone impact with Skimmer propulsion,' said the Skimmer operator.

'Confirmed,' said SAI. 'Xtracts moving into position.'

'You've got to be kidding me,' said the security and communications officer. 'Look.'

They watched through the camera system. A mini submersible with two people in it could be seen approaching. It raced towards them.

'They're going to try and board us,' said the Skimmer operator. 'Why on earth would they do that? We're a hundred metres down.'

'I'm guessing that since they tried to make us surface and it hasn't worked, boarding is the next option,' said the security and communications officer. 'We can't stop them from entering the topside airlock, but we can delay them.'

'What about using the escape pods? Where are those damn Sea Hunters?' asked the Skimmer operator.

A shudder went through the Skimmer.

They looked through the camera system.

An Xtract drone had blocked the approaching pirate drone trying to ram them. In doing so, it had been knocked back into the Skimmer. It was now motionless.

'Damn it,' said the Skimmer operator. 'Get that Xtract drone back on its docking clamp. I mean SAI, secure disabled Xtract drone and return to docking clap.'

'Confirmed,' said SAI. 'Secure Xtract drone and return to docking clamp.'

Another Xtract drone could be seen securing the disabled one and taking it into the recess and onto a docking clamp.

'We'll bring it through the moon pool later and get a repair drone onto it,' said the Skimmer operator.

It was at that moment two new signatures appeared on the navigation hologram in the centre of the SAI console.

'Sea Hunter drone vessels approaching,' said SAI. 'Ten miles and closing.'

'Still at least fifteen minutes away,' said the Skimmer operator.

As they were watching what was going on through the camera system, the mini-sub turned around and headed back towards the pirate sub.

'Look, they have turned back towards their sub,' said the communications and security officer. 'What's spooked them? Not us, that's for sure. They must have picked up the Sea Hunters. Not enough time, I guess.'

They watched as the mini-sub was recovered. The two drones also returned to the sub and docked on its hull. In no time at all, it was gone. The pirate sub would get away before the Sea Hunter drone vessels arrived.

'SAI, recover the remaining Xtracts,' said the Skimmer operator.

'Confirmed,' said SAI. 'Recovering remaining Xtracts.'

'Get that repair drone to finish fixing the sheared coupling and connection to the spool,' he said over comms to the Xtract bay. 'Confirm what the problem is and the time to repair and recover the rest of the communication streamer. With the damage to the rim drive, we'll have to make the jump to the Harvester from here using the overdrive.'

The Skimmer crew got on with assessing the damage to the rim driven propulsion and the streamer coupling and spool and preparing to make the jump to the Harvester. Once back at the Harvester moon pool, they would then repair and reboot the rim driven propulsion and get it back online.

***

The Sea Hunters had arrived on location. They were too late to do anything about the pirates. The Hunter unit drone vessels had scared them off. They were securing a perimeter around the Skimmers' position. Pursuit of the pirate sub was secondary to securing the safety of the Skimmers and personnel at sea. Since the Skimmer was in distress, pursuing the pirates was not an option.

Max and Alex were now both at the SAI console. The drone vessels, having established a perimeter polygon were now circling both them and the Skimmer below. They were positioned above the damaged Skimmer a hundred meters below. Comms had been established.

'Do you need assistance to get to the Harvester?' asked Max over comms.

'No,' said the Skimmer operator. 'We can make the jump to the Harvester instead of using the rim driven propulsion. We'll repair the damage and bring the rim drive back online once we get there. We can enter the moon pool on just one of the rim drives.'

'Any other damage?' asked Max.

'Just the streamer. It's sheared and the coupling to the spool has been damaged but we can fix it.'

'Right,' said Max over comms. 'We will remain on location until you are gone. On return to the Harvester, I will meet with you for a debrief. I need to file a report on all this.'

Max ended the communication. Turning to look out at the distant horizon he watched as the drone vessels continued to circle their position.

'From what Rick said, I'm guessing that overdrive is going to get a lot more useful given the increase in piracy incidents out here,' said Alex.

'As discussed previously. Why would pirates want to damage a Skimmer?' asked Max.

They both thought for a moment.

'I see two possibilities,' said Max carrying on. 'One being it's not the pirates but a group using the pirates as a cover for some other purpose. Second, that purpose could only be related to either of the two things. Wanting this Xtract tech Rick has discussed with us or that the Skimmer overdrive system has become more highly valued than stealing nodules. Either way, it can't just be the pirates themselves. Something has changed out here.'

'Let's recover the patrol drone and dragonfly drone again and get out of here,' said Alex. 'Once back at the Harvester, we can meet with Lee and Ying Yue and get their thoughts on all this. We also need to contact Rick again and find out more about where the Skimmer program is at. If his people are advancing the Skimmer overdrive program, it has implications for us and for the dragonfly program.'

'Sir,' said the duty officer. 'The Skimmer has made the jump to the Harvester. Pirate sub is long gone, and the location is now clear.'

'Stand down operations,' said Max, 'Recover the patrol drone and dragonfly drone then depart for Harvester,' said Max.

'Yes, sir,' replied the duty officer.

'We'll do our inspections at the Harvester instead of at sea,' said Max. 'As you said Alex, let's also speak with Lee and Ying Yue.'

'SAI,' said Max. 'Request Cam to meet us in the mess.'

'Confirmed,' said SAI. 'Request Cam to meet in the mess.'

'Let's get some food as well,' said Alex.

'Too right,' said Max stretching. 'All this excitement has worked up an appetite.'

They left the duty officer to monitor their transit to the Harvester.

It felt all too convenient, thought Max to himself. The pirates, ramming and boarding attempts. He trusted his gut feeling. Something was not right with all this. *Best guess,* he thought to himself, *is that someone else is using the pirates as a cover to carry out their own agenda. Question is,* he thought, *what is that agenda and what is the outcome they are looking for, whoever it is.*

Chapter 5

Early in the morning, Ngarra's Skimmer made its final approach to the Harvester. They watched through the camera system as the Skimmer moved under the giant hull of the Harvester. Pausing, it started its ascent to the moon pool above.

They left the surrounding marine life behind.

Yellowfin tuna parted.

The giant steel hull swallowed them whole.

Dim lights on the side of the moon pool passed them by as they rose to the surface.

It was always mesmerising to watch.

Like something out of a science fiction movie.

As they broke the surface, a gentle wave slid off the top and circled the moon pool. The Skimmer finally settled, and the docking clamps secured them in place.

The outer hull shields retracted, the camera system deactivated, and they looked out. Jonny, Ngarra and Jesse, watched as the robotic arms activated on each side of them. The first of the Skimmer nodule trays were slowly removed and the offloading process started.

'SAI, request all crew to meet in the rec area for a brief,' said Jesse.

'Confirmed,' said SAI. 'Request all crew to meet for a brief in the rec area.'

'Let's go folks,' said Jonny as he took off his interface lenses and SAI made the announcement. 'Food and some downtime.'

'Who said anything about food,' said Ngarra.

'An army runs on its stomach and so do I,' said Jonny.

'Well, you could certainly run a whole army on what you eat,' said Jesse as she looked him up and down.

Her intense stare was always unnerving. The crew had got used to it, though. They hassled her sometimes about looking like she came straight out of the old Matrix movies from decades ago. And she had a personality to match.

'Harsh,' said Jonny, smiling. 'Now you're starting to sound like Stella. One of her on here is enough.'

Jesse smiled. A cold and calculating smile. It always seemed there was an intent behind it. She still didn't talk much about her background. Despite the crew's best efforts, like Rick back at the Xed Ocean Academy, she remained a bit of an enigma.

'I'll get Connor,' said Jesse moving off to the information hub. 'Meet you lot down there.'

Jonny and Ngarra left the SAI console and walked down to the rec area.

'Strange woman,' said Jonny, as they descended the stairs. 'I might have to start calling her mother.'

'Tell me something I don't know,' said Ngarra, smiling at Jonny's remark. 'But I guess there must be a good reason the Academy picks certain types of personalities for security and communications roles.'

They meet Stella and Chang at the base of the stairs coming up from the Xtract bay below. Together, they walked across to the table and sat down, waiting for Jesse to come down with Connor.

'Well, here we are again,' said Jonny sitting down. His stomach grumbled.

'What was that?' asked Ngarra, smiling and looking Jonny up and down.

'Here they come,' said Stella. She was tempted to say something to wind Jonny up. She resisted the urge.

'Let's make it quick,' said Jonny rubbing his belly and looking at Stella half expecting some sort of smart remark from her.

'Okay, listen up,' said Jesse as she came down the stairs with Connor and they sat down. 'We will spend the night on the accommodation deck.'

'Are you sure?' asked Stella with a worried look on her face.

'This place has got weird lately. An airy silence is around. As if something is going on here and nobody wants to talk about it.'

'A Stella bubble,' said Jonny.

Everyone laughed.

'They're trying to avoid you,' said Jonny, carrying on.

'Always the comedian Jonny boy,' said Stella with a wicked smile on her face.

'Jonny, listen, I'm serious,' said Jesse. 'Stella shut it. Focus guys. This is serious.'

Stella rolled her eyes and the crew quietened down.

Jesse gave her a cold look.

It was their way of coping, Jesse thought to herself, *to make light of a tense situation.* It had got them through some tough times before.

'I will speak with Ying Yue,' said Ngarra carrying on. 'She will surely tell us what's going on.'

'What about Connor's tech?' asked Chang.

'It's in its final stages and ready to roll out. Doesn't it seem weird to you guys that all those threats we had to deal with previously have stopped?'

'It stopped when Sue left though,' said Jonny. 'Maybe it was all about her.'

'And what about the Sea Hunters?' asked Ngarra.

'You're a bit biased when it comes to them, Ngarra,' said Jesse.

'I suppose I am,' said Ngarra with a smile, 'but with good reason, given what they did previously.'

Although it now seemed the Sea Hunters had their backs, Ngarra was still cautious. Nothing was quite what it seemed, and he was the last person that would willingly just go along with whatever he was told. Besides, Jesse knew more than she was letting on.

'It would be naïve to think that a threat no longer exists,' said Jesse as she looked at Ngarra. 'Sue went with Chang's father. That would mean she must still be around. I would like to think she still has some influence. I'm just not sure how. I would guess the PLA Navy is still up to something. Unless, of course, Sue has gone rogue and is carrying out someone else's agenda entirely.'

Chang was listening intently, and his face slowly went red. The crew could see his frustration mounting.

'Hell, she shot my sister!' exclaimed Chang.

'Why would my father even entertain the thought of having her around? Something isn't right with that. Damn him!'

Chang had got himself worked up over all the talk about his sister and their father. He was angry and it showed.

'I'm sure he has his reasons,' said Jesse as she motioned him to relax. 'Ying Yue seems to know what she is doing.'

Chang shook his head and was about ready to get up and storm off.

'Maybe it's her, Ying Yue,' said Jonny. 'I mean whatever is going on that has made things feel weird around here.'

'Damn you!' yelled Chang finally getting up and slamming his fist on the table.

'It's my sister, you nut. She has nothing to do with it!'

'The blind leading the blind,' said Jonny calmly smiling at him.

Chang stood there glaring at him, fists clenched. It looked like he was about to launch himself across the table at Jonny.

'Cut it out, you two, now,' said Ngarra. 'Jonny, that's not called for. Let's not jump to any conclusions until we have talked to them.'

Ngarra looked intently at Jonny and then at Chang.

Jonny shrugged his shoulders. 'Just trying to put forward ideas,' he said.

'Do I have to mother you two and send you to your rooms,' said Jesse.

'I'm out of line,' Jonny said to Chang, 'sorry, mate.'

'I'm not your mate,' said Chang angrily as he reluctantly sat back down, ignoring Jonny.

'Okay everyone,' said Jesse. 'Now that we have our heads about us, let's make our way to the accommodation. I will get in touch with Harvester security and arrange a catch up with Lee and with Ying Yue. She will probably want to see you, Chang.'

Chang nodded his head.

'Sure,' he said, breathing a sigh of relief.

'Okay then, let's get on with it,' said Jesse,

Jesse got up and went to the SAI console. *I hope this lot keeps their cool,* she thought to herself as she went up the stairs to the SAI console. At the SAI console, she spoke to Harvester security over comms. A meeting was arranged over a meal.

In the rec area, the others went and got their overnight bags.

They returned to the rec area and waited.

Jonny helped himself to a snack and gave some to Connor.

Ngarra went and stood at the entrance and waited. He looked out over the gangway and along the moon pools.

Stella motioned Chang to follow her. He shrugged his shoulders and followed reluctantly. Despite his attitude towards women, for some reason, he had grown close to Stella. *Perhaps she reminded him of his mother,* she thought to herself. His attitude towards women had shifted somewhat lately.

They walked forward along the narrow esplanade skirting each side of the enclosed overdrive. They stood and looked out into the distance along the moon pools.

'Do you trust your sister?' asked Stella cautiously.

'What sort of question is that?' asked Chang turning towards her and trying not to get wound up again.

Despite his attitude toward the crew and his anger over the family, she was the one person that he would listen to. Chang had grown to trust Stella.

'Just wondered,' said Stella, gesturing it was no big deal.

'Of course,' replied Chang. 'Why wouldn't I?'

'I'm curious,' said Stella. 'I mean, what would motivate her to be stuck out here for so long working in that lab?'

Stella was intuitive. She felt uneasy around Ying Yue. Not that she would tell Chang that. It was almost as if Ying Yue was pretending to be someone she wasn't. *That calm demeanour hid something deeper,* she thought to herself.

'Dedication to her work,' said Chang. 'She's just like her mother.'

Chang grimaced at the thought and was about to say something more.

'Come on, everyone,' they heard Ngarra say from the gangway. 'We're off. Let's go.'

Snapping out of thoughts about his sister, Chang shrugged his shoulders dismissively at Stella.

'Let's talk about it later then,' said Stella.

'Whatever,' said Chang.

They walked back to the rec area. Jesse had come back down from the SAI console. Everyone was waiting to go, carrying the few things they would need for the night.

Stella and Chang picked up their bags and followed them.

They all walked down the gangway and along the boardwalk.

A Harvester security officer met them and escorted them to the nearest lift that would take them to the accommodation level.

They passed robotic arms that were slowly offloading nodules from Skimmers onto the conveyor.

Along the way, they passed another Skimmer that appeared damaged.

'What happened?' asked Ngarra as they stopped to look. The Harvester security officer insisted they move on.

They could see another crew member from the Skimmer watching as a repair drone worked on the rim driven propulsion.

'Rammed,' he replied. 'Wouldn't believe it, but pirates rammed us. We thought they were even going to board us before the Sea Hunters arrived and scared them off. We made the jump here using the overdrive.'

'Move on,' said the Harvester security officer impatiently.

Jesse nodded her head but decided to ask a few questions anyway.

'Why would they ram you?' asked Jesse, thinking about the brief they had got from the Xed Academy.

'Who knows,' he replied, shrugging his shoulders.

'Let's hope we don't get rammed as well,' said Ngarra as he looked at Jesse.

She motioned that they would talk more about it later. The Harvester security officer was getting impatient with them.

'We're off to accommodation,' said Jesse to the Skimmer crew as they moved off. She looked over at the repair drone working on the rim drive. 'Come see us if you have time. It would be good to know what happened in more detail.'

'Will do,' he said.

Jesse didn't think he would follow up on it. Crew tended to keep to themselves out here. Jesse motioned them to move on before the Harvester security officer started getting physical and pushing them on. They said goodbye and walked over to the lift and entered it.

From a distance, the Harvester security guard stood silently watching their every move.

'Wow, he seemed nervous,' said Stella.

'Who,' said Ngarra, 'the security guard or the crew on the damaged Skimmer?'

'The security guard,' said Stella as the lift closed.

'Holy smoke,' said Jonny as they took the lift. 'It's becoming like the wild west out here lately.'

'Thank god, we have a cowboy such as you to look out for us,' said Stella.

'Too right folks,' replied Jonny. 'Now saddle up and get in behind.'

The others laughed at his antics.

They relaxed and chatted about other things.

Typical Jonny, thought Ngarra. But he was right. The increased pirate activity, the change in behaviour, ramming, the weird silence and feeling about the Harvester each time they came to offload now. Something was not right.

The lift stopped and they exited into the accommodation foyer and walked over to the reception.

***

After checking into their rooms for the night and dropping off the few belongings they had with them, they went to the restaurant for a meal.

'Nice that we aren't sleeping onboard the Skimmer for a change,' said Chang as he sat down with a plate of food. 'The number of times over the last year we have had to stay onboard has sucked.'

'Jonah did say to stay on our Skimmer,' said Jesse as she sat down, 'but given our situation and your sister, we can assume it will be okay. Your sister will be here shortly. And yes, it has been great not being chased around the ocean lately.'

'What about her research?' asked Connor. He had been quiet. Listening intently his mind was racing with thoughts and ideas. Jonny came back with a plate of food for him and also sat down.

'The mimic drones. I was thinking maybe it's so quiet around here because they got it to work. If the system, I mean what if the Harvester was now running everything itself. Wouldn't it be quiet? All anyone would need to do is monitor it all. They wouldn't be in control of anything anymore.'

'What if it wasn't intentional?' asked Chang as they all ate.

'Good point,' said Jesse. 'A lot of assumptions, though. No control sounds like losing control. There's a difference. The law of unintended consequences when it comes to AI technology.'

'Yeah well, you wouldn't want mimic drones to shut humans out of the equation would you,' blurted Jonny with a mouth full of food. 'If what they have created is that infectious surely there would be an off button?'

'Depends on what the intent of it all is,' said Jesse.

'But even the best of intentions when it comes to automation and AI can have unforeseen consequences,' said Stella.

The crew all nodded their heads in agreement.

'Wow, everyone agrees on something for once.' Jonny smirked.

'Don't get used to it,' said Chang.

'Speaking of mimic drones,' said Jesse as she interrupted the conversation before it went sour. 'There she is.'

Ying Yue had walked into the restaurant. Spotting them, she waved and walked over.

They all greeted her. Stella got up and gave her an infectious hug and holding her hands said how great it was to see her again.

'How's the team,' she said as Chang got up, greeted his sister, and grabbed a seat for her. 'I'll get some food and come back.'

While she went and got some food, the others carried on eating.

They discussed the differences between Connor's work and Ying Yue's.

Seeing her walk back over Jesse reminded them not to discuss the details of the technology Connor had developed in front of her.

'How's father?' asked Chang as Ying Yue sat down.

'Are you okay after being shot at?' asked Stella.

'It's been a while but that's a big deal.'

Chang frowned at Stella for interrupting the conversation with his sister.

'Fine to both questions,' she said, smiling softly and motioning to Chang that it was okay.

Stella couldn't help thinking of Ying Yue as the smiling assassin. Ironically, that's what she thought of Sue as well. But now her attention was focused on Ying Yue. She trusted her gut. Something didn't feel right about Ying Yue, but she couldn't put a finger on what it was.

'It seems airily quiet around here lately,' said Stella. 'I mean, besides the accommodation deck it's like a ghost ship.'

'We are very efficient,' said Ying Yue. 'My lab project is well advanced and incorporated into Harvester operations now. Our increase in efficiency is significant.'

'So, the mimic drone program has taken over everything,' said Connor.

'I wouldn't put it that way,' said Ying Yue smiling again. 'It's simply a source code that allows integration across all the assets. It removes the need for independent control. It's an AI that essentially attaches itself to any operating system, replicates itself and links it with every other piece of hardware.'

Connor was listening intently. He wanted to say something, but Jesse motioned him to keep quiet. Ying Yue saw the exchange but said nothing.

'Perhaps a little different to your technology, Connor,' she said, trying to get him to say something.

'Perhaps,' said Connor glumly. *It's dangerous*, he thought to himself. 'My technology is not about creating a collective. Human oversight of Gilgamesh and the red queen sequence is still an integral part of its control. One sphere for each Skimmer.'

Chang was feeling a little grumpy. It felt like they were picking on his sister.

The tension could be felt around the table.

'Come on folks,' said Jonny as he tried to lighten things up. 'You could cut the air with a knife around here.'

Jonny grabbed a knife and waved it in front of them, slicing the air and handing them a piece each. There was laughter all around and the conversation did indeed lighten up.

For a short time, talk turned to family, holidays, and life ashore, but the evening was getting on.

A short time later, Ying Yue stood up.

'I must get going,' she said standing. 'I have things to attend to.'

'Yes,' said Ngarra, 'and Jesse and I still have to meet with Lee about the increase in piracy activity.'

'Chang,' said Ying Yue. 'Let's catch up in the morning before you head off.'

'Okay,' he said in reply.

Ying Yue walked off leaving them to it.

'We are off to see Lee then,' said Ngarra as he stood with Jesse. 'You lot can do as you please. See you in the morning at the usual time.'

Ngarra and Jesse walked out of the restaurant to the foyer. They asked reception to contact security and escort them to operations to meet with Lee.

After a brief conversation over a comms link, the receptionist motioned to a security officer standing in the foyer quietly talking to another officer to come over.

'Follow me,' he said.

Jesse thought he looked a little nervous.

They walked into an elevator and it took them to the operations deck. In silence, they waited until it stopped. Exiting the lift, they followed the security officer and walked through operations.

Ngarra felt uneasy. He looked at Jesse and she nodded.

It was so quiet, Jesse thought to herself. Just a few personnel at their monitoring stations. And even those people stared blankly at the monitoring system in front of them. There didn't seem to be much going on. But the moon pools were as busy as ever. As was the drone deck. Ships still came and went, being loaded out with nodules. Maybe Connor is right, that mimic drone program of Ying Yue's was designed to do exactly what he said, infect and take over everything. It removed the human element from the control of AI.

'Ngarra, Jesse, how are you?' asked Lee as they entered the meeting room.

Ngarra was startled out of his thoughts and almost jumped in surprise. Jesse looked at him and wondered what he was thinking.

'It's so quiet around here given how busy things actually are,' said Ngarra.

The security guard left and stood outside and waited.

'Please, have a seat,' said Lee, ignoring the remark.

He looks a little nervous as well, Jesse thought to herself.

'Have you heard anything about why these pirates have started to ram Skimmers?' asked Ngarra as he sat down.

'No,' said Lee, 'but there is concern that it will have an impact on our offloading schedule for ships. If your crew aren't meeting extraction quotas set by contractors, it has a knock-on effect.'

'Even the Sea Hunters are stretched in dealing with the change in tactics by these pirates,' said Jesse.

'What about that technology of yours?' asked Lee.

'It's rolling out across all Skimmers would surely help. I mean the Xtracts would respond to any such threat wouldn't they?'

'We don't actually know for sure,' said Jesse. *How does he know about the roll-out?* She thought to herself, *or is it just a leading question?*

'In theory, yes,' Jesse continued. 'Because it would compromise competing and being rewarded for nodule extraction and loading the trays. But it hasn't been implemented yet.'

'Interesting. I guess you'd better find out then,' said Lee. 'How does it work?'

'Extraction quotas can still be met,' said Jesse as she ignored his question and quickly changed the subject.

'Of course,' said Lee, noting that she wasn't going to answer the question.

'The Skimmers can also use the overdrive to make the jump to the Harvester if the rim driven propulsion is offline from being rammed,' said Jesse. 'Your quota targets will not be compromised.'

'Nice piece of kit that overdrive,' said Lee. 'A shame it's all tied up with patents and proprietary rights when installed on those Skimmers. Someone obviously had it all in mind when they designed those Skimmers.'

Jesse continued to ignore the leading questions and comments.

'The point being,' said Jesse. 'That on arrival, the lost time at sea and downtime in bringing the rim driven propulsion back online while in the moon pool is compensated for by using the overdrive to make the jump.'

'As in, there is no time or not much time when making the jump,' said Lee, smiling.

They all smiled at the comment.

'Well, not much anyway,' said Jesse. 'Depending on how it's executed.'

Jesse continued to resist the temptation to respond in detail.

'If damaged, do you agree that the Skimmers will need longer in the moon pools to make repairs?' asked Ngarra.

'Of course,' said Lee, 'but that is something our Chief Operations Officer will discuss with Jonah and Rick at your crew monitoring centre and look into. I assume our Chief Operations Officer will speak with them directly. It is fortunate that Chang works for your crew and we have a history now. Given previous circumstances, that is. Otherwise, we would not be having this conversation.'

'We can appreciate that,' said Ngarra, 'and thank you for meeting with us.'

'On that note, I have things that need doing,' said Lee as he stood up. 'I'm not sure I've really helped you with anything.'

'At least, there is a growing awareness of the impact the increase in piracy and change of tactics is having on mining operations in "the Area",' said Ngarra.

Everyone stood up and went to exit the meeting room.

'If indeed it is the same pirates we are dealing with,' said Lee.

A curious comment, thought Jesse as they left, *why would he say that? He is not privy to the briefs we have been given.*

'Operations in "the Area" are going to change in many ways I would think,' said Lee carrying on with his line of thought. 'Even here we are always working towards greater efficiency.'

They thanked Lee for his time and the security officer took them back through operations to the lift and then back to the accommodation deck. The security officer checked in at the reception. Ngarra and Jesse left him and went to their rooms to get some rest. Tomorrow, they would be off again on their next mining run.

Chapter 6

The next morning, before leaving for their mining location, everyone was up early and getting something to eat. The crew were apprehensive about dealing with the increased risk of piracy. They hoped that Connor's technology might somehow remove some of that risk or at least mitigate against it.

'Where's Jonny?' asked Ngarra as they sat eating.

'Have you got that book?' asked Stella, smiling.

'What do you mean?' asked Ngarra, giving her a curious look.

'Where's Wally?' she said.

Everyone laughed.

'Very funny,' said Ngarra. 'Do you all remember that book or various versions of it?'

They all nodded and talked about it. Except Chang. He had no idea what they were all going on about. Stella explained it to him.

Connor looked blankly at them and shrugged his shoulders. He didn't get the joke.

'Sometimes I just don't get you guys,' said Connor as he returned to eating.

'Anyway,' said Stella. 'Jonny boy is still in his cabin in la-la land.'

Stella jumped up, grabbed a cup of water, and raced off.

'No not again, don't you dare,' said Jesse as Stella raced off. 'Remember what happened last time?'

Stella didn't wait to listen.

The rest of them waited for the antics that would follow.

There was some yelling and a playful scream and then they heard running.

'You're dead,' said Jonny as he raced into the rec area close behind Stella. He grabbed her and picked her up, lifting her over his shoulder.

'Put me down, you oaf,' she said laughing.

Chang who did not usually participate in such antics, decided to help.

'Come on, Jonny. Stella, I got you,' he said, walking up to her and quietly pouring a cup of water over her head.

'Chang,' she yelped, trying not to laugh, 'you pooh!'

'Bro, are we mates now?' Jonny laughed.

'Don't get used to it,' said Chang as he went to sit back down.

Jonny let go of Stella.

Without a pause, she grabbed Chang's hand as he turned to go and sit back down. She side-stepped, leapt forward and used her legs to scissor drop Chang.

As they hit the floor, Jonny quickly grabbed both of their legs and lifted them up.

'Put us down,' said Stella as they dangled just off the ground.

'You guys need to lose some weight,' he said, lowering them onto the deck.

Chang went red in the face. A little embarrassed at his predicament.

'Funny guy,' said Stella as she got up and poked his stomach, making a squelching noise.

The others watched and laughed again at the antics.

'Right,' said Ngarra as the laughing subsided. 'Fun's over folks. Let's get this show on the road. We have nodules to mine and trials to run.'

'I'll make sure Gilgamesh is ready to go,' said Connor as he took off to the information hub.

'Connor, get on comms with us in the Xtract bay,' said Stella. 'We need to sync the Xtracts with Gilgamesh and make this red queen thing into a permanent arrangement.'

He nodded his head as he bounded up the stairs. Chang and Stella walked down the stairs to the Xtract bay.

'I won't be far behind,' said Jonny as he raced off to get dressed. He was still in his boxer shorts.

Ngarra and Jesse walked up the stairs behind Connor and into the SAI console.

'SAI, prepare to depart for the mining location,' said Ngarra.

'Confirmed,' said SAI. 'Preparing to depart for the mining location.'

The navigation hologram appeared in the middle of the SAI console. Ngarra entered the new coordinates and they both watched as SAI calculated the course. The outer hull shields were closed and the external camera system activated.

'Sorry about that, folks,' said Jonny as he raced in and put his interface lenses on. He informed Harvester's operations that they were leaving. He scanned the route SAI had projected and made some of his own adjustments.

Watertight bulkheads were all now closed. SAI confirmed that the Skimmer was watertight, and all systems were nominal. Rim driven propulsion was bought online and Ngarra ran some cross-checks with SAI.

'Let's hope we don't have to use the overdrive to outrun these pirates,' said Jesse.

'More like let's hope they don't find us while mining and tethered to the streamer,' said Jonny.

'I kind of hope we do,' said Ngarra. 'Use the overdrive, I mean. We are behind with our trials and Rick is pushing ahead with the testing schedule now.'

'True,' said Stella. 'An excuse to really put it through its paces.'

'Fine by me,' said Jonny. 'Let's tic-tac-toe and show these pirates who's boss.'

Jesse smiled at the analogy and thought about reports in previous decades in the news and media that used that wording to describe what was once coveted zero-mass or interial mass reduction propulsion technology. With the advent of patents and disclosure, that was no longer the case. Public science had been given the injection it needed. The world was becoming a very different place now.

'Skimmer is watertight and all systems nominal,' said SAI.

'Xtracts online, no problems here,' said Stella over comms. 'We have synced with Gilgamesh and the red queen is active.'

'SAI, depart for the mining location,' said Ngarra.

'Confirmed,' said SAI. 'Departing for the mining location.'

The rim driven propulsion powered up.

The docking clamps released them.

They watched what was going on outside through the cameras that projected everything on the screen. The Skimmer slowly submerged into the moon pool. The dimly lit conveyors and robotic arms slowly disappeared.

The water in the moon pool engulfed their Skimmer. Lights shone dimly as they passed them by. They descended and exited out of the bottom of the giant hull.

The Skimmer stopped at a hundred metres depth, paused, orientated itself to its destination and then took off, clearing the Harvester security perimeter.

***

A while later, and in transit to their mining location, the crew took some time to relax.

'Right,' said Jonny, taking his interface lenses off. 'We have a bit of time before arriving at our mining location. I need sustenance,' he said, rubbing his belly again.

'We just had something to eat. You're always eating,' said Ngarra.

'You guys did. I was busy working out,' he joked.

'You had better maintain your well-rounded strength that goes with all that eating,' said Jesse. 'Those pirates will make a nice juicy meal out of you otherwise,' she said smiling.

Jesse's dry sense of humour took a bit of getting used to. At times, her words cut like ice. Other times soothing and reassuring. No wonder they had started referring to her as a mother.

'Are you saying I'm fat?' asked Jonny jokingly.

'I'm offended.' He lifted his arm and tightened his muscles, showing off.

'I'm going to check on Connor,' said Jesse as she waved a dismissive hand at him and walked out of the SAI console. She went down the right-hand side between propulsion and life support towards the information hub.

'Right you are then,' said Ngarra as he shrugged his shoulders at Jonny. 'SAI, retract outer hull shields.'

'Confirmed,' said SAI. 'Retract outer hull shields.'

The camera system turned off and the outer hull shields retracted to reveal the blue-green void of the photic zone in front and above passing them by. Below, the eternal blackness always loomed large, ever waiting to engulf them it seemed.

Ngarra and Jonny walked out of the SAI console and down the stairs to the rec area.

'I'm going forward to think,' said Ngarra as they reached the bottom of the stairs. 'You can be on call for the first watch.'

Jonny nodded his head and went and got some food. Having missed breakfast, he was hungry.

Ngarra turned and walked forward along the narrow esplanade that ran either side of the enclosed overdrive propulsion system. He walked past the enclosed

61

overdrive that stretched up to the SAI console above and to below and forward of the Xtract bay monitoring console.

He looked out into the blue-green void. It was a feeling everyone never got over. Watching the ocean sliding by. It was always surreal. A person could stand there for hours just looking into nothing.

What about these pirates? he thought out loud. *Why had their behaviour changed?* The increasing aggression and damage of Skimmers was an ominous sign that something was going on. And now, suddenly, Rick wants to push ahead with the overdrive trials and complete them. *Are the two related in some way? Does he know something? And why is it so quiet on the Harvester?* The crew in there looked worried; almost frightened.

Ngarra was an intuitive person. He was deeply rooted in his aboriginal culture and entrusted with the oral knowledge of his ancestors and the dreaming. Something was unfolding before him. He could feel it. He was meant to be here at this moment.

Ngarra continued looking out into the blue-green void. He carried on thinking.

These Skimmers seem to have a connection with the dreaming. Something that happened to Australia a long time ago. Hundreds of thousands of years ago. Alcheringa and the Golden One, an ancient creator, an ancestor known to indigenous Australians; the star people on earth. He felt it pull. A connection with an arrival from the stars. Australites, the tektite mineral that looked like a button. It was shaped from molten glass as it entered the atmosphere. And these Skimmers and their overdrives. Past, present, and future seemed to come together. *What did it all mean? The dreaming?*

Ngarra was now totally lost in thought about the dreaming. He jumped as SAI made an announcement and a proximity alarm activated.

'Subsurface vessel detected,' said SAI.

'SAI, confirm, does it have a signature?' asked Ngarra.

'Confirmed, no identified signature,' said SAI.

Probably a pirate sub, he thought to himself as he raced off towards the SAI console.

'SAI, open Skimmer wide comms,' he said on the way.

'Confirmed,' said SAI. 'Skimmer wide comms open.'

He passed Jonny in the rec area. Seeing Ngarra in a rush, Jonny got up and quickly followed him up to the SAI console.

'Everyone, pirate sub detected. Pirate sub detected. Take up your positions.'

Ngarra raced into the SAI console with Jonny not far behind him. Jesse came rushing in from the information hub.

'SAI, arm ARC array. Confirm Skimmer is watertight. Close outer hull shields. Activate Xtracts.'

'Confirmed,' said SAI. 'ARC array armed, Skimmer is watertight, outer hull shields closing, Xtracts activated.'

'Stella, Chang,' said Ngarra over open comms. 'Cross-check Xtract status and confirm sync with Gilgamesh.'

'SAI, urgent request to Xed Skimmer crew monitoring to speak with Jonah and Rick.'

'Confirmed,' said SAI. 'Eel drone and grid buoy proximity nominal. Live feed available.'

A pause followed and then the message board activated. A duty officer appeared.

'We picked up your proximity alarm,' said the duty officer. 'Your crew vitals have spiked.'

'A pirate sub is closing us,' said Jesse. 'Get Jonah and Rick.'

'Requesting them now,' replied the duty officer.

Rick was already in the complex and came over to the monitoring station.

'Transfer this to the main screen,' he said to the duty officer as Jesse watched on.

'Will do, sir,' Jesse heard the duty officer reply.

'What's your situation?' asked Rick.

'Unidentified signature detected and closing us. We are assuming it is a pirate sub. We have powered up the Xtracts and ARC array to defend ourselves.'

'As you know their tactics have changed,' said Rick. 'They will likely try to damage and board you.'

'We can slow and launch the Xtracts and use the ARC array and torpedoes,' said Jonny, looking over Jesse's shoulder.

'No,' said Rick.

'You can't compromise your mining operation,' said Jonah breathing heavily as she appeared on camera. 'I was out in the sim centre and just got here.'

'We can handle it,' said Ngarra.

'No,' said Rick. 'You must use the overdrive and disappear. You need to get on with mining and not get caught up in all this.'

'The pirate ship is within ARC torpedo range,' said Jonny.

'Proximity alert. Three unidentified signatures detected,' said SAI.

'Damn it,' said Ngarra as he went to use open comms. 'They have launched their two drones. Jonny, get SAI to slow the Skimmer, Stella deploy six of our Xtracts, and Connor make sure Gilgamesh has control.'

'You need to get out of there,' said Rick as he watched what was going on. 'Use the overdrive!'

'No, this is an opportunity to run Gilgamesh,' said Ngarra. 'The Xtracts will react to the threat posed to their power source from the Skimmer. This red queen thing Connor has developed is permanent now.'

'It's not the time,' said Jonah. 'You need to get to your mining location. The Sea Hunters will have picked up your proximity alarm anyway. Doing it on-site is another story. Not in transit.'

'Confirmed Sea Hunters have been notified,' said the duty officer. 'They are too far away to be there in time.'

'Okay, okay,' said Ngarra with a sigh. 'Stella, stand down on the Xtracts.'

'Pirate drone inbound,' SAI announced. 'Course and speed constant, impact imminent.'

'Damn it,' said Ngarra. 'Jonny use the ARC defensive array. Try and knock it out.'

'SAI,' said Jonny. 'Target pirate drone with ARC array.'

'SAI, initialise overdrive,' said Jesse. 'Arrival location is the mine coordinates.'

'Now?' questioned Ngarra.

'My call,' said Jesse.

'Okay, okay,' said Ngarra, 'but we haven't followed protocol. We'll get overspeed on the rim drive powertrain.'

'No time,' said Jesse. 'Reboot and calibrate at the Harvester.'

'Good and do it now,' said Rick over comms. 'Get out of there before anything happens. We will talk later.'

The message board went blank.

'Overdrive initialised,' said SAI. 'Energy field nominal, inertia compensation and mass reduction confirmed, arrival coordinates confirmed, frequency discharge imminent.'

A hologram showed the countdown as the capacitor discharge ring around the base reached the correct frequency for electrical discharge. Below, the semiconductor ring-spun the mercury plasma vortex, which had ionised. A massive polarised electromagnetic field was generated. The capacitor ring would discharge into it at a high frequency from the direction of the location coordinates. Opposite was another tube that would discharge at an even higher frequency, compensating for inertia. Relative to their surroundings their mass would be reduced or cancelled. At the correct intensity and duration of discharge, they would literally 'bounce' to their location coordinates. The extreme acceleration would result, but the crew wouldn't feel a thing.

A shudder was felt through the Skimmer.

'System disruption,' said SAI. 'Recovery at eighty percent.'

'Damn it,' said Jonny. 'An indirect hit. Pirate drone still inbound.'

'Get us out of here,' said Jesse. 'Now!'

'SAI, execute discharge,' said Ngarra.

'Confirmed,' said SAI. 'Proceed with discharge.'

'Arriving at mining coordinates shortly,' said Ngarra.

The crew watched the navigation hologram and looked outside through the camera system as they made the bounce. The outer hull shields had been closed due to the piracy threat.

Everything around them seemed to turn into a blur of waves. It was quite disorientating to watch. For a brief period, it all rushed past them. Then for a moment nothing, then the blue-green void and the black depths below reappeared.

'At mining coordinates,' announced SAI. 'Overdrive nominal. Rim driven propulsion drive is suboptimal. Powertrain overspeed.'

'Man, I would still like to get a look and know more about how that thing actually works,' said Jonny.

'We can discuss it more later,' said Jesse. 'Focus.'

'Eyes on, Jonny, and monitor SAI's approach,' said Ngarra. 'SAI, move into position and deploy the communication streamer.'

'Confirmed,' said SAI. 'Move into position and deploy communication streamer.'

'Stella and Chang,' said Ngarra over comms. 'Activate Xtracts and prepare to deploy to the seabed.'

'Roger that,' said Stella over comms. 'Let's hope there aren't any pirates in the vicinity of our mining operation. I want to know more about this overdrive too.'

'Later folks,' said Jesse. 'Right. Once those Xtracts are deployed, let's all meet in the rec area for a debrief.'

'SAI, retract outer hull shields,' said Ngarra.

They watched as the camera system deactivated and the outer hull shields opened. Outside, they looked down either side of the Skimmer as it made a slow flat turn. SAI scanned the location as the Skimmer straightened up and made its final approach. Coming to a stop the communication streamer was deployed and started its descent to the depths below.

Jonny took his interface lenses off and looked outside as well.

'Always love watching those Xtracts power up,' he said. 'When the pilot lights come on, it looks like a Christmas tree out there. Bets on for which one goes first this time.'

They watched as the rows of lights lit up along each recess. The crew had their bets on which Xtract would detach first. As usual, they had got SAI to randomise detachment. The idea had spread amongst the crew and provided for ongoing entertainment within and between the Skimmer crew.

'Yes! Number five is alive and in the bag,' said Jonny with a pump of his fist.

'Bugger,' said Stella over open comms. 'That puts you in the lead.'

One by one, the Xtracts moved slowly over the Skimmer wings and nodule trays. Pausing briefly off the edge of each Skimmer wing, they slowly descended alongside the communication streamer to the depths below. In a few hours, they would start reappearing with their first load of nodules. Everyone was keen to see how Connor's new technology would work. Gilgamesh, red queen and the Xtracts.

Chapter 7

In the rec area, Ngarra's crew were in a heated discussion about the potential for Connor's technology to deal with the pirates if they got caught out during a mining operation. The Xed Academy wanted to roll it out across all Skimmers, but Chang was adamant that it still wasn't a proven technology.

'If pirates are encountered when the streamer is deployed,' said Connor. 'The Xtracts will perceive them as a threat and respond. An interruption to competing to mine nodules and gain an advantage over each other in delivering them to the Skimmer in return for power will be perceived as a threat.'

'But you don't know that for sure,' said Chang. 'A bunch of simulations and a few of your red queen trials have been used to accelerate learning. It's still like a child.'

'But it works,' said Connor, getting up and walking around, waving his arms in the air. 'Gilgamesh is designed to be non-central. It's like a mesh cast over the Xtracts. Each Xtract learns from the other through competition. Every time and over multiple iterations. Gilgamesh uses the red queen to continually run iterations and permutations.'

'So, during an encounter,' said Stella, 'what you are saying is that if one Xtract does something that decreases the probability of maintaining optimal power then every other Xtract learns from that and together they each adjust to try and gain an advantage.'

'Sort of,' said Connor, 'each Xtracts knows that the more nodules it provides to the Skimmer, the more energy or power they will get in return. If something gets in the way of that they will respond, learn, and adapt. I'm just not sure how.'

'Like learning on the run,' said Jonny. 'You have just provided a framework. Gilgamesh is the frame and the red queen is the tool. So, the actions of each Xtract is learnt from. It is then passed to all others as either a decrease or an increase in maximising the opportunity to get more power from the Skimmer and collect more nodules.'

'Pretty much,' said Connor. 'I just help the process by injecting scenarios into Gilgamesh and altering parameters when there are not any real-life ones to learn from. Like the squid.'

'Makes sense,' said Ngarra. 'I guess we will see how that goes when we encounter pirates.'

'So ultimately we can lose the communication streamer altogether then,' said Jesse, 'but that isn't going to happen anytime soon. It's a contractual requirement and out of our control at present.'

'Well, according to you,' said Chang, 'Rick has other plans for the Skimmers and all this testing of the overdrives that have been installed on them.'

'Speaking of that,' said Jonny, 'so is this overdrive like a fusion reactor?' asked Jonny.

'Well, not really,' said Jesse. 'The source of power runs the magnetic semiconductor plate, capacitor ring and drive cooling system. It could be provided in any number of ways. A micro-reactor, for example. But no fusion occurs in the gas phase of the mercury vortex. The plasma is monomeric but magnetically confined. It's the electrical conductivity of the plasma that allows it to be contained through interaction with a magnetic field. In a vortex, the inward magnetic pressure offsets the huge pressure of the plasma pushing outwards. A lot of physics and thought behind understanding exactly how and why it works, though. A discussion for another time.'

'That just contains it though,' said Stella. 'How does it generate this field around us that allows us to bounce or jump? I mean, relative to what's around us, how do we have zero-mass? We still actually have mass, don't we?'

'I think it's because when an electric pulse is discharged into the mercury plasma vortex at a very high-frequency mass is cancelled relative to our surroundings,' said Jesse. 'Sound or extreme frequency and vibration carries mass. It's like we have our own repulsive energy field. Like gravity is repulsive.'

'So, the mercury plasma generates this field and the discharge into it cancels our mass relative to our surroundings by carrying it,' said Stella.

'Something like that,' said Jesse. 'Think of it as a sound wave carrying mass. Relative to our surroundings we have either reduced or near zero-mass because of this high frequency vibrating energy field that is generated. An observer just sees us at the start and end of a bounce over a distance. An observer just sees a rapid and coloured blur in between as we move.'

'So, what is it about mercury then,' said Jonny. 'Why use mercury?'

'I know,' said Stella. 'It's a poor conductor of heat. It's also a mild electrical conductor and has a low boiling point of just three hundred and fifty-six degrees. It's a low-temperature plasma and doesn't react with the tiled iron containment and shielding.'

'Yes, and possible because it's not magnetic,' said Jesse. 'I think it is all about the interaction between an electric current at a very high frequency and the generation of a polarised energy field. Perhaps two opposing currents pass through the mercury. The current from the spinning magnetic semiconductor flows through the ionised mercury plasma from the centre of the inward spiralling vortex to its edge. The discharge current moves across it perpendicular to the direction of this field. It can be orientated to the arrival coordinates for making the jump. It has both a vertical and a horizontal counter-rotating component.'

Jesse looked at the crew. They were still a little confused. They had had many conversations about how the overdrive drive worked. Each time, they seemed to understand a little more about it all. They had attended the classes at Xed Academy on all this. *She was still getting her head around it,* she thought to herself. The training at the academy was one thing but having intimate knowledge of its workings and the physics behind it all took time to understand.

'Yeah but what is it about mercury that allows that to happen,' said Ngarra. 'I mean at the atomic level? I'm curious, that's all.'

Jesse thought about it some more.

'I think it goes something like this,' she said, 'there are significant relativistic effects for atoms with large atomic masses. So, when an electron spins there is an increase in mass. This means that for mercury there is a contraction in the outer electron shell. It is a filled shell and because of this very stable as a gas or plasma. It's almost like being a noble gas such as argon. As a plasma, mercury is stable and generates an enormous amount of energy. So, a huge change in mass and thus charge occurs from a massive change in electron spin. Electrons are spun out of their orbits.'

'So,' said Stella. 'An inward spiralling vortex combined with an outward spiralling current generated from stripping electrons from atoms by the magnetic semiconductor plate at its base generates a powerful electromagnetic field. The high-frequency discharge across it from the capacitor ring can is then used to essentially carry the mass of the Skimmer within this field. Relative to our surroundings we have reduced our mass.'

'Sort of,' said Jesse. 'I'm still getting my head around it all by myself.'

'We don't get squashed like a bug on a windscreen then,' said Jonny, 'No mass equals no inertia. And to make sure, we discharge an even higher frequency opposite to the direction of travel. Like bouncing a bug off a wall then. Without squashing it I mean.'

Jonny had a wicked grin on his face.

He got up and raced across the rec area and flattened himself against the bulkhead like a flapping butterfly. Everyone laughed.

'I've had enough of all this mechanics and physics of overdrives,' said Jonny as he flapped around against the bulkhead. 'My head is spinning.'

Everyone laughed at him again.

'What?' he asked, looking confused.

'Spinning,' said Stella as she laughed at him. 'Electrons, shells, and an increase in mass. You certainly have a lot of that, mass I mean.'

Everyone laughed again.

Jonny raced over and was going to pick Stella up and hang her upside down again.

'Jonny, enough,' said Ngarra. 'Let's eat. All this talk about the overdrive is doing my head in.'

Ngarra, as usual, was impatient to get on with things. The tendency to lose focus over extended periods of concentration on one task was linked back to the problems he had with his ADHD. He preferred to leave the detailed science and engineering to the others.

'Best thing you've said so far today,' said Jonny.

The crew went and got some food and the conversation turned to more light-hearted topics.

***

At the Xed Academy, Rick was informed by the duty officer that Ngarra's crew had got away from the pirates. They had successfully used the overdrive but overspeed on the powertrain for the rim drive had caused some problems.

He had a meeting with Jonah before they both appeared before the Council to discuss increasing concerns about piracy.

Rick left the crew monitoring and communication complex and walked through the sim centre and learning hub and out onto the campus grounds.

It was busy as usual.

Students were coming and going from the sim centre. Lost in thought, he made his way to the admin building and up to Jonah's office.

On his way, he kept thinking.

As requested by his people, he had pushed forward the Skimmer overdrive trials. Between Connor's technology, the change in piracy behaviour and concerns about what GlobeCorpMining was up to out at that Harvester his people wanted to move ahead with the next phase. The Cygnus project was the goal but what would Jonah think about it all? They still had to meet contractor requirements for crewing the Skimmers and extracting nodules.

Rick entered the admin building and walked through the large foyer into the wide-open central space that stretched from the floor to the glass-covered roof high above.

He walked over to the lift and took it up to Jonah's office.

Exiting, he walked along the mezzanine and looked out over the wide-open space and down to the floor below. From each level, people were coming and going. Above and through the glass, he saw taxi drones come and go from the drone port on the roof.

Arriving at Jonah's office he entered and said hi to her secretary. She got up and walked through with him to Jonah's office. She was standing with a coffee in hand and looking out over the campus.

'They got away okay,' said Rick as he walked up to her.

Her secretary went and got Rick a coffee as well.

'So I hear,' she replied. 'This change in piracy behaviour is concerning. I don't want my crew to be hurt just because of a few nodules.'

'I think it's more than that,' said Rick. 'As I said. We need to push forward with the overdrive trials and finish them.'

'We have the Council meeting shortly,' said Jonah. 'Questions will be asked.'

'We have other plans for the Skimmers,' said Rick. 'Between my people and the Skimmer contractors and owners, there is a significant push to move to the next phase.'

'But we still have an obligation to GlobeCorpMining to deliver nodules,' said Jonah.

'I'm not saying we compromise our source of funding,' said Rick, 'but we need to push ahead with all this. The Skimmer contractors have agreed. Besides, it will counter the interruptions to meeting extraction targets from the increasingly aggressive behaviour of the pirates.'

'True,' said Jonah. 'The overdrive being a permanent feature will make a big difference.'

'And from what Connor has told us,' said Rick, 'the technology for the Xtracts is in its final stages. That can only help us in moving to the next phase.'

'It's time for the Council meeting,' said her secretary as she walked over with Rick's coffee.

'Right, let's go in then,' said Jonah.

They walked through to the meeting room and stood around the circle waiting for the Council members to appear.

Members appeared on either side of them. An image of each was projected.

The usual members were present.

'Greetings everyone,' said Jonah.

'Here we are again,' said Rick.

'Indeed,' said the Council member for Australia. 'Lately, your reports seem to indicate a growing concern about piracy activity in "the Area".'

'Not only that,' said the member of the UAE. 'It's the change in behaviour. Intentional damage of Skimmers and attempts to board them.'

'Tactics have definitely changed,' said Rick.

'I am concerned for our crew,' said Jonah. 'We need more assurance that security in "the Area" is up to the task.'

'But why damage Skimmers?' asked the member for Oceania.

'It isn't sustainable if all these pirates want is access to an ongoing supply of nodules that they can steal while the streamer is deployed. Maybe their interests have changed.'

'What if the piracy operation has been infiltrated by a third party with another agenda?' asked the member for Australia.

'Exactly,' said Rick. 'It seems technology may be the new commodity here. I mean either Connor's Xtract technology or perhaps even the overdrive propulsion system. Given the situation, my people are moving the trials and testing forward.'

'What about Chang's father? The Chief Operations Officer of GlobeCorpMining,' said another member. 'Maybe he is behind it.'

'I doubt it,' said Jonah. 'Too much to lose and besides, he always plays the long game.'

'I agree,' said Rick, 'but he did take Sue with him after that incident on the Harvester. She shot his daughter Ying Yue. We don't know what happened to Sue after that. My guess is that somehow she is tied up in all this.'

'Excellent point,' said the member for the UAE. 'It makes sense that the PLA Navy would have an agenda regarding this technology.'

'If you are correct,' said the member for Australia. 'Then we need to be careful.'

'We need to put my crew first,' said Jonah. 'I can appreciate the involvement in the overdrive trials and adoption of Connor's technology across the crew, but they aren't soldiers, they're civilians and young ones at that.'

'By bringing forward the overdrive trials,' said Rick. 'We mitigate that risk. It means the crew can always get away.'

'Not when they are tethered to the communication streamer,' said Jonah.

'So, let's move on adopting Connor's Xtract technology across all Skimmers then,' said the member for Australia. 'We can keep the streamer as a backup. It only gets deployed if the technology is compromised.'

'That could do it,' said Jonah.

This is great, Rick thought to himself. Accelerating both the Xtract technology and overdrive program will please his people immensely. He could bring the next phase forward out there in that vast expanse of ocean. Preparation for their goal.

The other Council members present discussed what was going on and all agreed that it was the best way forward. A brief discussion also followed about how to implement it.

'What about the Skimmer contractors?' asked one of the other Council members.

'They have nodule extraction targets to meet with those Skimmers. Some are leased out and some are owned by them.'

'It's a condition of using them and they are aware of the potential here,' said Rick. 'They are onboard with what we want to do. They signed up to the fact that a research program was part of the deal. It can only benefit them in the long run.'

'I still think my crew are being put second in all this,' said Jonah. 'If someone dies, it will not look good for the Xed and the Ocean Academy at all.'

The Council discussed the implications of a fatality and how they might overcome it.

While they were doing this, Jonah took a moment to think.

Rick has an entirely different agenda when it comes to the ocean Academy Skimmer crewing program, she thought to herself, *he still wants to split it out as a separate entity. Maybe he is right and that would protect my life's work and my crew. One degree of separation.*

She thought about it some more while the others were discussing the crewing program.

'It's agreed then,' said Rick as everyone finished talking and quietened down. 'We will adopt the approach suggested regarding this Xtract technology of Connor's. And as I said, bring forward the overdrive trials. It will mitigate against the increased risk of piracy in "the Area" given their change in tactics. Irrespective of who's behind it all, which will protect the crew for now. I will do some digging and see what I come up with regarding the thought that this Sue is somehow involved in all this.'

The Council members all nodded and said goodbye. Their images disappeared, and Rick and Jonah were left standing alone again. A brief discussion followed between them about the crew and the required timings to implement what was needed.

Rick left and returned to the sim centre to complete other work.

'Are you okay?' Jonah's secretary asked after Rick had left.

'I'm concerned,' said Jonah. 'Nothing is certain. Except that mining must continue regardless of anything. For that to happen, no one will compromise their ability to operate in "the Area". That, at least, is the overriding factor in all this. We need to measure any agenda against it that others might have and determine what the likely outcome might be.'

'How do you protect what you have built here,' said her secretary. 'I mean, it's an educational institute linked to the needs of industry.'

'By remaining transparent and open and sticking to our mandate,' said Jonah. 'No secrets. If we remain in the public eye, we can't be touched.'

'That doesn't mean things won't change,' said her secretary.

'No, it doesn't,' said Jonah, 'but at least whatever the outcome, we can continue our work.'

The conversation carried on. Jonah and her secretary discussed how to keep Xed viable and focussed on what it was originally set up to achieve.

Perhaps, she thought to herself, *Rick was right about separating the crewing program from all this.* The danger was though that she would lose control of something she had poured her heart and mind into to set up. And what about Chang's father and GlobeCorpMining? Time would tell.

Chapter 8

Rick was in crew monitoring with the duty officer in charge and had called Jonah in to discuss a developing supercell in detail. They were in the meeting room on the mezzanine. Looking out through the glass over the floor below at the main displays on the wall in front it showed projections of a developing supercell.

'We have enough time for all current Skimmers on mining runs to return to the Skimmer and offload,' said Rick. 'Then we get them to return to a location as one group; not spread out across mining tenements.'

'What about the streamer?' asked the duty officer in charge.

'Some will try and deploy it even though they are not meant to during a supercell. If something went wrong and pirates were around and it shears off, we will be in for a large Xtract recovery bill from the contractors.'

'I wish we had been a little further ahead in adopting Connor's technology across all Skimmers,' said Jonah. 'Then it wouldn't matter. The Xtracts would find their own way to and from the Skimmer. They wouldn't need an Xtract communication streamer.'

'Let's get through this supercell first,' said Rick. 'Then we can move to the next phase. Same goes for the overdrive trials we have brought forward due to this piracy issue.'

'If you look at the projections of the supercell,' said Rick as he used the console in the meeting room to manipulate the main display, 'you will see that we can get the Skimmers to mine here,' he said pointing his finger at the screen in the meeting room. 'We can spread them out across this particular tenement in "the Area" until it has passed.' He plotted a polygon and outlined the location they were talking about. 'I will inform Max so the Sea Hunters can make plans to support the operation.'

'We need to brief the crew again,' said Jonah.

'The duty officer in charge will do it,' said Rick.

The duty officer nodded in response.

'Lockdown protocol,' said Jonah to the duty officers on the floor below over comms.

The duty officer looked up and where they were standing and nodded. They had been looking at the main screen and images being displayed by Rick from the meeting room above.

'Skimmers must finish their mining run and return to the location and coordinates designated by us,' said Rick over comms. 'They must hold off deploying the streamer or Xtracts until further notice.'

'You know that some will still carry on with mining,' said the duty officer in charge. 'They will take the risk.'

'Of course,' said Jonah, 'but the issue is piracy.'

'The real concern,' said Rick, 'is that with the change in tactics any attempt to ram and board a Skimmer during a supercell could very well shear off the streamer?'

'Any significant damage that compromises life support systems and a Skimmer would be forced to surface,' said Jonah. 'The SAI would prioritise the safety of human life.'

'We need to assume that there will be a piracy incident during this supercell,' said Rick. 'Just by grouping them together, we are inviting trouble. As indicated, I will speak with Max about all this and where we are going to group the Skimmers.'

'What about the overdrive?' asked Jonah.

'As we discussed at the Council meeting, The Skimmer crew could just use that to get away.'

'Assuming they have not deployed their streamer,' said Rick. 'Like we discussed previously, that is the problem.'

'Damn it,' said Jonah as she thought about it all. 'As much as we insist, some of our crew are going to use it aren't they?'

'You know the Skimmer crew better than anyone,' said Rick. 'They are young, enthusiastic and ambitious. It will happen.'

'So, we wait for the inevitable then and hope we have everything in place to deal with it,' said Jonah. 'Sounds like a recipe for disaster.'

'The Skimmer SAI will not compromise life support systems no matter what,' said Rick. 'Preservation of human life is its first or primary objective no matter what. A Skimmer will surface in the middle of that supercell if needed. The crew cannot override that.'

'That leaves us with the escape pods then,' said the duty officer in charge. He had been listening carefully to the conversation.

'Good point,' said Rick as he looked across the floor below at the others on duty at their stations. 'The goal here is making sure the crew stay down and don't surface. If they use the escape pods, another Skimmer can pick them up through the moon pool.'

'So, a number of different outcomes to think about,' said Jonah with a sigh.

'Not really,' said Rick. 'It still boils down to just a few realistic possibilities. We need to be prepared for them, for both the Skimmers and the Sea Hunters' response.'

'More specifically,' said Jonah. 'What if this change in piracy tactics is all about the overdrive technology? Or worse, what if it's about Connor's technology or even both?'

'Two things are important here,' said Rick. 'Either these so-called pirates want to steal an entire Skimmer, or they just want to take Connor's technology for themselves. Either way, it's a perfect opportunity to try. Right in the middle of a supercell in "the Area".'

'We have to hope that the Sea Hunters will be in a position to deter such a move then,' said Jonah.

'Right,' said Rick. 'This is the brief I want you to give to all Skimmers,' he said to the duty officer in charge.

Rick outlined in detail the brief to go out to all Skimmers in 'the Area'. The duty officer listened and then left. He went back down to the main floor area and briefed his duty team. They set about briefing all Skimmer crew on what was to happen.

'Let's contact Ngarra and Jesse directly,' said Jonah. 'Given Connor's technology that is onboard I want to talk with them about all this.'

'Good idea,' said Rick as they left the mezzanine and walked down the stairs to the floor below.

Rick got another duty officer at a workstation to contact Ngarra's skimmer. A pause followed as eel drone and grid buoy proximity was checked. A live feed was available, and the message board opened.

'Hi, Rick, Jonah,' said Jesse as her image appeared. 'All good here. We are at our next mining location. We will be making our run to the Harvester in the morning.'

'Hi,' said Rick. 'I take it you are aware of the supercell forming in the convergence zone?'

'Yes,' said Jesse. 'We have time to return and offload at the Harvester though. We will then proceed to our next location.'

'Change of plans,' said Rick. 'We have informed the Harvester and another brief is going out to all crew as we speak.'

'We have major concerns about piracy and the potential for something to go very wrong during this supercell,' said Jonah.

'I want all Skimmers working closer together for the next run,' said Rick. 'It makes it easier for the Sea Hunters to be on scene if something goes wrong.'

'We have the overdrive,' said Jesse, 'and you have brought forward the trials.'

'Not if you are tethered and then rammed and disabled,' said Rick.

'Skimmers aren't supposed to be tethered during a supercell. They are meant to hold positions and not deploy Xtracts,' said Ngarra.

'Yes, but not everyone does it and we have been lenient on that to meet contractor requirements,' said Rick.

Ngarra smiled and looked at Jesse. Even they had, at times, carried on mining during a supercell. It was an unspoken rule and they would likely try this time as well. The risk being that if something went wrong and the streamer sheared off, they would lose the Xtracts.

'The Sea Hunters will likely deploy interceptors during the supercell,' said Rick. 'They will be able to patrol the general area we are grouping Skimmers in for this. The Hunter vessels themselves will standoff. They will be out of the main path of the supercell.'

'It's a shame we are not adopting Connor's technology,' said Ngarra. 'I mean deploying the sphere. Deploying Gilgamesh and the red queen across all Skimmers. We wouldn't need the communication streamer then. It would just be used for monitoring them when needed.'

'That thing Connor has constructed with SAI, Gilgamesh as he calls it, is ready, I assume,' said Rick. 'To be safe though, the streamer still has to be used. However, if for some reason you need to deploy Xtracts and you must dump the streamer, they will find their own way back if something goes wrong. My advice though is to hold the position in lockdown as protocol dictates.'

'And if there is a piracy incident, we use the overdrive,' said Jesse.

'Yes, given the streamer should not have been deployed,' said Rick knowing full well they would likely deploy it and do some mining. 'You can still use the overdrive to reach extreme speeds without making the jump. Inertia compensation will kick in, regardless.'

'Ha, it wasn't that long ago we did that,' said Ngarra. 'To escape I mean. Remember the Sea Hunters chasing us down during that incident?'

Rick smiled or at least tried to. It looked like more of a grimace. *Different situation,* he thought to himself. Things have moved on. His people also wanted more disclosure about what was really going on. *In time,* he thought to himself. Connor's technology had been timely though, and they, his people, were very interested in its integration with the project. Project Cygnus.

'Yes,' said Rick as he looked at Jonah in response to Ngarra's comment, 'but let's focus on what is happening now. If you can get back to the Harvester sooner, then go. Better for you to be in position and holding out while this supercell passes through "the Area" than delayed.'

'Will do,' said Jesse. 'That briefing to all the crew is coming through to us now. We will talk again.'

The screen went blank.

'Right,' said Jonah. 'I'm heading back to my office to catch up on some work before the day gets on too much.'

'I've got work to do here,' said Rick. 'Then I need to check over training schedules at the sim centre.'

'Talk later then,' said Jonah as she walked off.

Jonah exited the crew monitoring and communication complex and headed out through the sim centre and learning hub and exited the building. It was busy. Students were coming and going, moving between the Xed and the Ocean Academy.

The more she thought about it the more she thought that maybe Rick was right. She continued thinking about it as she walked along the path to the admin building.

Separating out the Skimmer crew program and the sim centre could be the right move, she thought to herself, *but he's still not telling me everything. And what would GlobeCorpMining think of it all? Was this all about protecting the program and its further development from too much influence by the Chinese or was it something else entirely?*

Jonah entered the admin centre and walked through to the centre of the building. Looking up she could see the glass dome high above. A few drones flew over it coming and going from the drone port above. Above her and around the sides, people were walking along the mezzanine between offices. She walked over to one side and entered a lift, taking her to the level her office was on.

In the lift as it rose, a sense of foreboding flooded her body and she shivered. *The calm before the storm,* she thought to herself.

'In more ways than one,' she said out loud to herself.

She smiled to herself as the lift stopped and she exited. *Why is it that I feel a bit helpless in all this?* she thought, *as if nothing I can do is going to change what is going to happen or the outcome of all this. The universe wants this to happen.* What exactly 'all this' had, still eluded her.

Jonah entered her office and her secretary got up and made her a coffee. Her secretary knew her well and anticipated she would want a coffee.

'Always reading my mind,' said Jonah.

'Of course,' she replied, 'I think I've been here too long.'

'Never,' said Jonah, smiling. 'Get yourself one.'

'Oh, I'm ahead of you on that count today,' she replied.

Jonah smiled and watched her return to her desk. She looked out over the campus and the distant horizon. *What is going on out there?* she thought to herself. The complicating thing in all this was Chang's family connections and her relationship with Chang's father as Chief Operations Officer of GlobeCorpMining. They were significant funders of the Skimmer crewing program as well. And then there is the link between Connor's technology and Chang's sisters' work. Something didn't seem right with it all. Rick may worry about his overdrive trials but perhaps it was bigger than that. Her concern was holding onto a technology that guaranteed the future success of the Xed and the Ocean Academy crewing program.

Jonah's thoughts continued to wander, hoping that amidst all the growing chaos a solution to everything would present itself.

Chapter 9

The Sea Hunters had arrived at the Harvester to do some Skimmer inspections. The Hunter unit consisting of the main ship and its two drone vessels cleared the Harvester security perimeter and moved into position. Ngarra's Skimmer had already left the Harvester for their mining location.

While the team carried out inspections of Skimmers, Max and Alex had arranged to meet with Lee about piracy in 'the Area'. Alex and Max were in the drone bay getting ready to fly across to the Harvester in a patrol drone. Cam and his inspection team would take another drone across.

Hunter Command had also told them to pay more attention to the overdrive logs. Change was afoot and no one quite knew what was going on.

'Right Cam,' said Max as they prepared to leave. 'Let's get your inspection team in a patrol drone. We will take another. You stay onboard the Harvester overnight. We will come back.'

'Roger that,' said Cam. 'Maybe some snooping as well,' he said, looking at them and grinning.

'Indeed,' said Max. 'Rumour has it that something is going on inside that giant floating bathtub.'

They walked over to the two patrol drones on their docking clamps and climbed in. The inspection team strapped in and the docking clamp moved the patrol drone out onto the drone deck. Max and Alex boarded the other patrol drone, strapped in and watched as Cam's drone-powered up and took off. The docking clamp raised, released the drone and it pitched forward and took off across the security zone to the Harvester.

'Flying today?' asked Alex as the docking clap moved them out onto the drone deck.

'Of course,' said Max, 'nice day for it.'

He put his interface helmet on as did Alex.

Max powered up the drone and the docking clamp raised and released them. He used some thrust and got a bit of height, pitched the drone forward and accelerated, clearing the side of the vessel.

He angled the drone down and flew low across the water towards the Harvester.

The Hex tower was raised, and Harvester operations cleared them for approach and landing.

As they approached the huge Harvester drone deck, they angled up towards the leading edge.

Hovering off to the side, they watched as Cam landed his patrol drone. The Harvester docking clamp grabbed it and lowered it into place.

'Coming in,' said Max over comms to Cam.

'Nice day for it,' said Cam in reply as his inspection team exited the drone.

Max and Alex could see Cam's inspection team standing on the drone deck next to their patrol drone.

Max bought their drone in fast, reared up and hovered into position. The docking clamp grabbed them. As it secured them, he powered down the drone.

The docking lamp lowered them into position.

'I never get sick of that,' said Max as he took his helmet off and they both exited the drone.

'One of the perks of the job,' said Alex, smiling. 'The toys just get bigger as you get older.'

'Indeed,' said Max, smiling as they walked over to where Cam and his team were standing.

'Right, boys,' said Max as he stretched and folded his arms. 'Cam, get your team below and start inspections. We'll catch up with you over a meal tonight before we fly back and discuss details.'

'Sounds good,' he replied. 'Right, let's go,' he said, turning to his team as they walked across the drone deck to one of the exits.

Over at the hex tower, they could see a figure standing on the observation deck.

'Looks like Lee,' said Alex as they walked.

It wasn't a busy day. A few transport drones were docked on clamps and the odd Harvester patrol drone came and went.

'I would like to get this meeting out of the way,' said Max. 'I wouldn't mind going to the moon pools myself this time. If something is afoot, then maybe a walkthrough will give us more insight. Then we can catch up with Cam.'

They walked up the stairs of the Hex tower.

'Gentleman,' said Lee as they approached him. 'It is good to see you once again and in more positive circumstances.'

'Strange times though, isn't it,' said Max. 'I hope Harvester operations are going well for you.'

'That's one way to put it,' said Lee with a look of concern on his face at the comment.

Strange indeed, thought Alex to himself, *he seems a little nervous*. Max glanced at Alex and he acknowledged that the response from Lee was odd.

'I take it you want to meet straight away?' asked Lee.

They both nodded.

'Let's go and talk over something to eat,' said Lee.

'As usual, your hospitality is second to none,' said Alex.

Lee smiled and led them on.

Walking into the hex tower, it lowered, taking them below to the drone bay. Exiting, they followed Lee and a security officer across to the lift. It took them below to operations and to the restaurant they usually met in over a meal.

It seems airily silent, thought Alex to himself along the way, *subdued. It was as if everyone around them were on edge.* Previously, when they were aboard, it was always busy. People coming and going, chatting, and going about their business.

The security officer stood to one side at the entrance to the meeting room. They used the same meeting room every time. It was off to the side of the restaurant.

Getting some food from the buffet they returned and sat down.

'It's so quiet here,' commented Max.

'We have a lot on at present,' said Lee as he ate. 'Our crew is under a lot of pressure,' he said, not looking at them. 'That's all.'

'How is Ying Yue?' asked Alex.

'Oh, she's fine,' said Lee again, not looking at them. 'Busy in her lab. Like I said we have a lot on right now.'

Alex looked at Max. Lee seemed irritated by the line of questioning.

'I take it you are up to speed on the increase in piracy incidents in "the Area",' said Alex. 'The change in tactics and ramming Skimmers. We think it might be to try and board them.'

'Yes,' said Lee. 'GlobeCorpMining informed us. Ying Yue's father is looking into it for us. The Skimmer contractors must be concerned.'

'Everyone is concerned,' said Max. 'Safety of the Skimmer crew is paramount. But we can't be everywhere. One wonders why pirates would want to board a Skimmer when all they need to do is steal nodules from trays while Skimmers are tethered to their communication streamers.'

It was a leading question to test Lee's reaction. They both watched and for a moment, everyone ate in silence. Lee seemed to be thinking about his response.

'Perhaps it is not the pirates,' said Lee cautiously. 'Perhaps it is someone else using them as a cover.'

'Anyway, have you heard from Sue lately?' asked Alex.

An awkward silence followed. Max looked briefly at Alex and thought, *well played.*

'As far as I am aware,' replied Lee. 'She is working at the naval facility ashore. She is also under the watchful eye of GlobeCorpMining as well. They have offices at the facility.'

What was the relationship between the PLA Navy and GlobeCorpMining? thought Max to himself, *what does Ying Yue's father have to do with it and where does Sue fit in?* It was all very convoluted.

They continued to eat in silence until finishing their meals.

'Well,' said Max, pushing his empty plates back and resting his arms on the table. 'We should get going,' he said, looking at Alex. 'We need to catch up with our Skimmer inspection team during the day before heading back to our vessel.'

'I'm sure you do,' replied Lee.

A look of relief could be seen on his face. Max wondered what he was not telling them. *A lot,* he thought to himself. The meeting seemed over before it had even started.

They were about to get up when a Harvester officer interrupted them. He looked nervous as well. *What it is with these people lately?* Max thought.

'Sir,' he said, looking at Lee and glancing at Max and Alex. 'Met-ocean scans have picked up a cell developing in the convergence zone. It's a big one, a supercell. Modelling predicts we are going to be on its path.'

'I'm coming,' replied Lee.

The Harvester officer nodded his head and disappeared.

'The Harvester is designed to handle a supercell,' said Lee, 'but we need to prepare. I assume you will too.'

'Indeed,' said Max. 'Interesting development.'

'Change of plans,' said Alex.

'On that note, we really do have to get going,' said Max.

Max's smartwatch buzzed, and he looked down at it.

'Seems our lot have picked it up,' he said looking at Alex. 'Let's meet with Cam and then get going.'

They got up and thanked Lee for his hospitality. The security officer led them to the lift and back to the drone bay.

Along the way, Alex contacted Cam and told him to meet them at the patrol drones urgently.

The hex tower was lowered. The security detail left them, and they took the lift it surrounded up to the drone deck.

Cam was already there and standing next to the patrol drone. The Harvester security detail that had escorted him were standing off to one side waiting.

'That was quick,' said Alex looking across to where Cam was.

'Sounded like it was more than urgent,' said Cam, smiling.

'We have a situation,' said Max as they stopped by the patrol drones. 'A supercell is forming in the convergence zone. We need to get back and plan a course of action. But you still get your team to finish inspections. Be back onboard 2000 tonight.'

'Bugger,' said Cam. 'Something isn't right on this Harvester. Something has changed. I've got a nose for these things.'

His two offsiders nodded their heads in agreement.

'Another time,' said Alex. 'We need to decide where we want to be to ride out this supercell.'

'See you back onboard,' said Max as he and Alex boarded their patrol drone and strapped in.

Cam tipped his cap and stood back as the drone powered up and the docking clamp raised. Releasing the patrol drone, he watched as it tilted forward and raced across the deck and over the side. He looked on as it flew low over the water back to the Hunter vessel.

On the patrol drone, Max and Alex considered their options.

'A bit frosty wasn't it?' asked Max as they flew towards their vessel.

'Lee is hiding something,' said Max, 'that's for sure.'

'Let's see if we can find out what happened to Sue,' said Alex.

'Yep,' said Max. 'Once we have this supercell sorted. It will be a big one. Those Skimmers will all hunker down for it.'

'Here we go,' said Alex as they approached the Hunter vessel to land.

They came up beside the stern and slipped sideways across the deck. The docking clamp raised and grabbed them. Max powered down the patrol drone as it lowered and secured them into position.

The docking clamp moved them into the drone bay and into position. Removing their harnesses and interface helmets, they both climbed out. A waiting technician proceeded to check over the drone.

'Sir, operations are tracking the supercell developing in the convergence zone,' said the drone bay duty officer poking his head out from the control room as they walked to the stairs at the rear.

'Thanks,' said Alex. 'Yes, we got the message. Stand by for instructions.'

Alex and Max headed up the stairs to operations.

They walked into a flurry of activity.

Duty technicians had various charts and weather maps displayed on the screen and in holograms. Modelling was being used to determine the path and intensity of the developing supercell.

'Sir,' said one of the technicians, 'the Harvester is directly in its path. Current Skimmer operations are spread out. They will also be in harm's way. Not as bad as the Harvester, though.'

'I see,' said Max as they looked over the projections. 'It's a big one for sure. Fifty-metre swell height, plus fifty below sea level for the roll. Those Skimmers will ride it out at a hundred metres' depth untethered just in case the streamer shears off. No mining.'

'Even though they are not meant to mine some will,' said Alex. 'They will deploy the communication streamer and carry on mining just to meet their load schedules.'

'True,' said Max. 'However, we need to standoff. We must ensure we are out of its direct path but near enough to the Skimmers to respond if needed.'

'The Skimmers will be grouped in "the Area" for this,' said Alex, 'but as you said, some will continue mining. What about the interceptor drones? They can keep an eye on things down there.'

'Those pirates will be a worry,' said Max as he thought about what Alex had suggested. 'They will take advantage of the situation.' He stretched, folded his arms, and thought for a moment. 'We can handle a thirty-metre swell without too many issues. But fifty metres?'

'That's why we stand off and rely on the interceptor drones.'

'Sir,' said one of the duty officers. 'Incoming communication request from the Xed Academy.'

'Open message board,' said Max.

'Gentlemen,' said Rick as his image appeared.

'Rick,' said Max. 'We were just talking about you. This supercell.'

'That's what I am contacting you about,' said Rick. 'With the increase in piracy and change in tactics, there is a danger they will take advantage of this supercell. We will group the Skimmers out of its direct path. Will you be able to stand off but still reach them?'

'Great minds think alike,' said Max, smiling.

'As long as we are not stuck in a fifty-metre swell,' said Alex.

'As you know, their tactics have changed,' said Rick. 'I am concerned they will attempt to board a Skimmer during this supercell.'

'We have three interceptor drones and breaching pods,' said Max. 'If we deploy them between us and the Skimmers, they can monitor them.'

They watched as Rick considered what was being discussed.

'While grouped together, some will refuse to not deploy their streamer,' said Alex. 'They will carry on mining.'

'In terms of response times,' said Max. 'It depends on how long this supercell takes to move through. We need to stand off. We need to be far enough away to avoid the worst of the supercell. Given the duration, the interceptors will run low on power and eventually return. We are still trailing an alternative power system. But it's not fully operational. We will stagger them.'

Alex nodded in agreement.

'Okay,' said Rick. 'A bit of planning to do at both ends then. I will be in touch.'

Rick's image disappeared from the message board and for a moment, the whole operations centre was silent.

'Right,' said Max, 'I want this vessel and the drone vessels in position and ready when this supercell hits. Watertight from now until I say otherwise, monitor that supercells development, intensity, and path and prepare two interceptor drones and a boarding party. Find a box on that chart and a vector we can move along safely without being in the direct path of this thing or too far away from where the Skimmers will be. It's going to get rough over the next few days.'

'Yes, sir,' replied the crew on duty in the operations centre.

'That's an understatement,' said Alex, smiling.

The others chuckled and chatted to each other.

'I suggest you all pop a pill now,' said Max. 'It's going to get ugly.'

'Pull up a navigation hologram of all current Skimmer mining locations,' said Alex to one of the duty crew.

'Hmm,' said Max as they looked at it. 'There's enough time for most Skimmers to take a load to the Harvester and return to their next mining location. But to ride this out and for safety and security, Rick said Xed crew monitoring will get the Skimmers grouped closer together. Let's plot a safe course for us first. We will just have to wait and see where the location will be for grouping Skimmers.'

'Time is getting on,' said Alex. 'I'm going to grab some food and go to the drone bay to catch up with Cam when he gets back from the Harvester with his inspection team.'

'Sounds good,' said Max. 'I will go to the SAI console and check in with the duty watch-keeping officer.'

He turned towards the duty officer in charge of operations.

'Linger with intent outside the Harvester security zone until further notice and wait for Cam's return,' said Max.

'Yes, sir,' they replied.

The duty operations officer in charge contacted the SAI console informing the duty watch-keeping officer of what needed to be done.

Alex and Max left the operations team to get something to eat first.

The others started preparing for the supercell and contacting the rest of the crew about what was going on.

'It's going to be pretty rough on everyone,' said Alex as they entered the mess, got something to eat and sat down.

'It's been a while since we have encountered a supercell,' said Max, 'but my real concern is putting a breaching pod boarding crew on an interceptor and in harm's way during this supercell.'

'If there is a piracy attempt lives could be lost,' said Alex. 'I mean, with the change in tactics, the ramming and boarding attempts.'

'Here's a thought,' said Max. 'What if a Skimmer has to surface? We would have to do a surface rescue.'

'Not if the Skimmer crew used an escape pod,' said Alex.

'Good point,' said Max. 'Now we're talking.'

'It's getting late,' said Alex as he pushed his meal aside. 'I'm going to head down to the drone bay. Cam will be here soon. I will brief him on all this.'

Max nodded as Alex got up and took his plate with him.

'Right you are,' said Max. 'I'll head to the SAI console shortly. I'll get a weather update from the team as well. Let's have a morning brief with everyone tomorrow straight after breakfast. It will be our last chance to enjoy the fair weather. Over the next few days, this will all unfold for better or worse.'

'I'll arrange it before turning in,' said Alex as he walked off towards the drone bay.

The escape pod idea was good, he thought to himself. If there was an emergency and a Skimmer surfaced during the supercell, they would launch their escape pods and head to another Skimmer for recovery.

Alex reached the drone bay. He had some time before Cam arrived back. Walking out onto the drone deck he looked across at the Harvester in the distance. For the most part, life at sea was enjoyable. A bit of rough weather now and then but endless horizons of the ocean more than compensated. *Besides,* he thought to himself, *when they did get ashore between patrols, he appreciated it that much more.*

Chapter 10

It was very early in the morning. Ngarra's crew were up well before dawn to leave for the Harvester with a load of nodules. A sense of urgency prevailed. They had shortened their stay at the mining location. The coming supercell meant they had to get to the Harvester, offload and proceed to another location before lockdown.

Ngarra was at the SAI console with Jesse. They were checking the met-ocean reports.

The last of the Xtracts returned from the depths below, dropped their nodules into the trays and attached to the docking clamps.

'It's building,' said Ngarra as he manipulated the hologram in front of him. 'Here's its trajectory, here we are, here's the Harvester and our next location. We are to proceed there and ride it out.'

'At least, with being a hundred metres down we won't get much of it,' said Jesse. 'It's getting to and from that Harvester and getting into position that we need to worry about.'

'We'll be underway soon enough,' said Ngarra.

'I don't fancy hanging around that Harvester too long anyway,' said Jesse. 'It's fairly quiet and no one says much. Something isn't right.'

'We'll have to catch up with Ying Yue again sometime and ask her what's really going on,' said Ngarra.

They watched as the last of the Xtracts moved silently across the Skimmer wing. The Xtracts entered the recess, docking on their clamps.

'Are we using the overdrive then?' asked Jesse.

'Most Skimmers will be using it for this,' said Ngarra. 'So yes, it means we can get into position for lockdown with plenty of time to spare.'

'Communication streamer is not far off being recovered and secured,' said Chang over comms from the Xtract bay. 'Xtracts secured. One is being bought into the maintenance bay for servicing.'

'Roger that,' said Ngarra. 'We will be making the jump this morning to save time.'

'Love it,' said Stella over comms.

'Love it?' questioned Ngarra.

'I mean, using the overdrive more,' said Stella. 'More time mining and less time running around this ocean between the Harvester and each mining location. Are we actually making the jump or just using the energy field to go really fast?'

'Making the jump,' said Ngarra.

'I like to think of it as more of a bounce,' said Stella over comms. 'Like the first part is the build-up, the discharge into the field. The second part of it is us arriving at the end of the bounce without moving through the physical distance in between.'

'Good analogy,' said Jesse over comms, 'the wall we bounce off is the higher energy discharged into the field that cancels out inertia . It allows us to make the jump without being squashed like a bug on a windscreen.'

'You should ask Jonny about that,' said Stella laughing. 'His second career in acting is waiting for him.'

The others smiled remembering his antics in the rec area earlier.

'Who would have thought,' said Ngarra, 'mercury plasma contained inside an iron casing with a circular magnetic semiconductor at its base to create a polarised vortex, and what is essentially a bunch of giant capacitors set at thirty-degree intervals in a ring around it discharging into it.'

'I really would like to have looked behind this bulkhead,' said Stella over comms as she looked forward from the Xtract bay console.

'We haven't needed to,' said Jesse over comms. 'Once we use it more often, we will. Walking around it above from the rec area forward to the viewing area I often think about it. The day fast coming when it will be used constantly to get around between mining runs.'

'Can't come fast enough,' said Chang over comms. 'Running around the ocean sucks big time.'

'Let us know once you have recovered that Xtract for servicing and the moon pool and airlock is secured,' said Ngarra over open comms.

Ngarra and Jesse looked outside again. They watched as one of the Xtracts left its docking clamp. It moved slowly across the Skimmer wing, paused briefly, and disappeared underneath the Skimmer towards the moon pool.

'We have a bit of time before making the jump,' said Jesse. 'Let's get some food and check-in with the others.'

'I bet you that's exactly where Jonny is,' said Ngarra as they left the SAI console.

'I'll grab Connor,' said Jesse. 'He will be tied up with Gilgamesh.'

Ngarra walked down the stairs to the rec area.

Jesse walked down one side of the Skimmer between propulsion and life support to the information hub to get Connor.

***

In the Xtract bay, Chang and Stella watched as the Xtract was recovered to the maintenance bay for servicing.

Through the camera system, they could see its surface in the moon pool. A docking clamp secured it and lifted it up and out of the moon pool. It moved along and into the airlock, which then closed and adjusted to one atmosphere of breathable air. The airlock opened. The Xtract was moved into the maintenance bay. The airlock and moon pool closed. SAI armed them both ready for departure.

'Hey, you two,' said Jonny as he came down the stairs and through the watertight bulkhead to see what was going on. 'Coming up for some food before we leave. We are going to make the jump to save time with this supercell forming above us.'

'Must be hard for you,' said Stella. 'I mean making the jump means no downtime in transit to feed whatever that is growing inside you,' she said, poking his stomach and laughing.

Chang grimaced. Despite having got over their differences, he still thought Jonny was painful to be around. Some people just bugged him no matter what. Jonny was one of those people.

The vibe between Jonny and Chang was a little tense. Stella tried to lighten the mood.

'An alien.' Jonny laughed rubbing his belly. 'I've been probed.'

'Must have had a sex change too then,' joked Stella. 'When are you due?'

'Well, these ancient aliens were great at manipulating DNA and seeding humanity weren't they?' asked Jonny.

'Not much hope if it's your seed.' Stella laughed. 'The only useful genes you have are blue ones, boy. Humanity is lost.'

'I look to our first nations for hope then,' said Jonny bowing. 'Not you girlfriend, our indigenous friends. Like Ngarra, the first among his people. No hope for you, girl.'

'Could you two just stop,' replied Chang gruffly. 'This endless banter is boring.'

'Ha, boring is what you are.' Jonny laughed. 'I'd die from being tortured by moaning if there were more than one of you down here.'

'Funny guy,' said Chang harshly. 'Hiding your anxiety over being fat are we?'

'I'm mortally offended by your derogatory comment,' replied Jonny with a wicked smile. He made a grandiose gesture stating. 'As a modern youth, I have been taught to have no resilience, no respect for authority, and no boundaries or work ethic. So, everything offends me and I'm not accountable. Life is easy.'

The sarcasm in his voice was aimed at Chang. Whether he got it was another story.

'Yeah well, luckily Xed doesn't tolerate that from its new entrants now do they,' said Chang with a sting in his voice. 'Not sure how you got in then,' he said with a wicked smile.

Jonny did one of his warrior moves and pretended to be shocked at the same time. Chang jumped back, reacting to his stance.

'Come on, boys,' said Stella. 'Enough of this. Too much testosterone in here. Let's go to the rec area and eat before we make the jump.'

Stella pushed them both to go up the stairs.

'The repair drone is doing its thing,' said Stella as she watched it from the Xtract bay console. 'Anyone would think I'm your mother down here.'

'Whatever,' said Chang dismissively.

The Xtract was suspended from the docking clamp in the maintenance bay. A repair drone was working on the mounts for its loading bucket.

They walked up the stairs through the watertight bulkhead and into the rec area.

Jesse, Ngarra and Connor were there.

'Not often you beat me to it,' said Jonny as he helped himself to some food.

'Losing your fighting edge are you?' asked Jesse.

'Not many edges left to see,' said Stella laughing.

The crew all burst out laughing, including Chang.

'I'm well rounded in all areas of life,' said Jonny laughing. 'I must admit that was damn funny, Stella. But this hulk of muscle has got you lot out of some pretty tight situations.'

'That is true, for sure,' said Jesse.

Jonny got into a few postures as if he were on show at a body competition.

'Strike a pose,' said Stella. 'Go, boy! Where's your vogue now?'

The laughter continued as they all got some food and sat down.

Connor, of course, didn't know what to think.

'The crew thinks I'm well rounded, Connor,' said Jonny. 'I'll take you all on any day.'

'Sure,' said Connor looking at everyone. 'Anyone would have a hard time taking you down in a fight.'

'Too right, Connor,' said Jonny as he pointed his utensil at them all around the table.

'Gilgamesh can take on most things you know,' said Connor. 'It can learn by itself now and adapt. The red queen sequence works. If you could find a giant squid to attack them, I'll prove it to you. You can handle a giant squid, can't you. Jonny?'

'Connor, you're not trying to be funny are you?' he asked in reply.

Connor managed a smile. But he looked up to Jonny and thought he might actually be able to fight a giant squid.

'Actually, if we do get attacked by these pirates,' said Connor, 'and the Xtracts were deployed, they should respond and adapt. Gilgamesh would see the interruption as a threat. It's a type of relationship, like in nature. Like I said before, the Skimmer, SAI gets its nodules and the Xtracts get their power. It's all about access to resources, competition for food and survival of the fittest.'

'Yes, it is all about the food,' said Jonny, rubbing his stomach.

The others laughed but Connor was quite serious.

'What's more,' said Connor, 'with the red queen sequence, the Xtracts will quickly learn and adapt to such an encounter while it is actually happening.'

'Is it SAI or Gilgamesh now running the show,' asked Stella, 'or is it both?'

'Both,' replied Connor. 'SAI runs the Skimmer. It doesn't think for itself, though. Gilgamesh, on the other hand, is like a child. It can learn without human input, but it needs guidance and direction.'

'Isn't that dangerous?' asked Ngarra.

'Not really,' said Connor. 'Unless, of course, you locked out the human oversight I have built into it. A link. You can't delete that ever. I can't delete certain parts of the mesh, which prevents that from ever happening. Locking out human oversight, I mean.'

'Sounds painful being linked,' said Jonny jokingly, putting a hand on his heart.

'If Gilgamesh had feelings,' said Ngarra. 'It might be upsetting that you can simply wipe parts of its memory that it has acquired from learning with the click of a button.'

'It doesn't have feelings,' said Connor. 'It isn't sentient or self-aware, it's still a machine you know. Once SAI and I came up with the red queen sequence, we had to have a way of controlling it. Otherwise, yes, we would have created a monster. Like a child with no parental oversight and therefore no control or self-regulation as it grows older; a friend rather than a parent. We are not its friend, we are its Master, its parent, its teacher.'

'So, SAI could be integrated into it then,' said Jesse. 'I mean Gilgamesh?'

'Technically speaking, yes,' said Connor, 'but I have left that wall up. The Skimmers aren't ours or should I say Xed's, but the Xtract technology is. I am working on an independent power source as well.'

'That could well change,' said Jesse as she thought about project Cygnus.

Rick would want to know more about all this, she thought to herself. All security and communications officers were aware of the bigger picture. It could be important. She had to talk to Rick about it. The overdrive trials had been brought forward. Testing would increase across all the Skimmers. Even with the contractor's limited knowledge of all this, the owners of the Skimmers and the people that installed the overdrives would love it. *I don't think Jonah fully realises the implications of this technology,* she thought to herself.

'Right, let's get going,' said Ngarra. 'SAI, prepare to depart to Harvester. Initialise overdrive.'

'Confirmed,' said SAI. 'Prepare to depart for Harvester. Initialise overdrive.'

The crew got up and put all their plates and utensils in the dispenser. They moved off to their stations and made ready to make the jump to the Harvester.

***

At the SAI console, Ngarra was checking the overdrive schematics that were displayed. Jesse was watching what was going on. Jonny cross-checked their relative arrival coordinates with the Harvester. They didn't want to accidentally arrive in it, just near it. That could be fatal.

'SAI, confirm Skimmer is watertight,' said Ngarra.

'Confirmed,' said SAI. 'Skimmer is watertight.'

'Stella and Chang,' said Ngarra over open comms. 'What's our Xtract status?'

'All recovered, moon pool and airlock armed, one in the bay, streamer secure and samples recovered,' replied Stella.

'SAI, close outer hull shields,' said Ngarra.

'Confirmed,' said SAI. 'Outer hull shields closing.'

They watched as the ocean disappeared and the external camera system activated.

Jesse continued looking at the overdrive schematics. The circular magnetic semiconductor at its base was online. The inward spiralling mercury vortex was spinning inside its iron sheath, and a heated gas plasma had formed. Polarity was confirmed, negative at the top and positive at the bottom and the powerful energy field generated perpendicular to the spin axis was on display. The discharge ring capacitors were displayed, showing their status as well.

'SAI, confirm coordinates for arrival at Harvester.'

'Confirmed,' said SAI as the coordinates were displayed for their arrival position.

'SAI, confirm energy frequency for discharge into plasma vortex and inertia compensation. Confirm alignment of powertrain with rim driven propulsion.'

If this wasn't done correctly, it caused overspeed on the rim drive. That got the other crew into trouble. It would go offline and then must be recalibrated and rebooted to use it.

'Confirmed,' said SAI as the calculation for the required discharge was cross-referenced against the magnitude of the discharge needed to arrive at the coordinates and compensate for inertia.

'We are ready folks,' said Ngarra.

'Always get nervous,' said Jonny. 'I don't like the thought of being squashed like a bug if it all goes wrong.'

'You won't as there is always a failsafe,' said Jesse. 'The whole thing will not proceed without inertia compensation. It's always a given. It won't work otherwise. We'll be fine. I'm still getting used to all the terminology though.'

'I feel like an animal in a test lab,' said Jonny.

'It was all worked out long before they exposed humans to all this,' said Jesse, 'but that's another long back story that is part of the Security and Communications course. We're at the sharp end of it all now.'

'Yeah well let's just get it over and done with,' said Jonny. 'I can appreciate that the discharge is to the jump coordinates relative to us but the fact that opposite it is a more powerful discharge that we essentially bounce off and it negates inertia is just scary.'

'That's one way to think about it,' said Jesse. 'Relative to people outside it looks like we went from point to point instantly. In here, it's a bounce. The second part of the bounce sees us arrive at our location. The difference being that all that force is in the same direction rather than equal and opposite. Newton's equal and opposite reaction appears turned on its head.'

'As you said, Jesse, that's one way to look at it,' said Ngarra.

'Well, maybe Newton's laws still apply in a funny kind of way but within this bubble, we have generated,' said Stella over comms.

'They do actually,' said Jesse. 'Okay let's go. Stand by.'

'Where's Einstein when you need him?' asked Jonny. 'And the dudes we learnt about at the Academy with their suppressed torsion physics work.'

'SAI, execute jump to arrival coordinates,' said Ngarra.

'Confirmed,' said SAI. 'Execute jump to arrival coordinates.'

They watched the navigation hologram as the overdrive did its thing. The discharge happened. It went across the polarised plasma vortex at its base. The discharge occurred relative to the coordinates the Skimmer had orientated itself to. Another discharge occurred in the opposite it. Seconds went by, a moment of nothing, a void consisting of energy encased them; occupying the space between atoms and stripped subatomic particles. The camera system showed the surrounding ocean blur into streaks.

'At arrival coordinates,' announced SAI as the surrounding ocean reappeared.

'Thank god for that,' said Jonny as he breathed a sigh of relief.

Jonny looked at the navigation hologram and zoomed in on their position. They were about thirty minutes out from the Harvester.

'SAI, engage rim drive and proceed to Harvester,' said Ngarra.

'Confirmed,' said SAI. 'Engage rim drive and proceed to Harvester.'

The Skimmer got underway. Power was diverted to the rim driven propulsion system. The crew had correctly aligned the powertrain for the jump. No overspeed was induced.

Chapter 11

The Skimmer was on the final approach. Jonny had his interface lenses on and was watching as the Skimmer quietly slid under the hull of the giant Harvester.

Through the camera system, Ngarra and Jesse watched what was going on outside.

Marine life circled the giant hull.

Their Skimmer stopped below a moon pool entrance.

It began to rise.

They were in the chute rising to the surface of a moon pool.

Lights in rows dimly lit led the way to the surface.

With a final heave, the Skimmer surfaced, and a wave rolled gently around the moon pool and settled. The docking clamps closed on each side and secured them.

The outer hull shields retracted, and they looked into the distance along the conveyor on each side of them, the robotic arms stretching away in either direction.

A few other Skimmers had also made the jump to offload so as to get to the next location in time for the lockdown and coming supercell. Outside, the sea state was starting to deteriorate.

The Harvester was also in the process of locking down. Soon the conveyor would halt, and the robotic arms would be secured. The moon pool area would be made watertight.

As they were looking outside at the robotic arms offloading nodule trays, the message board activated, and a Harvester security officer appeared on the screen.

'All Skimmers must offload and exit their moon pool by 0600 tomorrow morning. After this time, the moon pools will be in lockdown and not accessible. If you stay, you will not be allowed to leave the accommodation level.'

The screen went blank.

They turned back to watch outside as the nodules slowly moved along the conveyor.

'Everyone,' said Ngarra over open comms, 'let's meet in the rec area for a briefing now.'

Just as they were about to leave, the message board activated again.

'Incoming message request from Sea Hunters,' said SAI.

'SAI, open message board,' said Ngarra, turning around.

Jesse and Jonny stopped, waiting to see what it was all about.

'Greetings folks,' said Max as his image appeared. 'I have been talking to Rick. He told me you were due back at the Harvester. My team is doing inspections. I assume you have had the briefing about what is going on. I wanted to catch up about your technology and piracy in person. Let's meet in accommodation on the Harvester. We will come back across on our patrol drone and meet with you shortly. We are all out of here by morning. We have been delayed from departing. Cam and his team are still onboard and will come up with you. They are completing inspections.'

Sure enough, they looked out and could see an inspection team walking towards them along the boardwalk next to the conveyor.

'Okay,' said Ngarra. 'We will see you shortly.'

The screen went blank again.

Jesse went and got Connor.

They all moved off and walked down the stairs to the rec area.

Stella and Chang were already there waiting.

'Right folks,' said Ngarra. 'The Sea Hunters are here, and Max wants to speak with us personally about piracy and technology. Not sure what they want but he said they have spoken to Rick. An inspection team is walking towards us and will take us up to accommodation to meet him. Max said they are flying back across in their patrol drone now.'

'What about my sister,' said Chang. 'I would like to catch up.'

'Let's get this sorted and then contact Lee and your sister for a quick catch up,' said Jesse. 'I'm sure everyone is flat out getting ready for this supercell, though. It will be tight.'

They heard voices and footsteps coming up the gangway to the rec area. The entrance was open.

'Ladies and gents,' said Cam as he walked in. 'My team here will do their usual thing. Then we'll head off to meet up with Alex and Max. They're coming back across just to see you lot. We were meant to be out of here by now so time is short.'

'I'll take them around,' said Jonny as he got up and left to show the inspection team what they needed to see.

'This is a particularly nasty supercell,' said Cam as he stood waiting.

'It appears so,' said Jesse.

An awkward silence followed.

They looked at Cam. Ngarra didn't really like the Sea Hunters but it seemed they were becoming increasingly intertwined with them. Between piracy and the technology everyone seemed to want to get their hands on, and the overdrive trials, they all seemed to get pulled evermore into whatever was going on.

'You lot have had a bit of a rough time,' said Cam, while they waited.

'That's one way to put it,' said Ngarra.

The crew, of course, didn't recognise Cam from their earlier encounter with an intruder onboard their Skimmer while in the moon pool.

Connor, on the other hand, thought his voice sounded familiar but he wasn't sure why. He was looking at Cam intensely.

A short time later, the inspection team returned. They had filled out their paperwork and collected the samples, which were now in a pelican case.

'Let's go then,' said Cam as he motioned for them to come with him.

They all exited the Skimmer and walked down the gangway to the boardwalk. A Harvester security detail watched them intently as they walked to the lift.

'I'm sure his voice sounds familiar,' said Connor as he whispered to Jonny, while they walked behind everyone else.

'Funny you should mention that,' said Jonny. 'I thought he seemed familiar as well. I mean we know who he is and have seen him on occasion, but it's more than that.'

One of the Harvester security details had walked over and met them at the lift. They all entered the lift and it took them to accommodation.

As they exited the lift. Cam spotted Alex and Max sitting off to one side in the main foyer.

'Greetings you lot,' said Max as they walked over to him. 'Take a seat.' 'This is becoming all too familiar,' said Jonny. 'We're almost family now.'

Max gave him a blank look, paused, and then smiled. 'Sure,' he said, 'family.' He then looked at Chang intensely.

A stifled laugh followed as they all sat down.

Chang squirmed in his seat. He wasn't sure what to think about it all.

Cam and his team left to finish inspections and then return to the Hunter vessel.

'Now,' said Alex, 'we don't have much time, but a lot is going on. We have this supercell approaching, the increased risk of piracy and the change in their tactics. We will standoff and monitor the Skimmers while this supercell comes through. We have been asked to keep a close eye on your Skimmer in particular. Rumours are afoot that, for some reason, the combination of your Xtract technology and this overdrive propulsion system is something highly valued by others. The supercell is an ideal cover to try and do something.'

'Surely pirates wouldn't be behind it all,' said Jesse. 'What if it's someone pretending to be the pirates as a cover?'

'Exactly,' said Max. 'We think there is a connection with what happened here on the Harvester the last time we crossed paths.'

'You mean when my sister Ying Yue got shot,' said Chang. 'That damn Sue deserves everything she gets. And where was my father in all that? Too little too late.'

Ngarra glared at him and motioned for him to calm down.

Chang shrugged his shoulders. He had been in enough trouble before and didn't really care.

'The thing is,' said Alex, 'that no one is quite sure what your father did with Sue. We know she went ashore to their facility, which is located inside a Chinese navy base. As to what she is up to, no one knows.'

'If my father has anything to do with it and it puts my sister in danger again, I'll kill him,' said Chang angrily.

'Cut it out,' said Jesse. 'Let's talk about it later.' She motioned for Chang to go and cool off.

Chang got up and walked away.

Max looked at Jesse, trying to gauge her position on everything. *Always cool, calm, and collected,* he thought to himself. What did she know about all this?

'We anticipate that something will happen,' said Alex. 'You have to be prepared and able to adapt.'

'We have the overdrive,' said Jonny. 'We can get the hell out of dodge if it comes to that.'

The others smiled.

'Such a way with words,' said Max.

'You better believe it, bro,' replied Jonny.

Max smiled at his colloquialism. *The goal had changed for the Sea Hunters,* he thought to himself. Rather than try and secure the technology Rick now wanted them to protect the crew. Something about advancing plans for his people's program with these Skimmers.

'If you are tethered to your streamer,' said Alex, 'then you will be vulnerable. If damaged, they will attempt to board. It happened recently to another Skimmer. We think it was a test run to see if they could do it.'

'Well, technically we are not meant to deploy the streamer during a supercell,' said Ngarra. 'Mining is halted, and we wait it out.'

Ngarra certainly didn't want to admit that they also deploy their streamer during supercells and carry on mining. They could be written up and get an infringement notice.

'But people bend the rules,' said Alex, 'and we are lenient on that. Always have been. It's at our discretion.'

Ngarra smiled. Skimmers were well known to carry on mining during a supercell when they shouldn't. If the streamer sheared off, they would have one expensive recovery bill for Xtracts from the contractor.

'That's it really,' said Max. He lent back and stretched his arms then folded them on the table in front of him. 'Our interceptor drones will be patrolling within the vicinity of the grouped Skimmers.'

'Right, we have to get going,' said Alex looking at his smartwatch and then at Max. 'We need to get back to our Hunter unit and prepare to move into position before this supercell hits. And you lot need to get on and get out of here and in position as well with the other Skimmers before lockdown.'

'We are going to catch up with Ying Yue first and leave after,' said Jesse. 'Chang wants to see her. Something is off on this Harvester. Don't you find it airily quiet? You could cut the air with a knife.'

Alex and Max looked at each other. A quiet signal passed between them not to say anything.

'Cam hasn't said anything,' said Alex, 'and we haven't been on here enough to notice.'

Alex and Max said their goodbyes, got up and walked through the foyer to take the lift to the drone deck. A Harvester security officer followed them.

Jesse went to the main reception area and asked a security officer if they could contact Ying Yue and ask if she wanted to catch up with her brother Chang before they left.

'That was awkward,' said Jonny, while they waited.

'Sure was,' said Stella. 'I feel like I'm living in a glass box and everyone is watching our every move.'

'Well, not your moves, girl,' said Jonny trying to make light of the situation.

'How's that baby of yours?' asked Stella sarcastically.

'Ouch,' said Jonny grinning. 'I'm offended.'

'Listen up you two,' said Jesse as she motioned for them to cut it out. 'Ying Yue is coming now. Let's move through to the restaurant and meet her there. Time is short. I don't want to be stuck on this heaving monster during this supercell.'

They moved through to the restaurant and got some food and sat at a table off to one side.

'Now this is more like it,' said Jonny as he came over and sat down with a plate full of food.

'Last supper,' said Stella sitting opposite.

'That's ominous,' said Chang. 'I feel a sense of foreboding about all this.'

'No one is taking Gilgamesh,' stated Connor.

He had been quiet until he spotted Ying Yue.

'Here she is,' said Chang as he got up to greet his sister.

'How is everyone?' she asked, walking up to them.

'Could be better,' replied Jesse. 'Hopefully, we get through this supercell without incident.'

'You look worried,' said Chang as she sat down with them to talk.

'Not really,' said Ying Yue. 'Just a lot on and not enough sleep.'

'How's your research?' asked Chang.

Connor listened intently, desperate to be included in the conversation and talk about his work.

'Moving fast now,' said Ying Yue. 'Too fast in some ways. Infectious you might say.'

That's an odd thing to say, Jesse thought to herself.

'Given the Harvester crew has to try and keep up with all the changes from our research,' said Ying Yue, 'they are starting to feel like robots and left out of it all if you know what I mean.'

Ying Yue had talked in strange ways previously when trying to communicate a message she didn't want others to hear or know, thought Jesse. She wondered what it meant.

'But you and Lee run the show now,' said Jonny. 'Just put the brakes on it all.'

'Too late for that,' said Ying Yue. 'We opened Pandora's box.'

'You wouldn't want to lose control then would you?' asked Jesse, still thinking about what Ying Yue was trying to say without saying it.

'Mimic drones and a self-driven mining operation would be great,' said Connor. 'Fully automated here on the Harvester. Everything connected, like some giant fungus grown from an infection after a virus has cleared the way. I mean the coding you have developed.'

I must speak with Connor, thought Jesse. *He has the mind to uncover hidden meanings and see behind things more clearly than the others.*

Ying Yue smiled at Connor's analogy. She knew he was into learning from nature about how AI might work. Intelligent design could be usurped to take control of everything.

'Are you saying everything in nature has an intelligent design that can be mimicked and coded for artificially?' asked Ying Yue.

'Exactly, but you wouldn't want to lose control of it,' said Connor. 'Like Gilgamesh.'

'Gilgamesh?' questioned Ying Yue.

'Thanks, Connor,' interrupted Jesse. 'Time is short, and we need to get a bit of sleep before an early start to beat the lockdown here.'

'That's what I call it now,' said Connor. 'You should see.'

'Connor, we have to go,' said Jesse quickly and motioning at him to stop.

Connor shrugged his shoulders.

'Come on, Connor, let's go,' said Chang seeing what was going on. 'Glad to see you, sister. Once this all blows over, we can catch up onboard again between mining runs.'

They all got up and said their goodbyes before heading back to the Skimmer. Ying Yue gave Chang a quick hug. He squirmed, a little embarrassed and then she hurried off back to her work.

'Ying Yue seems a little distant,' said Ngarra as they entered the lift and headed down to the moon pools.

A Harvester security officer took them down.

'I'm worried about my sister,' said Chang. 'Odd comments about her work. Almost like she has lost control of it.'

'Maybe she is under a lot of pressure to get her project implemented,' said Jesse.

Jesse noticed the expression on the Harvester security officer's face. She motioned the others to keep quiet.

The lift stopped and they exited and walked along the boardwalk next to the conveyor and robotic arms back to their Skimmer. The Harvester security officer stood and watched them walk back to their Skimmer.

The last of the Skimmers to leave the moon pools before lockdown could be seen in the distance. The sea state was continuing to deteriorate. The Harvester was moving more beneath them now. The ocean gathered its power ready to unleash it.

They walked up the gangway and into the Skimmer.

Standing in the rec area they continued to discuss what might be going on.

'I think it worked,' said Connor. 'I mean it worked better than she ever hoped.'

'What do you mean?' asked Jesse.

'Mimic drones,' said Connor. 'Maybe the Harvester crew no longer has control here. It's running itself. Wouldn't you be worried if you had been cut out of the loop altogether?'

'The law of unintended consequences,' replied Jonny. 'Be careful what you wish for, boy.'

'Well, whatever is going on we need to get out of here early,' said Ngarra. 'Let's get what little sleep we can and then go deep to ride out this supercell.'

The crew headed off and got some rest before making an early start and heading to the mining location the Skimmers would be grouped in during the supercell.

Chapter 12

At Xed, Rick was at the crew monitoring and communications centre. The duty watch team was coordinating the relocation of all Skimmers to one location within 'the Area'. Rick wanted to oversee operations. The day before, Rick and Jonah had briefed the crew on the situation. A message had been sent to all the crew. The Skimmers would stay in that location until the supercell passed. Concerns were mounting over piracy.

'The last of the Skimmers are in transit to the location,' said the duty officer in charge.

'Good,' said Rick. 'I just hope if anyone chooses to use their streamer and mine, those damn pirates don't show up.'

'And if they do?' asked the duty officer in charge.

'Potentially a Skimmer loses a streamer and we have to pay for Xtracts to be recovered for the contractor,' said Rick. 'Not to mention the threat to our crew given these damn pirates have decided to ram Skimmers and try to board them.'

'That Xtract technology, Gilgamesh, is it? It would ensure we don't,' said the duty officer in charge.

'Don't lose them you mean?' asked Rick.

'Yes, the Xtracts would return fine. But if a Skimmer is rammed and propulsion damaged, SAI will surface it. It's a huge supercell. The crew would have to use the escape pods. That's why we have grouped them. Skimmers can pick up another crew if they must through the moon pool. The surface will be hell for a while.'

Up on the main screen, they looked at the designated location. Markers showed where each Skimmer would be. A few remained in transit. Weather parameters showed a marked deterioration in surface conditions.

'Is the trajectory of the supercell certain,' said Rick. 'Anything that could alter it?'

'Almost certain, based on our calculations,' said the duty officer in charge. 'My team is monitoring it closely. The Skimmers are deep enough not to get caught up in surface and subsurface conditions.'

The duty officer in charge went through some modelling and projections of the path of the supercell in relation to where the Skimmers were located. Rick put his hands on his hips and stood watching and silently thinking.

'Maybe we are just making it easy pickings for these pirates,' he muttered to himself.

'What was that, sir?' asked the duty officer in charge.

'Nothing,' replied Rick. 'Just thinking to myself.'

It was a trade-off. Maximising the safety of the crew and allowing for some protection by the Sea Hunters if something went wrong. But it meant all Skimmers were in one broad location. It was inevitable that pirates were going to turn up.

While Rick was thinking, communication request activated on the main message board.

'Incoming message,' announced SAI.

Before SAI could even finish, the duty officer in charge responded.

'Urgent communication request,' said the duty officer. 'A piracy incident is underway.'

'Damn it,' said Rick. 'I think about it and it happens.'

The communication request had a tagline indicating that a piracy incident was underway.

'Eel drone proximity and grid buoy location nominal, live feed available,' said SAI.

'SAI, on screen,' said Rick.

'We've been rammed,' said the Skimmer communications and security officer. 'We had the streamer deployed and Xtracts down. They didn't board. Some minor hull damage has been sustained. Propulsion is okay and we remain watertight.'

'Damn it,' said Rick. 'Were you not meant to deploy during a supercell lockdown?'

'Yes,' she replied, 'but you know that doesn't always happen and people look the other way when we do it.'

'Tell me exactly what happened,' said Rick. 'Contact the Sea Hunters,' he said to the duty officer in charge.

'Two subs turned up this time,' said the Skimmer communications and security officer. 'They had four drones between them. Two made continuous passes topside and one eventually rammed us. The others we could see through the camera system. One had a docking hatch. It can carry personnel. The other two drones removed nodules from the trays, as usual. They left after that.'

'They are testing us,' said Rick as he considered his options, 'or should I say the Skimmers for a boarding.'

'I have the Sea Hunters,' said the duty officer.

'Standby,' replied Rick. 'First, get a message to all Skimmers to enact intruder boarding protocols.'

'Yes, sir,' he replied.

'You can still hold position through the supercell?' asked Rick as his attention turned back to the message board and the communications and security officer he was talking to.

'Yes, the pirates have moved on.'

'I'll be in touch then,' said Rick as he swiped the message board clear. 'Sea Hunters now,' he said to the duty officer in charge.

'SAI, on screen,' said the duty officer in charge.

Alex's image appeared.

'Rick, what is it,' said Alex. 'It's getting a little bumpy out here.'

'Piracy incident. Skimmer is okay, though. One of the drones has a docking hatch. They are testing the Skimmers for boarding. Defensive ARC arrays can't be used while the streamer is deployed.'

'We know,' said Alex, 'we are still at the Harvester and will deploy two of our interceptor drones to monitor the situation and act as a deterrent. We can't get there ourselves until the worst of this supercell passes through.'

'So, the interceptor drones are just a deterrent?' asked Rick.

'Yes,' said Alex. 'There is a window or period when all the Skimmers will be isolated from us due to the supercell. They will have to look out for themselves. The Authority has been briefed on the situation as have State Sponsors and contractors. Given the pirate situation has changed, emergency orders have been issued to us.'

'We have a team together here,' said Rick. 'Including the Sea Hunter liaison officer. If a Skimmer has its rim driven propulsion damaged, it will surface and the crew will use escape pods. However, if boarded at the same time we will have a big problem.'

'As in what?' asked Alex.

'Whatever drone is in use by these pirates and attached to the Skimmer will be sheared off. Our crew have been briefed and will enact intruder boarding protocols.'

'Escape then?' questioned Alex.

'Yes, the escape pods are to be used,' said Rick. 'A directive has been issued to proceed to another Skimmers moon pool for pickup.'

'Got it,' said Alex, 'but what's the point?'

'The point?' questioned Rick.

'Of a forced boarding of a Skimmer by these pirates,' said Alex.

'We are close to deploying the Xtract technology across all Skimmers,' said Rick, 'and we are advancing the overdrive trials. Someone wants it all, I guess. Can't think of any other reason. Flogging minerals from the trays when a Skimmer is tethered to a communication streamer is easy pickings. It can't be our usual pirates.'

Alex was prying to see how much Rick might know.

'Who then?' questioned Alex.

'Not sure,' said Rick. 'I have an idea, though. I'm going to catch up with Jonah and update her. Got to go.'

Rick swiped the message board clear and for a moment, there was silence. The calm before the storm. Everyone paused and looked at Rick.

'Right,' he said. 'Ensure all Skimmer crews know what to do in case of an attempted boarding. Lock it down tight folks. I don't want sheared streamers and lost Xtracts strewn everywhere out there. "The Authority" will have a field day issuing non-compliance and improvement notices for the Sea Hunters to enforce. It will just make the Sea Hunters' job harder in dealing with these pirates.'

Rick walked across the main floor past Skimmer crew monitoring stations and up the stairs to the enclosed mezzanine. He messaged Jonah on the way and they chatted briefly. She had been in her office all morning.

Exiting the sim centre complex, he walked across campus. He walked over to the admin building to meet with Jonah.

Absorbed in thought, he barely noticed staff and students greeting him along the way. A brief nod or raising of his hand was all they got.

His people would be concerned about the project, project Cygnus. The overdrive technology was key but since everyone had become aware of Connor's technology, the situation had changed. They wanted to advance the trials. They were pushing for a rollout of Connor's tech across all the Skimmers and jumping forward with the overdrive trials as soon as possible.

The law of unintended consequences, he thought to himself out loud.

Walking into the admin building his thoughts wandered. 'Embracing living in the unknown and the narrative rule of reality and quantum mechanics,' he muttered to himself.

He entered a lift and waited as it rose. He looked out of the glass panes into the enclosed space below. Above, he could see drones coming and going from the drone port. Below, people were walking about. The lift stopped and he exited and walked along the mezzanine to Jonah's office.

'Afternoon,' he said to the secretary as he walked in.

She greeted him and pointed to Jonah standing in her office, looking out over the campus with a coffee in hand.

'Rick,' she said. 'How's our crew after that piracy incident and is everything in place for this supercell? I was going to come down but got your message to meet.'

'Minor damage and being able to hold out until the supercell passes,' said Rick, 'but I don't think it's pirates. It must be more than that. The timing is too perfect. I mean, roll out of Connor's Xtract tech, bringing forward the overdrive trials. Something is off here.'

'Agree,' said Jonah, 'but how would these pirates even know? I want to contact Chang's father and discuss it.'

'Be careful,' said Rick. 'We don't know if he or someone connected to him, the subcommittee he reports to or the CCP itself or even the PLA Navy is involved in all this.'

'Piracy does seem to be a good cover,' said Jonah, 'but exactly who is it then?'

'Ask him prying and leading questions,' said Rick. 'Maybe Chang's father genuinely doesn't know what is going on.'

'Can't see that being the case,' said Jonah. 'He is held in high regard by the CCP subcommittee he reports to. He has full oversight of GlobeCorpMining.'

'But not of the military,' said Rick. 'They or a rogue group within it may have another agenda here.'

'So,' thought Jonah. 'Are you saying that they could be using piracy as a cover and the change in tactics is linked to them?'

'Maybe,' said Rick. 'Let's not say that, though. Let's keep it to ourselves. I'll sit in on this. But I'll be on one side. Don't let him know I'm here.'

'If he is available I will,' said Jonah. 'For me he usually is.'

Jonah used her smartwatch to contact Chang's father. A pause followed and a short text message came back. He was in a meeting and would contact her in an hour's time.

'He's busy,' said Jonah. 'I will catch up with him in an hour's time.'

'I will get back to the communication and monitoring centre then,' said Rick. 'The next forty-eight hours are crucial. Not much sleep and long nights.'

'I'll join you after I have talked with him,' said Jonah.

Rick walked out of the office and returned to the sim centre and crew monitoring and communications complex.

***

It had been about an hour and Jonah was standing at her desk overlooking the campus and going over paperwork. A never-ending pile of issues to address and sort out. The art of delegation was important, but she still liked to have oversight of everything going on. Especially when it came to her crew. The problems she faced with differing opinions about the future of the crew program and its links with the Ocean Academy and Xed worried her.

Her smartwatch activated. It was Chang's father. She swiped across it and an image of him appeared on the message board in her office.

'Jonah,' he said. 'Good to talk again. What can I do for you?'

'I appreciate your time,' said Jonah. 'As you are probably aware there is a supercell bearing down on "the Area" and our Skimmers will have to ride it out. We have them grouped in one location. Piracy is an issue and the Sea Hunters have a limited ability to get to them until the supercell passes.'

'Your point being?' questioned Chang's father.

'Well, one of our Skimmers just had a piracy incident. The tactics of these pirates have changed. They rammed a Skimmer and apparently one of their drones had a docking hatch on it.'

'Strange indeed,' he replied. 'Why would they want to board a Skimmer?'

'I thought you might have some ideas on that,' she replied.

'Pirates want nodules to sell,' he said. 'It's an easy target when tethered. Why would they want a Skimmer?'

'Are you saying they are testing to see how easy it is to board and take over a Skimmer and steal the entire load?' asked Jonah.

'Could be,' he replied. 'Maybe they are getting greedy and want an entire load of nodules.'

'It doesn't make sense though,' replied Jonah. 'It exposes the pirates to unnecessary attention.'

'Perhaps a cover for something else, then.' he said.

'What do you mean?' asked Jonah.

'If you're worried about your technology, we can help secure it,' he said. 'After all, having that kind of Xtract technology combined with a fully operational overdrive across a fleet of Skimmers is quite an achievement is it not?'

'Certainly,' said Jonah, 'but what would a bunch of pirates want with all that?'

'Your guess is as good as mine,' he said. 'Have you considered that perhaps it is not the pirates doing it? If tactics have changed that is.'

'We have,' said Jonah. 'That's why I am contacting you. I thought you might have some insight.'

'What are you implying, Jonah,' he questioned. 'That we are involved or know who is involved?'

'Certainly not,' she said, 'but you have had issues on the Harvester previously. I was wondering if there was any connection.'

'That has been eliminated,' he replied sternly. 'Sue has been reassigned ashore with the PLA Navy. What does that have to do with it?'

'Lee and your daughter are now in charge out there are they not?' asked Jonah.

'I don't appreciate your line of thought,' he replied sternly. 'If something is going on it has nothing to do with GlobeCorpMining.'

'I understand that,' said Jonah as she quickly changed her line of questioning, 'but we have a problem that just doesn't want to go away and someone or something must be behind it. Perhaps we can keep each other informed if anything comes up that may help solve it.'

'Let's do that,' he replied calmly. 'I must go, Jonah. I will look into this further for you, though.'

His image disappeared. Jonah was left wondering if she had pushed him too far and compromised their relationship. She thought not. They went back a long way and had been through ups and downs before. Still, something wasn't right, and she was convinced he knew something. Maybe he just wasn't prepared to say openly what he thought might be going on.

Jonah walked over to her secretary and informed her she would be at the crew communication and monitoring complex.

Walking out of her office and along to the lift, she couldn't help but think that the change was coming. The days of crew training up and rotating on and off skimmers in its current format between mining runs were numbered.

She entered the lifted and looked out at the people below coming and going as it descended to the ground floor.

She carried on thinking.

With those overdrive trials being pushed forward and the roll-out of this Xtract technology, everything was going to change around here, she thought to herself.

Maybe Rick will get his way after all.

Chapter 13

Chang couldn't sleep. After several hours of tossing and turning in his bed, he got up. It would be a few hours before the others were up and about. He walked into the rec area, got a drink, and sat at the table.

I wonder what is up with my sister, he thought to himself, *she seemed to have recovered fine after being shot.*

'Lucky,' he said out loud. 'Lucky she had that vest on.'

He carried on thinking.

He couldn't help it, but he was so angry with his father. He had got her into that situation. Sometimes he just wanted to punch him in the face.

It was no different to the blame he placed on himself for his mother's sickness. His thoughts continued to drift.

Despite being coerced into stealing Connor's technology, the crew seemed to have moved on from it.

He thought about this some more.

Perhaps adversity had even brought them all closer together. He liked to think so anyway. *Painful people,* he thought to himself, but he was growing to like them. The crew. An odd bunch. But was he any less odd than the others?

Chang smiled.

The thought was amusing.

He got up and walked along the narrow esplanade around the encased overdrive to the forward viewing area. He looked out along the moon pools of the Harvester.

All was quiet.

They were one of the last to leave before the lockdown. Even the conveyors had stopped now, and the robotic arms had been secured. He could feel the giant hull moving and the dampeners on the docking clamps compensating for it.

Where is Sue and why did my father take her with him? he thought to himself. *We haven't seen Lee around much either and the Harvester crew seemed nervous. What was his sister not telling them about all this? Something just didn't seem right here.*

'Good morning,' said Jesse coming up behind him.

Chang jumped but tried to act as though it was nothing.

'Thought I heard someone muttering to themselves up here,' said Jesse.

'You gave me a fright,' replied Chang. 'I was thinking about my sister. I couldn't sleep.'

'Once we get through this supercell, you can catch up with her again between mining runs,' said Jesse.

'Not sure I even feel comfortable around the Harvester at the moment,' said Chang. 'Something's off. Don't you notice it? My family knows something about all this. I'm sure of it.'

'A lot is happening,' said Jesse. 'Pushing the overdrive trials to completion sooner than expected, Connor's technology, this sudden increase in piracy and the change in piracy tactics. Then there are the mimic drones and your sister's research.'

'Do you think it's all connected?' asked Chang.

Jesse had a fair idea about what might be going on. She was privy to information others weren't. Being the Skimmer security and communications officer, she often used probing questions to check where her crew members thinking was at.

'I think that we are heading into trouble again and my damn family has something to do with it all!' exclaimed Chang as he raised his voice.

'What's all the noise,' said Stella as she walked up to them. 'The others are up now as well.'

'Nothing,' said Chang as he walked off gruffly and waved a dismissive hand at her and Jesse. He was feeling helpless.

'Family,' said Jesse watching him go. They followed Chang and walked back to the rec area.

'I see,' said Stella quietly as they walked into the rec area. She didn't want to press Jesse about it.

'Morning all,' said Jonny as he stretched and yawned seeing them walk into the rec area.

'You're up a bit early,' said Stella.

'You lot don't know how to keep quiet,' said Jonny. 'Besides we need to get out of here and hunker down.'

'That we do,' said Ngarra walking in as well. 'Grab some food and let's prepare and depart.'

'What about the mimic drones?' asked Connor as he came in and sat down with something to eat.

'It would be great to talk to Ying Yue and share thoughts on our programs. I have this idea you see, about Gilgamesh and their mimic drones.'

'We'll see, Connor,' interrupted Jesse. 'Let's focus on what's in front of us.'

'But this could change everything,' said Connor. 'True autonomy, self-repair and self-control at a whole of system level. I like the fungus analogy. Nature has much to show us, you know.'

'A fool's game,' said Jonny. 'Humans are at the top of the pecking order, not machines.'

'It's not a machine,' said Connor fiercely, 'it's Gilgamesh!'

Connor took his food and disappeared up the stairs to the information hub.

Jonny shrugged his shoulders. 'I wasn't talking about his work,' said Jonny.

'Leave him be,' said Jesse.

'He's so attached to that thing he has created,' said Jonny. 'It worries me.'

'It would worry me more if he wasn't attached to it,' said Ngarra. 'That's what worries me about these so-called mimic drones. Lack of human oversight.'

'Like I said, leave him be,' replied Jesse. 'He's put a lot of himself into it, that's all.'

'Let's get this show on the road then,' said Jonny as he stuffed his mouth full of the last of the food on his plate.

'Yep, let's do this,' said Ngarra as he quickly finished what he was eating.

He got up and put his plate in the dispenser.

The others followed suit.

Stella and Chang went through the watertight bulkhead entrance and down the stairs to the Xtract bay while Jesse, Ngarra and Jonny went up to the SAI console.

'SAI, prepare to depart to mining coordinates,' said Ngarra as he walked into the SAI console.

'Confirmed,' said SAI. 'Prepare to depart for mining coordinates.'

Jonny had already entered the new location given to them when they were briefed by the Academy crew monitoring about the supercell. He put his interface lenses on and zoomed in on the hologram to look at their route and the location.

'Looks like all the Skimmers that were spread out and mining in the path of this thing will be grouped,' said Jonny. 'Some are already there, others on the way. We are the last to depart from here.'

'SAI, display met ocean data for the next seventy-two hours,' said Jesse.

The hologram was overlayed with weather data. It looked nasty, to say the least. A fifty-metre swell and gale-force winds. At a hundred metres below, they would be just out of reach of the swell, which would penetrate the depths for some distance.

'The mother of all storms,' said Jonny.

'Chinese engineering,' said Stella over open comms. The comms link between the SAI console and the Xtract bay console was always open during departure and arrival. 'Lucky this beast of a Harvester is built to ride out supercells.'

'Still, I wouldn't want to be on the Harvester,' replied Jonny. 'Even with heave compensation and dampeners.'

'SAI, confirm Skimmer status for departure,' said Ngarra.

'Skimmer is watertight, rim driven propulsion online, all systems nominal,' said SAI.

'Just in time,' said Jonny. 'Once those docking clamps lock, we are stuck here.'

'SAI, depart for mining location coordinates,' said Ngarra.

'Confirmed,' said SAI. 'Depart for mining location coordinates.'

The docking clamps retracted, and rim driven propulsion powered up. The outer hull shields had closed, and the external camera system was activated.

Slowly, the Skimmer started to descend. The surface closed over them as they sank below, down into the moon pool and out below the Harvester. Rows of dimly lit navigation lights passed them by.

They stopped below the hull. It was dim outside. A dull hue given the deteriorating weather above. The Skimmer paused, orientated itself towards the coordinates and then took off, accelerating to cruising speed.

***

The Sea Hunters had also departed. They would move into position and standoff from the Skimmers out of the main path of the supercell.

On the way, they would deploy their two interceptor drones to monitor the Skimmers grouped together and hunkered down to ride out the supercell.

'Let's get those interceptor drones deployed as soon as we can,' said Max as he stood next to the SAI console and looked out over the deteriorating ocean conditions.

'We are going to move across its projected path and deploy them,' said Alex. 'Then head out to its leading edge. We will be out of the worst of it. It will still be a rough ride for twenty-four hours.'

'I want those surface drone vessels well out of the way,' said Max. 'Send them away. Box them in over here.'

Max pointed to a location on the navigation hologram of the supercell's path.

'SAI, depart from Harvester security zone towards entered coordinates.'

'Confirmed,' said SAI. 'Depart Harvester security zone for entered coordinates.'

The duty officer contacted operations and explained what was to happen.

Holding on, Max and Alex looked out over the ocean. The Hunter vessel and its two drone ships picked up speed. The vessel moved off in a wide arc, straightened up and headed off towards the entered coordinates. Behind them, the Harvester was slowly heaving to and fro as the sea state continued to deteriorate.

'The SAI console is yours,' said Max to the duty officer as they turned to leave.

'Yes, sir,' he replied. 'The SAI console is mine.'

'Let's get to the drone bay and pick up Cam along the way,' said Max. 'I want to discuss deploying these interceptors before we launch them.'

Alex and Max left the SAI console and headed back through operations. It was busy. The crew were looking at weather patterns, preparing to monitor the interceptor drones and send the drone vessels away. Others were checking vessel systems and confirming with SAI its status for the coming supercell.

The Hunter vessel would be closed up and watertight for the worst of it. Movement about the vessel would be restricted.

'Cam,' said Max as they passed a meeting room. 'When you're finished, come to the drone bay. Let's go over deploying these interceptors with the controller.'

'We're done here for now,' he said, getting up and telling his team they would finish later.

'Operations will monitor the interceptor drones through the grid buoys and eel drones as they watch over the Skimmers,' said Alex.

'Expecting trouble?' asked Cam as he walked out with them.

'You could say that,' replied Max as they made their way to the drone bay.

Alex, Max, and Cam exited the stairwell. On the well deck, the drone bay door was still open. It was the last to close once the interceptor drones had been deployed. Above them, the drone deck had been locked down and everything secured and made watertight.

They walked up the short flight of stairs and into the control room.

'Sir,' said the controller as they entered, 'two interceptor drones ready to be deployed.'

They watched as a couple of technicians did some final checks. No breaching pods were attached. The drones would patrol the area the Skimmers would be in while the supercell raged above.

'The interceptors will be out of range,' said the controller. 'We can monitor them through the grid. In autonomous mode, we will be relying on their detection and deterrence capabilities.'

'Nothing else should be in that part of "the Area" except the Skimmers,' said Max.

'And if there is?' questioned Cam.

'They have been programmed to defend the Skimmers, their Xtracts and themselves,' said the controller.

'We should have taken a breaching pod and boarded a few of those Skimmers for inspections during all this,' said Cam.

'Not our mandate,' said Alex, 'and we can't get to you if something goes wrong. Too much risk to you during this supercell and it's a waste of resources.'

'I don't want my crew stuck on those things during all this if something goes wrong,' said Max. 'You're no good to me on a Skimmer.'

'I could use a holiday,' said Cam, smiling.

'As could we all,' said Max.

'If those pirates turn up, the interceptor drones will assist the Skimmers in their defence,' said Alex. 'The Skimmer crew will just have to deal with it. Assuming they are not tethered, that is.'

'And if one of them is disabled and boarded because they are tethered and mining when they shouldn't?' asked the controller.

'Then we wait,' said Max. 'Nothing we can do until the worst of this supercell passes.'

'We've got the two surface drone vessels heading into position,' said Alex. 'They will be some distance off, though. It will take time to get them into position if something happens. Dependent on the weather, that is.'

'It will take us a while to move in and offer assistance even when the sea state eases,' said Cam. 'I mean, given the distance, we have to standoff for this beast that is bearing down on us.'

'It's the best we can do,' said Max. 'My crew and our safety come first.'

'Right you are,' said Cam.

Max stretched, folded his arms, and looked out at the technicians giving the thumbs up to the controller to deploy the interceptor drones.

'Pull up the navigation display,' said Max.

The controller swiped a screen and they all looked at their location.

'We should deploy them and then continue across the predicted path and wait it out here,' said Alex.

'Agree,' said Max

'We still have some time before the worst of it hits so let's make the most of it,' said Alex.

'Deploy interceptors,' said Max.

'Yes, sir,' said the controller. 'Deploying interceptors.'

They watched as the technicians stepped away and the docking clamps moved one at a time out through the bay door and over the well deck. In turn, each interceptor drone powered up and the docking clamp lowered it into the water. As each one was released, it shot out the back of the well deck and disappeared below the heaving seas. The docking clamps moved back into the bay and the large bay door closed. The Hunter vessel was now watertight.

Chapter 14

The bow plunged through the heavy seas. The direction of travel and how fast they could go was limited. To keep it bearable for the crew, they had to either head into the huge swells or away from them. Another wave smashed over the bow and the sea spray came up over the top of the vessel.

'It's a Monster supercell,' said Alex as he held onto something and looked at the navigation hologram in the middle of the SAI console.

'At least, we are on the outer edge of it,' said Max.

The duty watch officer held on and swiped a console screen and checked the path of the supercell.

'We can maintain our course and speed,' he said. 'It will limit the impact on the crew and keep us within range for a while longer of our interceptor drones monitoring the Skimmers.'

The outer hull shields were closed, and the vessel was watertight. Through the camera system, they watched as the vessel rode down the back of a giant wave and up the next. The wave crested and broke and the bow plunged through it.

'SAI, confirm the location and status of our interceptor drones,' said Max as he gripped the rails along the SAI console.

'Interceptor drones are on location,' said SAI. 'Patrol polygon has been executed.'

'Let's get to operations,' said Max. 'I want a seat through all this, and I want to look over options if things go pear-shaped with those Skimmers and pirates.'

'You have the SAI console duty officer,' said Alex.

Alex had been on watch for a while. It was common practice if more than two officers were at the SAI console for the ranking officer to take the watch from the duty officer so they could get some respite. It was more a courtesy than anything else, given that systems were mostly automated and run by SAI. It wasn't always the case, but it was appreciated when it did happen.

'I have the SAI cosnole,' he replied.

The duty officer carried on monitoring safety, propulsion, and navigation while Alex and Max headed off to operations.

'If any of those grid buoys go down, we will not be able to monitor the interceptors,' said Alex as they walked along the corridor and through to operations.

'Not to mention the Skimmers,' said Max. 'They will be on their own. I'm expecting trouble. Our interceptors can handle things in autonomous mode until we get there.'

They entered operations.

The few crew on duty were busy monitoring subsurface, surface and air domains, assets, weapons and engineering systems or the deployed interceptor drones.

'Laser comms signalling between the eel drones, grid buoys and us will be hit and miss through all this,' said Alex.

'We will likely lose monitoring the interceptor drones for a while,' said Max. 'What's the current operational mode of those interceptors?' he asked.

'Almost out of range and fully autonomous,' he replied. 'SAI has handed control to them. They are already boxed in, reacting to anything that is not a Skimmer or an Xtract.'

'Good,' said Max as he sat in the command seat.

Alex walked over to one of the crew and grabbed a rail. He looked over their shoulder at the tracking system for the interceptors.

'I don't know how much longer we will have eyes on them,' he said to Max. 'Real-time monitoring may be limited for a while.'

'Nothing much more to do but standby and wait,' said Max as he stretched back and swivelled the seat round to face forward. The vessel was pitching markedly now but with stabilisers, they had managed to minimise their role. 'I want a breaching pod crew briefed and ready, a surface sea boat crew on standby and a patrol drone and crew on standby,' said Max.

Alex contacted Cam and got him to organise the briefing and make sure assets were on standby.

'SAI, display and confirm defensive weapons system status,' said Max.

'Confirmed,' said SAI as the vessel's defensive weapons system display was brought up. 'All arrays online. Arming required.'

'SAI, arm all defensive weapons arrays,' said Max.

'Confirmed,' said SAI. 'All defensive weapon arrays are armed.'

A duty officer swiped their hand across a display and went through the various defensive system weapon arrays and assets and cross-checked their status with SAI.

'SAI, track and lock any subsurface, surface and air domain target and confirm identity,' said the duty officer as he overlaid the tracking systems.

'Confirmed,' said SAI. 'Target threat analysis and tracking active, defensive weapons array interface activated.'

'Who's up for a coffee,' said Max. 'Free jolly in a patrol drone for anyone that doesn't spill it.'

The operations officers on duty looked at him. They were not sure if he was serious or joking. It was hard to tell sometimes. The coffee cups were sealed.

'Come on folks, seriously,' said Max. 'It's a fun day at the fair on a roller coaster. Grab a coffee and enjoy the ride. When the shit hits the fan, then you can get your arses back in the hot seats. All we can do now is watch and wait.'

'And try not to throw up,' said one of them.

'Should've popped a pill like the rest of us then,' said Max.

The others laughed.

'You better go see the Medic then,' said Max.

He got up and left in a hurry.

When operational, the watches changed to twelve-hour standing watches. One night and the other day. Max always encouraged the crew to support each other through these long watches and to keep a degree of collegiality otherwise teamwork fell apart when things heated up.

The team smiled and relaxed a little. One went to the mess and got a round of coffee in sealed cups. He knew what each of them liked.

***

Ngarra's Skimmer was on the final approach. They were the last of the Skimmers to arrive at the designated location. They were to hold position while at the surface the supercell passed through 'the Area'.

Another brief had come through from the Xed Academy crew monitoring and communications about the threat of piracy. Another Skimmer, while tethered, had been confronted by pirates and rammed. Everyone working on Skimmers in 'the Area' was concerned and a little worried.

Ngarra's Skimmer moved in a wide, flat arc around the location of the arrival coordinates.

'Position coordinates are clear,' said SAI. 'On final approach.'

SAI finished scanning and the Skimmer straightened up and moved into position.

The Skimmer slowly came to a halt.

Ngarra, Jesse and Jonny watched.

'In position,' said SAI.

Jonny took his interface lenses off. 'We might as well mine,' he said to the others. Open comms was still active, so everyone heard him.

'Yeah.' Said Stella from the Xtract bay. 'Others will be.'

'I'm not so sure about it this time,' said Ngarra. 'Those pirates rammed another Skimmer. A small manned drone with a docking hatch was seen.'

'What are the chances though,' said Chang over comms, 'I don't want to sit here doing nothing for forty-eight hours while this supercell passes through.'

'We are alone out here,' said Jesse. 'Apart from the other Skimmers nearby even the Sea Hunters can't get to us straight away. There are only the interceptor drones patrolling as a deterrent.'

'I don't want to deploy the streamer,' said Ngarra. 'If it gets sheared off with Xtracts down, we could lose the lot and that will get us in a world of trouble with Xed.'

'Then it's the opportune time, ladies,' said Jonny. 'I mean to rely on Connor's tech without the streamer. The drones will look after themselves down there and return.'

Connor came racing in from the information hub. He had been looking over Gilgamesh and the red queen sequence. Hearing the conversation through the bulkhead entrance that was now open, he was excited by the prospect.

'Gilgamesh is ready for this,' he said excitedly. 'We know it works. Let's do it. With the red queen inserted, the only way to stop it is to turn the whole thing off. The transfer is permanent, and the only interface is through me. I can't change it. The interface between Gilgamesh, SAI and the Xtracts and myself can't be undone.'

'Do we still have oversight,' asked Jesse, 'I mean can we terminate the operation even though the Xtracts are truly autonomous? The last resort, given Gilgamesh, is still externally powered, is to just pull the plug on it all. Haven't solved that one yet.'

'I think I have found a power source that will work,' said Connor. 'Anyway, I made sure I can still define the parameters within which any operation or activity is to occur. However, once autonomous, the red queen sequence can't be accessed without unplugging and rebooting. I mean a complete system shutdown.'

'What's the worst that can happen,' said Jonny. 'An attempt to ram and board us. We use the overdrive and come back for the Xtracts later, deploy the streamer and recover them the old-fashioned way.'

'Come on, we can do it,' said Connor as he paced up and down.

'What if we deployed the streamer anyway?' asked Jesse.

'If Connor's tech is fully activated, we can drop the streamer and leave. We can use the Xtracts to recover the streamer later when we return. I mean, if a piracy incident occurs that is. If these pirates are ramming Skimmers, our propulsion could be damaged. They might attempt to board us. SAI may even surface the Skimmer if life support is compromised. The brief was to use the escape pods if that happened and transfer to another Skimmer and get away.'

Ngarra nodded in agreement.

'Okay, the decision is to do some mining,' said Ngarra. 'Let's deploy the streamer as a precaution. Our backup is that Connor's tech is fully operational and allows us to recover both the dropped streamer and the Xtracts if need be.'

'Yes!' said Jonny with a little fist pump.

'Fantastic,' said Connor excitedly. 'Finally, after all that work.'

'SAI, deploy streamer,' said Ngarra.

'Confirmed,' said SAI. 'Deploy streamer.'

'Stella and Chang,' said Ngarra over open comms, 'monitor the streamer's descent. Get those Xtracts online and ready to deploy. Then meet us in the rec area. Connor, you can brief us all on how all this is going to play out.'

Jonny, Ngarra, Jesse and Connor left the SAI console. They passed through the watertight bulkhead, down the stairs and into the rec area.

'This will accelerate the process so much,' said Connor as they walked down the stairs. 'For Gilgamesh, it's like evolution on steroids. I mean, the red queen that is. The learning will accelerate. In fact, I can't even determine what will happen after that. The whole will become greater than the sum of its parts.'

'After what?' asked Jesse as they walked across and sat at the table in the rec area.

The conversation carried on while they waited for Stella and Chang to come up from the Xtract bay.

***

In the Xtract bay, Stella watched as SAI deployed the communication streamer. It took an hour to reach the seabed four thousand metres below. It extended downward into the black depths below. She checked the status of each communication node strung along it as it deployed.

'Do you think those pirates will come?' asked Stella.

'I don't often worry about these things, but this is different.'

'Well, I don't think they are pirates,' said Chang. 'Look at what happened to me previously. Something else has to be going on.'

'Are you saying we are all in danger?' she asked.

'I think so,' said Chang. 'It just makes sense. It's an escalation of those previous attempts to coerce me into getting hold of Connor's tech. It's all connected somehow.'

'Let's discuss it some more with Ngarra once we finish this,' said Stella.

'For once I agree with you,' said Chang. 'Who knew women could be so intelligent,' he said sarcastically.

Stella ignored the comment.

Chang had largely got over his arrogance and misogynistic nature toward women and their gender. In fact, he had become somewhat protective of the crew after everything that had happened. He had seen that despite everything they still believed in him. He had to take a good look at himself. But he still felt a lot of animosity toward his father over his family. At least, he was more aware of the impact it was having on everyone around him. On occasion, the crew still bore the brunt of his anger.

'But are they the same people,' said Stella, 'I mean, this ramming? Not the pirates, but the same people that tried to get to you before?'

'I would have thought so,' said Chang as he remembered past events. 'Whoever they are.'

'You seem to be the centre of attention these days,' said Stella as she tried to lighten the mood.

'What do you mean by that?' asked Chang.

'You're spoiling my vogue,' said Stella, smiling.

'You're what?' asked Chang, raising his eyebrows.

'Uh, my style,' she said with an attitude. 'You know, all that attention you get is distracting everyone from me.'

'Woman,' said Chang gruffly. He managed a smile.

'You're not smiling at me are you, Chang?' asked Stella.

'I'll run the terminal checks down each side,' said Chang as he quickly moved off.

Chang wasn't one for smiling much and was a little embarrassed. Sometimes he didn't know how to take Stella.

Chang walked down the passage on each side of the maintenance bay along the inside of the external recess, checking the power status of each Xtract on its docking clamp.

'Green, yellow and red,' he said out loud to himself as he walked the length of the passage.

'Ah,' he said, stopping at one he could see indicating yellow. Power wasn't nominal. It needed more charging time.

'Comms check, hydraulics check, propulsion check, electrical check, and round and round we go,' he said, going through the check-off list for each Xtract. 'Every time we do this,' he said walking back to the Xtract bay console and passing through to the other side, 'I think why the hell am I doing it when you can just check it all from here. SAI has got this.'

'It's protocol and because you love it,' said Stella smiling as he disappeared down the opposite passage to do the same check-offs.

'Good to go,' he said after a short pause. 'Protocols and routines are my life here.'

He continued moaning about monitoring an AI and its automated systems.

Chang returned along the passage to the maintenance bay console. He walked back through the watertight bulkhead and across to Stella. They both look at the displays and then through the viewing screen at the maintenance bay beyond.

'Think of the bigger picture,' said Stella. 'What else would you rather be doing?'

'Other than hanging around out here underneath a supercell? I can think of a few things,' he said in a cynical tone.

'Me too actually,' she said smiling.

Stella was always trying to keep morale up. Like a mother hen, she thought of everyone as her children. She admired Jesse in her role, and she was much the same when it came to the crew. Although, Jesse was so serious all the time though. *A bit of a mystery that woman,* thought Stella.

'We could be doing lots of other things besides this,' said Stella. 'Be in the moment and live in the unknown. Who knows where all this is going to lead?'

Chang looked through the maintenance bay to the rear. The airlock was closed. *Might as well be in deep space hanging around some planet mining its resources*, he thought to himself, *what would be the difference?*

Chapter 15

The crew gathered in the rec area. The streamer had touched down and the Xtracts were ready to launch. The link between Gilgamesh, the red queen sequence and the Xtracts was permanent. It meant Connor's technology, the sphere of Gilgamesh, the red queen and all his work creating a self-learning mesh would take hold of the Xtracts. SAI would no longer have control of them unless Connor shut down Gilgamesh.

'Communication request from Sea Hunters,' announced SAI as they got something to eat and sat down. 'Eel drone and grid buoy proximity restricted, live feed not available.'

'SAI, on screen,' said Ngarra.

The rec area message board activated, and Alex's image appeared in a recorded message.

'For all Skimmer crew,' said Alex. 'Two interceptor drones are patrolling the lockdown area for the duration of the supercell. Advice is to cease mining. High probability of piracy incidents occurring during supercell. You are on your own for at least the next twenty-four hours.'

The message ended and Alex's image faded.

'At world's end,' said Chang in his usual grumpy voice. 'Sitting ducks, we are.'

'Such optimism,' said Jonny sarcastically. 'How did you become the chief happiness officer?'

The others tried not to laugh at the comment.

'Who pushed your button?' asked Chang raising his voice.

'Cut it out you two,' said Jesse before the situation escalated again.

Jonny shrugged his shoulders and made his usual warrior face at Chang. Ever the antagonist, the crew had got used to his antics.

'So, Connor,' said Jonny as he changed the subject. 'This is it then. Your love affair with Gilgamesh is about to have babies.'

The crew erupted in laughter.

'That was a good one,' said Stella as the crew stopped laughing and tried to keep straight faces.

Connor looked horrified. Being on the spectrum he took everything quite literally.

'If you're implying that there is some sort of biological component to this?' he questioned.

The crew erupted in laughter again. Jonny leant too far back and fell backwards onto the floor. The laughter carried on.

'You lot are just crazy,' said Connor looking questioningly at them all. Their sense of humour evaded Connor at the best of times.

'They are certainly that,' said Jesse catching her breath as she got up and helped Jonny off the floor. 'It's nothing, Connor. He meant your Gilgamesh is going to be like a mother to those Xtracts, guiding their learning.'

'Well actually, you are close with your analogy,' said Connor. 'More like Gilgamesh is cloning itself. They will all be Gilgamesh. It's a non-centralised system. Gilgamesh is more like a conduit, like the central nerve ring in a starfish, for example. But with human oversight. I mean I can switch it off if needed and influence the conduit or nerve ring if that's what you want to call it.'

'Sounds a lot like the Borg to me,' said Jonny.

'The Borg?' questioned Connor.

'Star Trek, the Borg,' said Stella.

Connor still looked confused. Analogies and synonyms didn't compute very well with him.

'Anyway,' said Jesse, 'Connor, why don't you brief us on this and then SAI can launch them.'

'Great,' said Connor. 'Up until now, Gilgamesh has synced with the Xtracts creating a link to the red queen simulation in the mesh. Now, instead of the Xtract programming being controlled by SAI, we deactivate it. SAI is now replaced by the red queen sequence. SAI can only monitor activity. The sphere of Gilgamesh takes over. It's permanent. We can't change it.'

'But like you said we still have oversight don't we?' questioned Ngarra.

'Of course,' said Connor, 'we can influence the learning by placing limits on the parameters within which the red queen functions. It's the learning itself that is the revolution. With red queen taking control, they will adapt and improve continuously by themselves now.'

'Nature's solution then,' said Jonny.

'Nature has a lot to offer,' said Connor. 'Take energy, for instance. How do you think some of that bell or flying disk technology came about during and after world war two?'

'Aliens,' said Jonny jokingly.

'Supposedly anyway,' said Jesse. 'Remember our training at the Xed Academy about the history behind all this?'

'You mean Viktor Schauberger and Nazi Germany,' said Stella, 'and others well before him like Maria Orsic and the Vril society. Then later you had Otis Carr and his work with flying disks. And look at those crash recovery disclosures and now there's this overdrive technology on these Skimmers . Maybe it's all connected. I mean where did that come from, the overdrive technology?'

'Our training included learning about Roswell, Antarctica and Operation High jump, Paperclip, van Braun, Apollo and the supposed extra-terrestrial presence,' said Jonny. 'Then there's the whole back story regarding Presients', intelligence agencies and signing of the National Security Act in the USA. And charismatic figures like William Tompkins and other people. Mining seems to be just one part of something much bigger. The builders?'

'Enough,' said Jesse. 'Now's not the time to get into all this. You learnt enough about it all during your training at the Xed and the Academy.'

'Right then, enough chitchat,' said Ngarra in agreement before they got into a long conversation about it all.

'Let's get these Xtracts deployed,' said Jesse.

'Yes,' said Chang. 'We might as well verify all this actually works while sitting here riding out this supercell.'

'The advice was not to mine nodules though,' said Jonny.

'Gone soft have we, Jonny?' asked Chang.

Jonny gave him a cold stare.

'Sure,' said Ngarra as he waved his hand at them to stop it, 'but the Xtracts will be independent. Like I said, if the worse comes to worst, we can detach the streamer and recover both it and the Xtracts later if we need to get out of here in a hurry.'

'Yeah, in a straight line to nowhere,' said Chang.

'Or a jump using the overdrive,' said Jonny. 'In that case, there is no straight line is there. No vector or direction. It's scalar and relative. Just leaving one place and arriving at another.'

They all nodded in agreement.

'Stella, Chang, you go to the Xtract bay,' said Ngarra. 'Jonny, come with Jesse and I to the SAI console. Connor, you go to the information hub. Confirm permanent transfer. Then we deploy.'

The crew got up and moved off.

Jonny, Jesse and Ngarra walked up to the SAI console.

They waited for the others to get in position.

'I'm going to verify the sync with the Xtracts now,' said Connor over open comms. 'You will need to confirm it by checking SAI no longer has control of the Xtracts. At the same time, I will confirm that red queen is in control.'

A pause followed.

They waited to hear from Connor.

'Go ahead,' said Connor over open comms.

'SAI, command override,' said Jesse. 'Deactivate control of Xtracts.'

'Confirmed,' said SAI. 'Command override verified. Deactivate Xtract control.'

'Connor, it's done,' said Ngarra. 'Cross-check with red queen.'

Another pause followed.

They waited in anticipation.

'Confirmed,' said Connor. 'You can deploy the Xtracts to their mining coordinates. SAI can only monitor them now.'

'Go ahead, Stella,' said Ngarra over comms.

'Onto it,' replied Stella.

Another pause followed.

Jonny, Ngarra and Jesse turned around and looked outside.

The outer hull shields were retracted.

They watched as one by one the Xtracts detached from their docking clamps.

The photic zone was exceptionally dark due to the storm raging above. The lights from the Skimmer and its Xtracts lit the surrounding area.

Silently, the Xtracts moved out over the Skimmer wings, paused, and descended to the black depths below.

'Right,' said Ngarra as the last of the Xtracts disappeared. 'Let's get back to the rec area. SAI monitor Xtracts. Scan and report on any other assets in range.'

'Confirmed,' said SAI. 'Monitor Xtracts. Scan and report on any other assets in range.'

'I'll stay here,' said Connor from the information hub over open comms. 'I need to oversee how Gilgamesh evolves. I have to monitor parameters.'

'Okay,' said Ngarra.

Ngarra, Jesse and Jonny walked to the rear of the SAI console, through the watertight bulkhead and down the stairs to the rec area and sat down.

Not long after, Stella and Chang came up from the Xtract bay and sat down with them.

'I guess all we can do now is wait for the supercell to pass,' said Chang as he sat down.

'And if those pirates turn up,' said Jonny. 'We get the hell out of dodge.'

'Agreed,' said Ngarra. 'We detach the streamer and use the overdrive.'

'So why has Rick advanced the trials?' asked Jonny.

'The situation has changed.' Said Jesse. 'Plans for the Skimmers and their further use have been brought forward.'

'I still have trouble getting my head around how it all works,' said Jonny. 'I mean the actual mechanics and physics of it all.'

'As security and communications officers, we have more of an idea than most from our training,' said Jesse, 'and we have all been taken through the concepts during crew training at the Xed Academy. We were trained in various theories. Remember, we discussed the application of the equations for the expansion of the universe when it comes to trying to understand how the overdrive works. And then also overcoming our misunderstanding of how the sun and indeed stars and black holes work. Externally driven processes, cosmic rays provide an energy source for fusion. It appears to be all about frequency, vibration, magnetism and electric fields.'

'Seriously,' said Jonny, rolling his eyes and grinning at Stella. 'I know we had to learn about all this. But how is it even possible? I mean the sun, black holes, the universe and linking it to understanding how overdrives actually work.'

'Our instructors said that one way to think about it is Einstein's cosmological constant,' said Jesse. 'It prevents the collapse of the universe, which was predicted by general relativity. It can do more than just hold the universe in a steady-state though, the constant I mean. It might also power the expansion of the universe. Then there was always ongoing discussion by our instructors about linking gravity with both relatively and quantum mechanics. I think correcting the misunderstanding of black holes was a key thought going around the

Academy, that gravity was both attractive and repulsive and understanding how that related to event horizons. And those singularities were not what we thought they were.'

'Okay,' said Jonny looking baffled and confused and using his hand to imitate his head spinning round and round. 'Now that's a whole lot of physics I still struggle with. But I'm a practical kind of man. The overdrive is an ironclad cylinder containing a mercury plasma vortex spun using a magnetic semiconductor plate at its base to generalise a field that negates our mass relative to its surroundings,' said Jonny. 'It's not a universe, sun or a black hole is it?'

'Sure,' said Jesse, 'but maybe it works like one, though. The overdrive worked even though people struggled to understand how or why it worked. Once they overcame the problem of orientation to a set of coordinates it, the rest is history.'

'What do you mean, works like one?' asked Ngarra as he looked at the others who all nodded their heads.

Jesse thought for a minute then carried on.

'In mainstream science, people always get stuck in their academic territory,' said Jesse. 'At the academy, we were taught that scientists didn't want to modify Einstein's equations. They looked to another physical cause that has the role of this constant. The dark energy of empty space or what they called vacuum energy. But in quantum mechanics, empty space is not empty at all. We were taught that it was where people started looking; trying to understand how the overdrive works I mean. Gravitoelectric-electric energy fields and controlling matter fizzing and popping in and out of the physical world. Torsion fields, angular momentum and hyperdimensional physics'

'Is that whole uncertainty principle thing we hear about?' asked Chang as he became much more interested in what Jesse was saying. He was trying to remember their classes on all of it at the Academy.

'You know the Heisenberg uncertainty principle, the more accurately you try and determine a particle position the less accurately you can determine momentum.'

'I suppose so,' said Jesse. 'According to our instructors, for a short period of time energy can be produced in empty space where there is no matter. Mass-energy equilibrium means a particle can be produced temporarily. It's called zero-point energy.'

'Yeah but during our instruction and training, I always struggled to get what all that has to do with the overdrive,' said Chang.

'Yeah,' said Jonny, looking totally confused. 'Me too. I'm not getting it here boys and girls.'

'Think of it is like this then,' said Jesse as she tried to get them to understand some of the physics. 'That experiment we learnt about in class where two metal plates are positioned a few micrometres apart. Fewer particles are produced between them than outside. It creates a difference in pressure that pushes the plates together.'

'So,' said Stella. 'Are you saying that what's inside the overdrive wants to collapse in on itself while at the same time pushing outwards? Are you saying the vortex does something similar. It produces negative pressure. I struggled with our instructors trying to explain all this to us.'

'You could think of it like that,' said Jesse, 'but remember we were taught that zero-point energy in and of itself is no good for producing the energy field needed to discharge into and make a jump on a Skimmer.'

'So,' said Jonny. 'The highly polarised mercury plasma vortex means all those excited electrons that are stripped and spun out of their orbits can produce the huge amounts of energy around us that is needed.'

'Exactly,' said Jesse. 'Because of torsion, the source energy of everything. The free energy occupying the space between all atoms and subatomic particles.'

'But what does vacuum energy particle properties, negative pressure and a polarised plasmas vortex of atoms and their displaced electrons have to do with understanding how the physics of this overdrive might work,' said Jonny raising his hands in the air, 'Apart from spinning my brain into mush.'

The others laughed at the analogy.

'Ahh,' said Jesse, smiling at them. 'Now we get to the bottom of it, or should I say the top.'

'Meaning what?' asked Chang who was now engrossed in the conversation.

'Our instructors said that one way to look at it is that pressure is a form of energy,' said Jesse. 'So general relativity predicts that both mass and positive pressure are gravitationally attractive. And that negative pressure is also predicted to result in gravitational repulsion in an inflationary universe.'

'My head is still spinning,' said Jonny as he whacked the palm of his hand on his forehead.

Again, there was a chuckle from the others as he banged his head a few times on the table.

'Come on, boy,' said Stella. 'Get with the program here.'

Jonny made a face at her.

'According to general relativity,' said Stella. 'A negative pressure creates a repulsive gravitational field. I get that Jesse, but what does that have to do with the overdrive? Gravitational attraction should cancel out gravitational repulsion.'

'No,' said Jesse. 'Remember in classes we were taught that mass which is attractive and pressure which is repulsive, affect acceleration of an expanding universe differently. And due to the increase in rate of spin in our vortex and resulting changes in mass, relativistic effects become huge.'

'I'm still lost,' said Jonny as he tried to remember their classes at the Academy and get his head around all the theory. 'So, the overdrive is gravitationally repulsive then. It produces a repulsive gravity field around the Skimmer due to negative pressure?'

'It's one way to view it,' said Jesse. 'Our instructors said to think of it as something like that. They showed us how it can be demonstrated in the Friedmann equations, the second one for the acceleration of the expansion of the universe. The pressure term is three times the size of the mass density term.'

'I remember,' said Stella. 'So, there is three times more negative pressure exerted as a force in a vacuum than there is produced by mass,' said Stella.

'Yes,' said Jesse. 'Because pressure has three dimensions. So, repulsion is three times stronger than attraction.'

'But our instructors also said that the amount of energy produced, or zero-point energy, in that repulsion is tiny,' said Stella. 'Zero-point energy is nt enough. Remember what they said, that the overdrive wouldn't produce a large enough repulsive gravity field just due to negative pressure and repulsion in a vacuum.'

'According to our course on all this and what the instructors said, I think that's where the highly polarised vortex comes in,' said Jesse. 'As I said before, torsion fields, angular momentum and hyperdimensional physics. The source of all forces is the enormous amount of energy created by spin, the energy that occupies all that empty space between atoms and subatomic particles. We have a vortex to harness it.

'God!,' said Jonny as he smacked the table with the palm of his hand in a comical gesture. 'Back to something I can get my head around a little.'

The others entertained his antics.

Jonny wasn't sure whether they were laughing at him or with him.

'Here's how I interpret what we were taught about all this,' said Jesse. 'Across the universe, there is a cumulative effect over distance for negative pressure and repulsion. But at a small scale in the overdrive, the lack of distance is compensated for by producing a stable high energy plasma vortex. The relative increase in mass due spin of subatomic particles is huge. A black hole in a tin can if you like. It's all about torsion or torsion fields.'

'My kind of language,' said Jonny. 'Keep it simple, boys and girls.'

Jesse smiled at him and nodded her head.

'The extreme rotation speed creates an outward pressure that stops the vortex of spinning subatomic particles from collapsing in on itself,' said Jesse. 'In this vacuum, however, the extreme inward pressure is just as great. So, you get the same gravitational repulsion you would see accumulate over large distances in space. In fact, you get enormous amounts of it. Thus, the repulsive gravity field around the Skimmer.'

'So, that means relative to our surroundings we have little or no mass then,' said Ngarra, 'like a hole or a bubble in space. We have no inertia either then. That's how the energy discharge into the field works to shift us then. Because the plasma is highly polarised a high-frequency energy discharge into it at right angles to the direction of the energy field shifts us in time and space. We have slipped out of phase. We are just more matter popping in and out of the physical world. It's an instantaneous shift of this bubble or hole in space with no acceleration and no inertia.

'I know they tried to explain it to us,' said Stella as she looked at Jesse. 'Is that how it works then? Is that why the discharge is on both sides? One aligned with our arrival coordinates and a greater one opposite to compensate for inertia and to stop us from being squashed like a bug.'

'But what about Feynman's equation that you talked about? For a zero-point energy universe, I mean,' said Ngarra as he also tried to get his head around all the theory. 'We were taught that vacuum energy means the universe would keep expanding. It would break his equation. Total energy must be zero. There must be a balance.'

'Here's yet another way to look at it.' said Jesse. 'Remember they told us to think of the vortex as being a soap bubble? Like the universe, it's elastic and proportional to its area. The film is always trying to contract but is resisted by the outward pressure of the air in the bubble. This is what a vortex does. The inward and outward pressure, I mean. So, like the universe, the vortex also has an equilibrium distance between its gravitational energy and mass-energy.'

'Is that this so-called Schwarzschild radius we learnt about in our classes,' said Jonny.

'Maybe,' said Jesse. 'I still struggle with the concepts myself that they taught us as well when trying to understand how all this works mechanically. The instructors were teaching us about the Schwarzschild radius of a black hole. In a black hole, there is a balance of energy between an object trying to leave it and gravity pulling it back. Like a spring when stretched, gravity is attractive and when compressed it is repulsive. If one mass moves closer to the other and is inside its Schwarzschild radius, then gravity is repulsive.'

'My mind boggles and I am even more confused now,' said Jonny as he put his hands on his ears like his brain was exploding. 'Again, how does that relate to understanding how the overdrive works? I mean, it seems there are different ways of explaining the theory behind how it all works.'

'According to what we were taught, gravity needs to be modified at the smallest scales to get general relativity to fit this theory,' said Jesse. 'Distances are in the region of the Planck length. It's about linking what works at large scales with very small scales, like spin and changes in mass in vortices of subatomic particles. For example, the earth's Schwarzschild radius is about nine millimetres. All its mass would have to be compressed to the size of a peanut to see repulsive gravity in action. The sun's one is about three kilometres. So, for large objects, repulsive gravity is always going to be hard to detect. But on a small scale at a quantum level, like within the overdrive vortex, repulsive gravity is going to be massive.'

'Well, boys and girls!' said Jonny as he slammed his palm on the table again. 'I have the answer for you all. To sum all this up, we are a black hole in a tin can that can be controlled, shifting us from one place to another by dropping into and out of the space between atoms and sub-atomic particles. We pop out here, we pop out there, fizzing and popping, we pop out everywhere.'

The others laughed and relaxed.

It had been an intense conversation about their training at the Academy.

'I like your analogy,' said Ngarra.

It was a difficult concept for the crew to get their head around. Different ways of thinking about how the overdrive worked.

Jesse looked at the crew and thought to herself, *with Rick pushing forward the overdrive trials, soon the crew would be using it regularly in tests and trials.* They all had a growing interest in understanding exactly how it all worked. Sure, the Academy taught them all the theory and concepts but many still found it hard to link the physics to what they observed when looking at the mechanics of it and what happens. Regardless, it worked, and people were still trying to figure out why.

'I don't know about you guys but my brain is fried from all that talk,' said Stella as she got up and wacked her palm on her forehead. 'I'm off to check on our Xtracts.'

'Tell me about it,' said Jonny as he motioned how his head was exploding from it all.

'Not much between the ears is there,' said Chang sarcastically.

'Says the person stealing other people's work,' said Jonny.

'Whatever,' said Chang as he realised his smart remark had backfired. His face went red and he got up and stormed off.

'Jonny, take it easy on him,' said Ngarra. 'Not called for. It's getting too much.'

Jonny shrugged his shoulders and nodded his head.

'I'll go talk to him,' said Stella as she left and followed Chang down to the Xtract bay.

'Leave it for a bit,' said Jesse. 'He'll cool off.'

Stella walked down the stairs to the Xtract bay below. 'Connor,' she said, passing him coming down from the SAI console above. 'How's the transfer looking?'

'Fine,' he said, 'as far as I can tell, the red queen is working. The Xtracts are adapting. Learning continuously to optimise mining operations by themselves without human input. I need an anomaly to occur to really see how they cope through.'

Stella continued down the stairs.

Connor walked over to the others.

'Everything is working,' he said sitting down. 'Gilgamesh is running the red queen and the Xtracts are learning to adapt by themselves to whatever conditions they encounter during mining operations.'

'That reminds me,' said Jonny. 'On the Harvester, you said something strange was going on. All this talk of autonomous self-learning in drones I mean.

What about those mimic drones, Ying Yue's project I mean? Could Chang's sister have done something?'

'Her approach seems to be based on inserting a computer virus into other drones and taking them over,' said Connor.

'Combined with their ability to mimic or then copy the behaviour and tasking of the other drone it sounds dangerous,' said Jonny.

During the conversation, Chang walked back in.

He had cooled off.

Stella had left him alone.

'I'm worried for my sister,' said Chang as he sat down. 'Where is the human oversight in that?' he asked, having heard what they were talking about.

'It would be like making a virus into a bioweapon and then spreading it. You lose control as it mutates among a population.'

'It's just a computer code,' said Connor. 'How's it going to alter itself? It's not a mesh with the red queen inserted in it.'

Connor had been thinking about it all, though.

'Well,' said Chang. 'Whatever is going on with that Harvester, I get the feeling something has changed.'

The conversation continued for a while. Chang's family was complicated, and his emotions often got the better of him, but he had calmed down again after Jonny's comment. Ying Yue's success, his mother's situation and his dad's career focus made it hard for him.

Chapter 16

The Sea Hunters were battling the huge seas whipped up by the supercell. Although not in the middle of it, even at some distance away, it was a rough ride. Everyone that wasn't needed on watch had been stood down.

Cam was in the well deck drone bay with his boarding party and a couple of technicians.

'I think this is the best place to be right now,' said one of them.

'The most stable for sure,' said Cam. 'It's the lateral movement, the roll that can get you. I popped a pill anyway. Going up and down isn't so bad. I hope our duty officer up there keeps her steady.'

'We all popped a pill,' replied another.

'You mean SAI keeps her steady,' replied another.

'The vessel pretty much runs itself,' said Cam. 'So yes, I guess.'

Everyone had to hold on to something to keep steady.

'Is the breaching pod ready to be connected to this interceptor?' Cam asked one of the technicians.

'Yes sir,' she said. 'Good to go.'

'And the sea boat?' he questioned.

'Ready as well,' she replied.

The technicians carried on with what they were doing.

Cam turned to his boarding party.

'We have to be ready for anything,' he said. 'Once the sea state reduces, we will turn about and head toward where the Skimmers are located. We know pirates are operating within the vicinity of the Skimmers.'

'So, it is highly likely they will steal nodules from a number of loads then?' asked one of them.

'You would think so,' said Cam, 'but according to Intel, their tactics have changed. One of the drones can carry a small boarding party. One, possibly two people, I think. They have also rammed a Skimmer.'

'Why would pirates board a Skimmer? It's high risk when they can just swipe a few nodules,' said the other.

'Whatever the reason, I have got us covered,' said Cam. 'Three of you will be on standby with the sea boat and the other two for the interceptor breaching pod. Worst case, a Skimmer is compromised and must surface. We have the sea boat for crew pickup if needed. Although, it seems they will use the escape pods and transfer to another Skimmer if that happens.'

'And the breaching pod?' questioned one of them.

'Like I said. If it gets messy, the Skimmer escape pods could be used. If the sea state is still too high, that is. Either way, Max wanted us on standby to provide support whatever the outcome.'

'What does that mean?' asked one of them.

'It means we also need to ensure that if used the escape pods are unharmed when in transit to another Skimmer,' said Cam.

'It might be all over by the time we get there,' said one of them.

'Then it really will be a rescue operation,' said Cam. 'That's all, folks. Our orders are to standby for deployment. So, go put your heads down and get some rest. Now we just have to wait.'

'Yes, sir,' they all said as they moved off.

'I'm off to the mess,' said Cam as he walked off with them. 'Then I'm lying down as well. This roller coaster is getting a bit much.'

The boarding party crew followed him up the stairs next to the control room. They passed the entrance to the patrol drone bay and proceeded up to operations.

'Cam,' said Alex coming down the stairs. 'Just the man I want to see. Come with me to the patrol drone bay. I want to discuss these dragonfly drone trials.'

'You lot carry on,' said Cam to his boarding party.

Cam had been looking forward to getting his down for a bit. Shrugging his shoulders, he turned and followed Alex back down and through the entrance into the patrol drone bay.

To one side was the strange-looking drone everyone was talking about. Once in the air, it generated a gravito electric-electric field that made it practically invisible. Cam and Alex walked over to it. A couple of technicians were looking over its propellantless propulsion system and holding something in their hands.

Alex waved one of them over.

'Deciphering this took a long time,' said Alex.

'So I hear,' said Cam. 'A touch pad with self-actuated code or software.'

'Well,' said Alex as they looked it over, 'without it, we could not get this thing to go anywhere. We could power it up but that was it.'

They took the code and walked over to the dragonfly drone.

'From what you said previously,' said Cam, 'the ring at the base encloses a corrugated surface that creates a pressure differential when injected with a mixture of water and air. That polarises the surface and the rods pointing up direct the resulting current and field that is generated. It creates lift.'

'That's correct,' said Alex. 'An adaptation of good old Viktor Schauberger's bell technology. It's the discharge rods to the sides that provide orientation to a set of coordinates when thought about. We couldn't figure out how to activate them until recently. You use the touch pads and look at a chart and think about where you want it to go.'

'Problem solved now then,' said Cam. 'What did you want me for?'

'Right, yes,' said Alex as they both gripped a rail as the seas heaved around them. 'In the coming months, we want to use this near the Harvester outside the security perimeter. See if they can detect it.'

'For what purpose?' asked Cam.

'Something isn't right on that Harvester,' said Alex.

'I know,' said Cam. 'Spying?' he asked, smiling.

'Sort of,' said Alex. 'We have been given a directive to closely monitor Skimmers coming to and from the Harvester for compliance, not just mining in "the Area". At least, that's the cover story.'

'And why don't we simply ask Lee and Ying Yue what is going on?' asked Cam.

'We don't want them to know that we think something is going on,' said Alex. 'Too many variables such as whether Ying Yue's father is involved and how much the PLA Navy has to do with it.'

'The dragonfly drone is a perfect solution then,' said Cam. 'Supposedly undetectable.'

'Unless, of course, they have the technology to detect it,' said Alex. 'We think it's all connected.'

'What is all connected?' asked Cam.

'The change in piracy tactics,' said Alex. 'Sue and the PLA Navy, what's happening on the Harvester, the game Ying Yue's father is playing.'

'Is he playing a game?' asked Cam.

'I thought he was pretty genuine. Sounds complicated.'

'It is,' said Alex. 'Anyway, I'll keep you briefed on this. It is need to know only okay.'

'Got it,' said Cam.

'Right, I feel like a cork in a bathtub standing here,' said Alex. 'I said we would meet Max in the mess after this and then get our heads down for a bit. Let's go.'

'Great,' said Cam. 'I was heading that way anyway before putting my head down for a bit myself.'

Passing by the patrol drones secured on their docking clamps, they went through the entrance and back up the stairs by the control room and through operations.

It was quiet.

Only essential personnel were on duty.

Everyone else was doing the best they could to lie low and ride out the supercell.

Alex and Cam held onto support rails as they made their way to the mess. Just a few of the crew were sitting quietly in the mess. Food was not a priority in this weather. A medic was sitting with a hot cup of soup in her hand and talking to Max.

'How's the crew?' asked Alex as they got a cup of soup themselves, came over and sat down.

'Coping,' said the medic. 'A couple in sickbay and the rest that are not on duty are in their cabins. I've been doing the rounds checking in on everyone and giving them a dose of this.'

She held up a solution.

'I popped a pill, but that stuff works wonders,' said Alex. 'The wonders of modern medicine.'

'Anyway, I'm off,' said the medic, getting up and taking her lead from Max. 'I'll check in with those on watch and make sure they are okay.'

Max nodded his head and the medic walked off to do her rounds.

'Right folks,' said Max. 'Besides upcoming meetings with engineering and supplies, let's make sure we are all on the same page.'

He lent back in his chair, paused, and looked at them.

'It's getting very busy out here,' said Max. 'Between this supercell, piracy, the Harvester and being informed that soon these Skimmers will be doing a whole lot of overdrive trials, I don't want us chasing our tails on all this.'

'Our immediate priority is this supercell and the piracy,' said Alex.

'Exactly,' said Max, nodding at Alex, 'but we need to have a plan in place. Even if that plan changes.'

'Our primary mandate under "the Authority" is to maintain security in "the Area" for Xtract mining operations,' said Alex. 'That means monitoring Skimmer compliance. This is our task.'

'Correct,' said Max, 'but we are coming under increasing pressure from Rick and the people he reports to. Anyone would think we are the military, which we are not. Well, not entirely anyway. We must be careful not to cross that line. It will all come back on us if something goes wrong. It's just too easy to blame us if anything goes wrong out here.'

'What you're saying then,' said Cam. 'Is that we have to make sure we always operate under our mandate within "the Area" then?'

'All activity in "the Area" is related to mining and by its very nature is civilian,' said Max. 'The military of various nations may well monitor what is going on, but they can't interfere. At least, not openly anyway.'

'And the grid can't be compromised,' said Alex. 'No one wants to be kicked out of "the Area".'

'Exactly,' said Max. 'I want you both to make sure that our mandate to operate within "the Area" is always at the front of your minds and applied to any operation carried out,' stated Max. 'That's an order.'

Alex and Cam nodded their heads.

Having finished sipping on their cups of soup they all got up.

'Let's move through to operations,' said Max. 'I want a brief on this weather system and timings. Let's go.'

Holding onto support rails, they walked from the mess back through to operations to meet with the duty officer. He and a few others were on watch. The rest stood down for the supercell.

They walked over to the met ocean station and looked over its various displays.

'Over the next twenty-four hours, we will get the worst of it,' said the duty officer as he went through different displays of the supercell moving through 'the Area'. 'We should be able to turn back towards the location of the Skimmers in the next twelve hours. Sea state will be down enough to turn about.' They looked over the displays and discussed their course relative to the location of the Skimmers and the supercell.

'How are our drone vessels handling it?' asked Alex.

'Fine,' said the duty officer. 'Better than us, given they are crewless and have a very low profile.'

They walked over to where one of the crew members was on duty. Calling up the status of the drone vessels they checked over the array of sensors and systems.

'No systems are down,' said Alex.

'Everything is enclosed,' said Max. 'Self-righting as well and unsinkable.'

'There is the capacity to crew them though is not there,' said Cam.

'A small crew,' said Alex, 'but rarely done and only for short periods in the company.'

'Right,' said Max. 'I'm off to the SAI console to check in with the duty officer of the watch. Then I'm getting my head down as well while we ride out the worst of this.'

Max left the others to it and walked through operations and into the SAI console. The outer shields were closed, and the camera system was operating. It was not a pleasant experience. The only thing to do was lay low and ride it out. And of course, pop a few pills.

As he entered, the duty officer of the watch was zooming in fine-scale on the navigation hologram, checking navigational safety and then zooming out with long-range sensors that SAI had. Not that he needed to as SAI was able to pick up on anything with the potential to cause an incident and impact vessel safety.

Chapter 17

On the Harvester, preparations had been made to ride out the supercell. It was built to handle such extremes of weather. It heaved slowly up and down as the huge seas rolled around it. The Harvester was in lockdown and nothing was allowed on or off the hulking mass as it rode the mountainous waves that surrounded it.

'What's the status on the moon pools?' asked Lee as he walked into the operations centre and over to the duty officer in charge.

'All Skimmers have exited the moon pools,' he replied. 'Docking clamps, conveyors and robotic arms have been locked. All personnel have exited the area and it is watertight.'

'And the drone bay and deck?' asked Lee.

'Drone bay doors have been closed and all drones lowered and secured on docking clamps,' said the duty officer. 'Drone deck lifts are raised and sealed. Nothing on the drone deck. Hex is lowered and the opening sealed. Drone bay and deck personnel entrances are all locked.'

'And deck levels?' asked Lee.

'All watertight bulkheads are closed between and within levels. We are watertight,' he replied.

'Good,' said Lee. 'Monitor and report any changes.'

Lee walked over to the officer monitoring met ocean conditions.

'What is the status of this supercell?' he asked her.

'The next twenty-four hours will see us through the worst of it,' she said, pulling up several models predicting its direction and intensity over time. 'Here is the eye,' she said. 'Once the wind and the sea state reduces to the threshold for operations, we can restart. At present, that's looking like at least forty-eight hours away.'

'That means by the time Skimmers start arriving to off-load and ships return to load out nodules it's going to be several days,' said Lee. 'Not a lot we can do about that.'

'Sir,' said the duty officer in charge, walking over.

He looked a little nervous, Lee thought to himself. In fact, a lot of personnel looked subdued and nervous lately. Even Ying Yue. He had to meet with her soon.

'Yes?' asked Lee.

'It might be nothing,' he replied, 'but it has been difficult to interface with the Harvester operating systems lately. We can monitor everything, given it is mostly automated. But for some reason, we keep being shut out of the system's user interface.'

'Meaning what?' asked Lee.

'The crew is nervous,' said the duty officer in charge. 'We don't seem to be able to easily alter or control operating parameters for the Harvesters plant. Nor can we easily alter or direct our assets, the subsurface patrol drones and airborne surveillance.'

'Interesting,' said Lee.

'It's like we are now one layer removed from a direct interface with the Harvester SAI,' he said. 'The crew just want to do their jobs effectively.'

'I am meeting with Ying Yue shortly and will discuss this,' said Lee. 'She will know more about it than me.'

Lee thought back to when Sue was onboard. He thought about her single-minded pursuit of the mimic drone program. She had almost killed Ying Yue over it. There was that time in the lab when they tried to use a copy of that technology of Connor's. Sue thought they had got hold of it, to interface with the mimic drone technology. At the time, it had concerned him. As did all this talk about modelling biological viruses to create unique computer coding. He was concerned about how it would be used when applying it to drone technology. The mimic drones.

'If it gets any more difficult,' said Lee. 'Contact me immediately. In the meantime, I want your team to run some diagnostics on our operating system. Run some interface scenarios on our SAI and do some testing.'

'Yes, sir,' the duty officer in charge replied, walking off.

Lee left to go and meet with Ying Yue in the research laboratory complex. He made his way through the mess to the lab research complex. A few personnel that were on duty greeted him as he walked along the passageway holding onto the rail. He ran his hand along it, tightening his grip now and then as the huge harvester slowly rolled from side to side and up and down.

The Harvester continued to heave slowly up and down as the giant waves and high winds blasted through 'the Area'. *At least, the Harvester was huge and heave compensators dampened the effect of the supercell,* he thought to himself on the way.

He walked through the entrance to the lab complex. Before going into the labs, he stopped at the platform overlooking the experimental Skimmer suspended above the moon pool below. Work had stopped due to the supercell. He saw Ying Yue through the lab screens. She waved and indicated she would come out.

Lee watched as Ying Yue went to the foyer and took her lab gear off.

'How are operations going?' she asked, exiting the lab area and walking over to Lee. He was now looking out at the Skimmer suspended above the moon pool below.

'I like coming here,' said Lee. 'Looking at that Skimmer and then down to the moon pool below I often wonder where all this is heading.'

'All what? What do you mean?' asked Ying Yue cautiously.

'All this drama is about that technology of Connor's and the Xed Academy,' said Lee. 'Then there's your research program and its implementation, and what happened with Sue. And Ying Yue's father's involvement, what the PLA Navy agenda is, those Skimmer overdrives and their use. It all must be connected somehow, surely?'

'I wouldn't know,' said Ying Yue cautiously. 'My family is important to me. They may be tied up in all this but that doesn't mean there is some sort of agenda going on, surely.'

Ying Yue thought about the situation. Sue may have been openly aggressive about her intentions and alignment with the PLA and its agenda, but Lee was more subtle. Lee reminded Ying Yue of her father. Calculating and calm no matter what. Her father was a company man. But she didn't really know much about his work life. She remained cautious about how much to say of her work on the Harvester.

Ying Yue's thoughts went back to the time Sue shot her onboard the Skimmer and how she had exposed what Sue was up to.

'You might be overthinking it,' said Ying Yue.

'That may well be,' Lee replied. 'What's the worst that could happen?'

'Is anything actually happening?' asked Ying Yue.

'I mean Sue is gone. The Harvester continues its operations and we have implemented the mimic drone program.'

'Yes, back to that,' said Lee. 'The crew seems concerned about this mimic drone program you have implemented. One of my personnel is running some diagnostics. They seem to think less control over operating systems has been created. Like we are one step removed from SAI and its control over everything. The crew are nervous about the implications it has for our human interface with SAI.'

'The mimic program is like a virus,' said Ying Yue. 'My mother spent many years working on the concept. It injects itself into the operating system of everything and creates multiple copies of itself. It replicates itself using the code within the operating system it infects and passes it on. It's not designed to disrupt, shutdown or destroy the AI running things. It takes over everything. It's like building a connected landscape in a virtual world. It just spreads and joins everything up. It's a bit like using the virus as a vector to inject a host, which it then uses to create a clear landscape. What comes after then joins everything up into a giant fungal network. Like one super organism with many different manifestations of itself. Or a single organism with multiple nodes that have different functions. That's what the mimic drone program is.'

'Interesting analogy and perhaps dangerous,' said Lee. He thought it sounded extremely dangerous. 'Is that such a good thing,' said Lee carrying on the conversation, 'where's the oversight or human interface? Direct control is removed.'

'It removes the need for us to code and control multiple assets separately and with separate AI's,' said Ying Yue. 'It provides for one massive common domain that runs itself autonomously. Like a fungal network.'

'But one without humans in direct control,' said Lee. 'The crew is nervous. If something goes wrong, they no longer have any direct control. You've removed the direct interface with the AI. It's like we must now ask it for permission to enter the operating system. We have no direct oversight over the optimisation of mining operations.'

'One thing has become apparent,' said Ying Yue as she considered Lee's concerns. 'It would be useful to get hold of that technology Connor has developed. Perhaps he has come up with something that overcomes your concerns about this.'

'Perhaps,' said Lee, 'but we don't have it, do we? I am not confident that what you have done does not pose a risk to the crew and our operation or indeed GlobeCorpMining,' said Lee. 'Being one step removed from the AI operating system is problematic. If any action by personnel is perceived as a threat to Harvester mining operations, The AI will lock us out. I don't know if you have thought this through enough, Ying Yue. Anyway, I'm going back to operations to look over diagnostics.'

Scientists! He thought to himself. A single-minded and sometimes dangerous thought process. Ying Yue was avoiding the question. It made him feel uneasy about the whole situation. Even the crew seemed wary of Ying Yue. Scientists. Always passionate about their project but unaware of the consequences.

Lee walked out of the laboratory complex and holding the handrail, made his way back along the passage, through the rec area and restaurant and into operations. He barely acknowledged the crew that passed him along the way. Deep in thought, he was worried about the mimic drone program.

Mimic drones were much more than just an integrated landscape, he thought to himself. Every asset, plant, and item were absorbed by the AI's operating system now. A single purpose, to optimise mining operations. He thought about how a giant fungus might work. The virus coding from the mimic drone program had essentially cleared a path for it, whatever it was, an empty landscape. Now, behind it like spores from a fungus, it spread, taking over everything. Almost like a genesis or beginning.

Arriving back in operations, he walked over to the duty watch crew running diagnostics on the Harvester and its SAI.

'What's the status of SAI?' asked Lee.

'Since Ying Yue activated the mimic drone technology, the Harvester SAI has set about integrating everything. It now continuously tries to optimise the entire operation simultaneously.'

'And is that a good thing?' questioned Lee.

'Initially, it appears to be,' replied one of the operating systems engineers. 'But there is, as you said, a problem.'

'And that is?' asked Lee.

'As you pointed out,' he replied. 'The human interface and oversight of SAI has been removed. We have no direct control over how far and to what extent this technology and program takes over and what it can and can't do.'

'What does that mean for us?' asked Lee as he thought again about his analogy to a biological virus that cleared the way and the fungus that moved in behind.

'We can monitor all the systems but if we want to alter or change anything, we can't. It locks us out. We must get permission to access it. It's like a risk optimiser that has gone crazy.'

'What if we in trying to get access to change something is a risk to optimisation of the system?' asked Lee.

'It will not let us in,' he replied. 'How it optimises itself may not be in the way we think it should be done.'

'I know Ying Yue said the mimic drone technology would change everything, but this is to the extreme,' said Lee. 'I need to talk with her father about all this. Perhaps we should pull the plug on it all and do a global reset.'

'Great,' he said. 'I'd rather be separate from such a system and have access. Now it does all the thinking for us like we aren't needed. That's why the crew might be nervous about all this.'

'Lucky for you then that the Harvester SAI does not understand what you are talking about,' said one of the operations personnel. 'As in unplugging it and going through a global reset.'

Lee smiled as did the others.

'If it becomes increasingly difficult to get permission to access our operating systems let me know straight away,' said Lee. 'And if crew safety and wellbeing are compromised, we are shutting this thing down and rebooting. I don't care what Ying Yue or her father says.'

'Yes, sir,' they all replied, returning to their work.

Lee walked off and holding onto a support rail made his way to a meeting room to get hold of Ying Yue's father. What were the implications of a totally autonomous SAI controlling everything? No human interface meant all they could do was monitor production and report. Up until now, servicing and maintenance schedules were also controlled by the crew. Tasks and repair drones were always assigned.

He walked into a meeting room and activated the comms link requesting an urgent connection with Ying Yue's father. He waited and a short time later, the message board in the meeting room activated.

His image appeared.

'Sir,' he said. 'I hope you are well.'

'Indeed, I am,' he replied, 'and you?'

'The supercell is uncomfortable, but we are well,' Lee replied.

'And the amount of downtime with locking operations until it passes?' he asked.

'Forty-eight to seventy-two hours at the most,' said Lee. 'However, I am concerned about the mimic drone technology.'

'My daughter has done well,' he replied.

'We are locked out of direct control of the operating system and SAI,' said Lee.

'It's a step-change in automation and drone technology and its integration,' he replied.

'But direct human oversight is removed,' said Lee.

'Optimisation of production is paramount,' he replied. 'Many years of work is behind all this.'

'Do you not see that if any of my crew attempt to alter the system now to meet our requirements that the SAI may not allow it?' asked Lee.

'Why would you need to anymore?' he replied.

Lee could see the argument was a pointless one. A long family legacy was behind what had been done. Biological viruses, to computer system program viruses, to fungal networks and their digital analogues and ultimately this mimic program.

'If something goes wrong, we will have to shut down and reboot,' said Lee. 'That's the only way now.'

'No,' stated Ying Yue's father emphatically. 'You will not shut down and reboot, ever! Ying Yue is to continue her work on that modified Skimmer in the hangar next to the lab complex and integrate the mimic drone program with it as well.'

'Yes, sir,' replied Lee. He had pushed it as far as he could. But something just did not seem right about it all.

'I have to go,' said Ying Yue's father. 'Follow Ying Yue's direction on this and report back to me as the project progresses.'

'Yes, sir,' replied Lee.

His image disappeared.

Lee was left thinking about what it all meant.

Obviously, something else was afoot, he thought to himself. He just couldn't figure out what the ultimate purpose was. With the supercell ragging outside and the Harvester climbing slowly up and down the huge swell, he decided to get some rest.

Chapter 18

On Ngarra's Skimmer, the crew were monitoring mining operations. The Xtracts were still collecting nodules from the depths below. They were not meant to mine during a supercell. However, with Connor's technology now activated they felt confident that if anything went wrong, the Xtracts would learn, adapt, and return to the Skimmer by themselves.

The crew were gathered in the rec area. Jonny came down from the SAI console. He was checking the progress of the supercell. Stella and Chang came up from the Xtract bay console.

'Another twenty-four hours and the worst of this supercell will pass through,' said Jonny as he got some food and sat down.

'The Xtracts are learning and adapting,' said Stella. 'This red queen sequence has done wonders, for Gilgamesh I mean.'

'Where is Connor anyway?' asked Chang.

'Hiding in the information hub with his child,' said Jonny.

They all laughed.

'A good analogy,' said Jesse. 'It still concerns me that we can now only monitor the Xtracts. SAI has no control over them.'

'Yes, but Connor can still direct the evolution of Gilgamesh,' said Ngarra. 'If an adaptation that is learnt using the red queen has unintended consequences, he can delete it or alter its parameters.'

'Like being a parent,' said Jonny. 'Ha, wouldn't it be great if you could just alter a child's parameters? Teachers would love that, wouldn't they? They wouldn't have to deal with all the issues a student brought to school with them from home and a lack of parenting skills or from the wider community.'

'Not that any of us would know,' said Stella. 'What's that saying that took hold in the 2020s? It was inappropriate to say students suffered from a lack of parenting skills. It was replaced with "it takes a school to raise a child".'

The others all laughed.

'Parents,' said Ngarra. 'Trying to be their friend and not setting any boundaries at home,' said Ngarra. 'No wonder they didn't cope at school back then. Must have been horrible for the poor teachers working within such an antiquated system that to the last stood in opposition to it all.'

'Anyway, getting back on topic,' said Jonny. 'If Gilgamesh and the Xtracts are now one isn't that going to cause an issue. I mean with the use of the SAI console interface when monitoring them.'

'No,' said Jesse. 'Connor's technology is governed by the interface between Gilgamesh and humans. The streamer now just monitors them.'

'As long as the streamer is out though,' said Jonny, 'and once we decide not to use it?'

'We can still deploy it at any time to check in,' said Stella.

'Unless it sees that as a threat as well,' said Jonny, 'and doesn't want to be monitored by SAI.'

'Can't see how that would occur,' said Ngarra. 'Besides it's better than being a plague upon the earth. Imagine what this so-called mimic drone program we keep hearing rumours of might result in. From what we have heard, it has a single purpose, to perpetuate itself for no other reason than to take over other systems and replicate itself at the expense of everything else.'

'Like Sue,' said Jonny. 'Taking over I mean.'

A nervous by everyone laugh followed.

'Funny guy,' said Stella. A serious look crossed her face. 'A dangerous woman.'

'That she is,' said Chang angrily as he remembered what happened. 'She damn well shot my sister!'

Chang had not been listening to the conversation much. He was drifting in and out of thoughts about his family.

'Well,' said Ngarra. 'Your father took Sue away. Who knows where she is now?'

Just as Chang was about to launch into an angry explanation about what he would do if he ever saw Sue again, a proximity alarm sounded.

'Long-range sensor detection.' Announced SAI. 'Unidentified subsurface vessel closing Skimmer.'

'What the hell!' said Jonny jumping up from his chair.

Everyone erupted into a conversation about pirates.

'Quiet!' yelled Ngarra.

Everyone was silent and looked at Ngarra.

'SAI, arm defensive array,' he said quickly. 'Retract the communication streamer. Bring propulsion online.'

'Confirmed,' said SAI. 'Defensive array armed, retract streamer, and bring propulsion online.'

'Let's go,' said Ngarra.

Everyone raced off to their positions. Stella and Chang went down to the Xtract bay, and Jesse, Ngarra and Jonny went up to the SAI console.

Watertight bulkheads closed behind them.

'What's going on?' asked Connor over open comms from the information hub.

'Unidentified subsurface vessel closing us,' said Jesse replying over the open comms link as they entered the SAI console.

'The Xtracts have detected the alarm,' said Connor. 'They are returning to the Skimmer, but it will take time. I am not sure what they will do in response now.'

'The communication streamer will take time as well,' said Stella over open comms from the Xtract bay.

'SAI, show navigation hologram broad-scale,' said Ngarra. 'Show location and vector of unidentified subsurface vessel.'

They watched as the navigation hologram appeared and adjusted itself.

'Confirmed,' said SAI. 'Unidentified subsurface vessel is a pirate sub closing from due north.'

'Damn it,' said Ngarra. 'Where's that interceptor drone that is meant to be monitoring our location? SAI, open communication link to Sea Hunters.'

'Confirmed,' said SAI. 'Eel drone and grid buoy proximity not optimal. Live feed not available.'

'Damn it!' said Ngarra.

The supercell had interrupted the laser signal communication network in their grid location. Ngarra proceeded to record a message to send.

'SAI,' said Ngarra. 'Record the message and send it to the Sea Hunters.'

A brief pause followed then Ngarra proceeded to record the message.

'SAI, priority message. A pirate sub is closing us. We are retrieving our streamer and Xtract mining drones. We will not get away in time. Request immediate assistance. End message.'

'Confirmed,' said SAI. 'Message recorded and sent to Sea Hunters.'

'SAI,' said Ngarra. 'Send the recorded message to the Xed Academy Crewing monitoring and communications.'

'Confirmed,' said SAI. 'Message sent to Xed crew monitoring and communications.'

'Stella,' said Ngarra over open comms, 'what's the status of the streamer and Xtracts?'

'Streamer is not even halfway, four Xtracts docked and waiting for the others.'

'We aren't going to make it,' said Jesse. 'It takes at least an hour to recover everything. Let's hope they just take nodules from the trays and get out of here.'

'For some reason, they have been ramming Skimmers,' said Ngarra. 'SAI, confirm the Skimmer is watertight and all compartments sealed.'

'Confirmed,' said SAI. 'All compartments sealed. Skimmer is watertight.'

'SAI, confirm the ARC defensive array is armed,' said Ngarra.

'Confirmed,' said SAI. 'ARC array is armed.'

'Jonny, get on top of this,' said Jesse. 'Let's go.'

'On it,' said Jonny, grabbing his interface lenses.

'We don't have much time,' said Jesse, looking at the navigation hologram. 'They are closing fast.'

They watched as the marker closed their position. On a fine scale, it also showed their own Xtracts coming into view, ascending, and docking on their clamps.

'Look, it has launched its two drones,' said Jesse. 'Nothing unusual so far. Let's hope they go straight for the trays. We can't use our defensive array with the streamer deployed.'

'Connor,' said Ngarra. 'How will Gilgamesh react to an external threat with this red queen thing of yours now active for these Xtracts?'

'Hard to say,' said Connor. 'Like the squid simulation, I showed you, I suppose. A threat to the Skimmer will be seen to compromise competition for resources, and nodules for power, and they will react. I only have the giant squid simulation to go by. Depends on how long it takes the group to learn and adapt. Red queen allows for rapid evolution and adaptation. That's the whole point. Let's hope it works for this.'

'Great,' said Chang over open comms having heard from the Xtract bay what Connor said. 'Let's just hope? Are you kidding me! Let's just blast them out of the water with the ARC array.'

'The streamer is not recovered. Our line of directed energy discharge is constrained,' said Jonny. 'We can't move and too many assets of ours are still in play.'

'Sitting ducks then,' said Chang. 'Where're my sister's mimic drones? Now there's a toy. It makes direct contact, attaches and infects, and takes over everything. Like clearing a path for what is to follow.'

'Dangerous if you ask me,' said Jonny over open comms as he braced himself for the onslaught. 'Here they come, boys and girls.'

At first, it appeared to be a standard piracy operation. The sub circled the Skimmer at a distance while the two drones attempted to take nodules from the trays. They returned them to the sub and deposited them into the empty missile silos lined with a sleeve that could be lifted out.

'That's not looking good,' said Jonny pointing at the change in direction and speed of one of the pirate drones. The one without the coupling hatch.

'Shit,' said Ngarra as they watched through the camera system feed, 'and look, the other drone is slightly bigger, and it has a coupling hatch. It could be manned. That's the one that was reported in the other incident.'

One of the pirate drones went past the nodule trays, along a Skimmer wing. It accelerated and angled upwards.

'It's going for the rim drive,' said Jonny.

'SAI, confirm propulsion is online,' said Ngarra.

'Confirmed,' said SAI. 'Propulsion online.'

'We can't move,' said Stella over open comms. 'The streamer is not recovered, and we have Xtracts docking.'

'We have to do something,' said Jonny, 'and fast.'

'SAI, command override,' said Jesse. 'Manoeuvre as ordered.'

'Command override confirmed,' said SAI. 'Manoeuvre as ordered.'

Safety protocols could now be overridden within parameters set to ensure SAI surfaced the Skimmer if life support systems were compromised.

The Skimmer shuddered and alarms went off. Everyone looked at each and for a moment everything seemed to slow down.

Stella was yelling over open comms. Connor was trying to talk over her and explain what the Xtracts were up to. Jonny was demanding that they hurry and manoeuvre the Skimmer.

Ngarra stood frozen amidst it all, his mind racing, looking for something to hold on to. He looked for something to focus on. He looked intently at the navigation hologram and watched all the activity. On the other side, he saw Jesse move to walk around to him. She seemed to be asking him something. He couldn't hear.

Like the dream time, standing still, he stared into the void. It seemed his ancestors stared back from the stars and a hand reached out, holding what looked like tektites. He remembered a dreamtime story about the sky people. He snapped out of it.

'Portside propulsion impacted,' announced SAI. 'No structural damage.'

'SAI,' yelled Ngarra, 'yaw to port at five degrees!'

'Confirmed,' said SAI. 'Yaw to port five degrees.'

The Skimmer shuddered. The streamer was still being recovered. An Xtract drone trying to dock was knocked out of position, stopped, recovered, and tried to move in again.

'It's coming around again!' yelled Jonny.

'SAI, yaw from port to starboard at five degrees continuously,' said Ngarra.

'You'll rip out the streamer!' yelled Stella over open comms.

'And damage Xtracts trying to dock,' said Chang.

'We've got another problem,' said Jonny. 'The other pirate drone with the docking hatch is approaching topside.'

'Damn it,' exclaimed Jesse, 'they're going to try and dock and board!'

'Guys, our Xtracts! Look,' said Jonny.

Through the camera system, they watched. The Xtracts trying to dock had stopped. Some had been knocked about as the Skimmer yawed from side to side. The other pirate sub drone was also approaching. It was going to attempt to ram propulsion again.

'I was trying to explain guys,' said Connor excitedly over comms. 'Red queen allows them to evolve quickly. To learn and adapt to an immediate threat to competition for resources and their reward system.'

They watched as an Xtract moved in front of the approaching pirate drone, between it and port side propulsion. The pirate drone altered course and clipped propulsion. A shudder went through the Skimmer.

'Portside propulsion rim drive compromised,' said SAI. 'Blades two and three have been damaged.'

The pirate drone turned in a slow arc and steadied, beginning its approach again. Meanwhile, the other pirate drone was getting into position above the Skimmer, trying to sync with the movement, yawing side to side.

'We're screwed!' yelled Chang over comms.

'Shut it, boy!' yelled Jonny over comms.

'SAI, increase yaw to ten degrees,' said Ngarra.

'You'll rip out the streamer,' yelled Stella, 'it's still not recovered!'

'Confirmed,' said SAI. 'Increase yaw to ten degrees.'

The Skimmer yawed from side to side. The noise of the streamer straining sounded throughout the Skimmer.

Through the camera system, they watched as two of their Xtracts blocked the approaching pirate drone that was trying to ram the Skimmer.

Perpendicular to the approaching pirate drone another Xtract crashed into it and sent the pirate drone spinning off course. The Skimmer Xtract had stopped dead in the water.

'Look,' yelled Jonny, 'another Xtract has attached itself to it and is holding position!'

'Connor,' said Jesse. 'Over open comms. You've outdone us all with this Red Queen and Gilgamesh.'

'It was always going to work,' said Connor. 'I just wasn't sure how quickly the learning and adaptation would happen.'

A shudder was felt throughout the Skimmer followed by a sudden decrease in the yaw rate and what felt like a large bump.

'The streamer has sheared!' yelled Stella.

'Docking sequence completed,' announced SAI. 'Airlock secure.'

'Shit, shit, shit,' said Ngarra. 'They've attached!'

It was chaos; the crew panicked about what was happening outside. While their Xtracts had protected propulsion, the other pirate drone had managed to sync with the rate of Skimmer yaw and dock.

Amongst the ensuing chaos, Jesse managed to send another recorded message to both the Sea Hunters and the Xed Academy crew monitoring that they were about to be boarded by pirates and their propulsion was damaged.

Chapter 19

An urgent communication had come in from Ngarra's Skimmer. All Skimmers had been grouped together across a board location within 'the Area' to ride out the supercell raging above them. Rick and Jonah were in the crew monitoring and communications centre. The duty officer in charge and the Sea Hunter liaison officer were also there.

'We don't have a live feed on the message board,' said the duty officer.

They listened to the message.

'Jesse looks concerned,' said Jonah. 'I don't like this at all.'

'An interceptor drone is operating autonomously,' said the Sea Hunter liaison officer. 'It will detect and assess the threat and eliminate it. I have had contact with the Sea Hunters. They also received a message from the Skimmer.'

'My crew is in a lot of danger out there,' said Jonah. 'What if they get rammed continuously? What happens if they are boarded? Pirates don't do this.'

'Last record that came in shows that the crew's vitals have spiked,' said one of the duty officers. 'Something significant is going on.'

'They can escape using the overdrive,' said Rick. 'We just have to hope they can recover the streamer and Xtracts in time.'

'But what if they have fully deployed it,' said Jonah. 'You know these crew. It is more than likely that they have already done a bit of mining while holding out until the supercell passes.'

'So, if we assume the worst,' said the Sea Hunter liaison officer. 'Then a streamer has been deployed and Xtracts are recovering nodules. A pirate sub then turns up and its two drones ram the Skimmer before it can recover its deployed assets and get away.'

'We know that Connor's technology has been rolled out,' said Rick. 'Gilgamesh's red queen. If it works, the way he said it would, then those Xtracts should adapt and respond to any threat to mining operations.'

'But why would a pirate sub want to use its drones to ram a Skimmer?' asked Jonah.

She was getting increasingly frustrated with the whole situation. Something just didn't add up. Chang's father seemed unaware of anything untoward out there. Or maybe he knew but couldn't say anything. GlobeCorpMining was certainly interested in Connor's technology. *And Rick, well he knows more than he is letting on,* she thought to herself. I wish he was a bit more open about all this. Maybe he couldn't speak up either. He seemed to be guided by the people he reported to.

'If they are caught out and unable to get away,' said Jonah angrily. 'How on earth are they going to avoid being rammed and boarded? And why boarded. Pirates have no use for such technology. They just steal nodules from trays and sell them on the black market.'

'We have to assume that the Skimmer will surface,' said Rick. 'SAI will not compromise life support systems, even if Jesse uses the override protocol to perform tasks SAI would not otherwise do.'

'Surface,' yelled Jonah, 'surface! They can't surface in the middle of a supercell!'

The others in the group jumped back. It was getting heated. The exchange between Jonah and Rick was intense.

'It would avoid them being rammed!' exclaimed Rick trying not to raise his voice at Jonah.

'And, if they are in fact being boarded it would cause the hatch seal between the Skimmer and the pirate drone to shear off. The pirate drone would not be able to reattach.'

'Rick,' said Jonah forcefully as she got in his face and lowered her voice. 'I have a crew confronted by a bunch of pirates that are not pirates being forced to surface, when they should not surface because they're in the middle of a damn supercell! What the hell do you think they are going to do? Enjoy the roller coaster ride! For Christ's sake, there must be a better option.'

Everyone stopped talking.

The ensuing silence was deafening.

'Come on, think you lot,' said Jonah, 'think!'

'The escape pods,' said one of the duty personnel. 'Didn't you go through that scenario before? They can use them to get away and board another Skimmer.'

'Now there's something useful,' said Jonah as she remembered their previous conversation about such a course of action. 'Get a recorded message to them stating what the preferred option is if they are forced to surface, whether boarded or not.'

The duty personnel nodded and got on with it.

A message was recorded and sent to Ngarra's Skimmer.

'You haven't answered my question, Rick.' she said, turning back to him.

'What do you mean?' he asked calmly.

'Damn it! Stop with the games, Rick,' she said.

'There is no game, Jonah,' he said, raising his voice. 'My only concern is the future of this place.'

'Connor's technology is just not worth anything to these pirates,' said Jonah. 'What's going on here? Whatever you are thinking, it is at the expense of my crew!'

'No! It isn't, Jonah,' said Rick as he looked at the Sea Hunter liaison officer and then the others on duty.

'The Chinese don't want the red queen to get out,' said Rick. 'They want their mimic drone program to take over. Red queen is a threat to them. You have no idea what is going on here!'

'Rubbish,' said Jonah. 'These Skimmers are the future.'

'Exactly,' stated Rick. 'They are.'

Everyone stopped, realising they all wanted the same thing.

'Do you realise the implications of combining the Skimmer SAI with Gilgamesh's red queen, its Xtracts and the overdrive,' said Rick. 'Maybe not but my people think the Chinese do and that's a problem.'

'What do a bunch of pirates have to do with it?' asked Jonah as she calmed down.

'The CCP, the subcommittee Chang's father reports to and the PLA Navy may not have the same agenda,' said Rick as he took a step back and took a deep breath. 'You may put a lot of trust in Chang's father. Perhaps too much. But given the investment GlobeCorpMining have made in the crew program for the Skimmers, I can understand why. But other forces are at play.'

'Are you not bringing the overdrive trials forward because of all this?' asked Jonah as she calmed down.

'We want to, but we also have to consider the implications this so-called mimic drone program has,' said Rick. 'Ying Yue may be Chang's sister, but she is also a company person. Others may have a different agenda for this infectious technology she has developed for the Harvester and GlobeCorpMining.'

'What is it that Ying Yue means in English again,' said Jonah. 'Reflection of the moon? Is there a dark side to all this? Are you saying we should watch more closely what's going on?'

'Well, someone previously made a lot of effort to try and get access to our people.'

Rick paused for a moment deep in thought then carried on.

'To get to Connor through Chang, I mean,' said Rick. 'I did what I had to protect him, and our crew and the technology.'

'I still don't understand the value of boarding a Skimmer and taking off with any such technology developed by us,' said Jonah.

They had both calmed down and were trying to come to some sort of agreement on a way forward.

'Because it's likely that it's not the pirates doing it,' said Rick. 'All I know at present is that it's a cover for someone or something else.'

'We can't afford to have contractor Skimmers compromised,' said Jonah. 'Even if they did agree to be part of the overdrive trials and plans for future mining operations when leasing or buying them. There are also maritime regulations and codes and standards for operating in "the Area" to consider.'

'The issue has always been that maintenance and servicing have been done at the Harvester,' said Rick. 'An agreement was reached with GlobeCorpMining about patented technology. However, outside influences are putting everything we want to achieve at risk.'

The conversation carried on.

Meanwhile, duty personnel reported on crew vitals. The Sea Hunter liaison officer contacted Max and Alex and explained what was going on. Rick and Jonah's heated exchange had finally resolved itself. They both wanted the same thing. With having different viewpoints, they often forgot that simple fact.

'Message from the Skimmer,' said the duty officer in charge as the others went about their respective duties.

Everyone stopped and listened to the message that had come through. It was as Jonah had feared. They had not been able to recover the steamer and Xtracts in time. With not being able to get away, they had been rammed and a boarding attempt was underway.

'Damn, damn and damn again,' said Jonah. 'Let's hope they carry out our advice if forced to surface.'

'Where's that interceptor drone?' asked Rick.

'Closing their position,' said the Sea Hunter liaison officer. 'It will provide a distraction for the pirate sub. If their drone is already attached to the hatch and airlock, it will be too risky to deploy any weapons systems. We can, however, eliminate the other pirate drone.'

'So, our crew are on their own then,' said Rick. 'Will the interceptor cover their escape in the pods?'

'It will. That's the plan,' he replied. 'Assuming that when boarded they are not stopped from getting away.'

'Get a message to all Skimmers,' said Jonah to the duty officer in charge. 'Prepare to receive escape pods from a compromised Skimmer. Anti-piracy operation underway.'

'What about the contractor that leases the Skimmer?' asked Rick.

'They can wait,' said Jonah. 'It isn't going to change anything. We will still have a mess to sort out afterwards.'

The duty officer in charge recorded and sent a message to all Skimmers to standby to receive escape pods from a compromised Skimmer.

'How's the supercell looking?' asked the Sea Hunter liaison officer.

'The worst of it will pass in the next twelve hours,' replied the duty officer.

He swiped his hand across the display of the supercell. Its trajectory appeared on the main screen to the front and above them. He overlaid crew vitals and positions of Skimmers located in a broad group one hundred metres below sea level.

'I hate this,' said Jonah. 'All we can do now is monitor the situation and wait for an outcome.'

'If Ngarra and his crew are half as good as you say they are,' said Rick. 'Then they will know what to do.'

'It's beyond their training,' said Jonah, 'but yes, they would be our top crew out there. That's why they are on Skimmer one.'

The duty officer got one of his team to organise some food and drink upstairs in the mezzanine area. No one was going anywhere until an outcome presented itself.

Chapter 20

On the Sea Hunter vessel, a duty officer in operations received an urgent message, requesting to speak with Max and Alex.

'Incoming message request from Xed crew monitoring and communications,' announced SAI.

'SAI, request Max and Alex to come to operations for urgent communication,' said the duty officer.

'Confirmed,' said SAI. 'Request Max and Alex to come to operations for an urgent communication.'

A short time later, Max and Alex entered operations. Walking in and holding onto a support rail they could see on the message board that it was from Rick at Xed crew monitoring and communications.

'Open message board,' said Max as he sat in the command chair and Alex walked over to the console.

'Max, Alex,' said Rick. 'Time is short. I assume you are aware of the evolving situation with our Skimmers and piracy?'

'We certainly are,' said Max. 'We have an interceptor drone out there. We are standing off as the sea state is too high to operate within "the Area" at present. We have set a course to minimise impact to our vessel and its crew.'

'One of our Skimmers, Ngarra's in fact is compromised,' said Rick. 'More than just taking nodules from trays, they have been rammed. One of the pirate drones is occupied and has an airlock hatch. They are going to try and board.'

'If we can get our drone vessels close enough, they may be able to help,' said Alex, 'but the sea state is still too high for them. Besides, once that pirate drone is attached to your Skimmer there is little we can do. We have to wait for the supercell to pass.'

'The fact that a pirate operation would want to board a Skimmer to take all the nodules doesn't make sense,' said Rick. 'Our crew is in significant danger out there.'

'Do you think it's related to Connor's technology and the overdrive project?' questioned Max.

'That is my thought,' said Rick. 'As to who's behind it, I could have a guess or two.'

'The drone vessels can use ARC torpedoes from a distance,' said Alex. 'Once close enough, they could at least deter the pirate submarine and the other drone ramming the Skimmer.'

Max nodded his head. 'Subsurface ARC weapons would be difficult to lock on a target anyway, given the sea state.'

'Still,' said Rick. 'We need you to get your Hunter unit to their location ASAP. We can't help the crew. They may be forced to surface. The crew will use the escape pods to get to another Skimmer in "the Area".'

'It will be a few hours yet before we are able to turn about and head towards that part of "the Area",' said Alex. 'Even then, it will be a rough ride for the crew. We will still have to wait to deploy any other assets to help.'

'Right,' said Rick. 'We are monitoring everything from here. Keep us posted on your status and whether the drone vessel ARC torpedo works.'

'Will do,' said Max.

Rick's image disappeared. The message board closed and for a moment Max looked lost in thought. His mind quickly ascertained what priorities and risks were involved for several options.

'If we alter course now and start our run back to the location where all those Skimmers are locked down, is it going to be safe,' said Max looking at the duty operations officer.

The duty officer pulled up weather projections and swiped his hand across them. He then used another screen to pull up the Hunter vessel schematics.

'Doable but one hell of a ride back,' he said looking over the details. 'However, by the time we get on location, the sea state will be down enough to deploy assets.'

'Make it so then,' said Max.

'Yes, sir,' said the duty officer as he contacted the bridge SAI console duty officer to make an announcement and alter course.

'Cam has everything ready for when we arrive on location, he tells me,' said Alex.

'Right team,' said Max as he leant forward in his command chair. 'Eyes and ears on. Bring up the two drone vessels and send them ahead. Let's get their folks and cause havoc for our pirates.'

The duty operations crew got back into their positions. They held on tight as the Hunter vessel turned about in the huge seas.

'And,' said Max as the Hunter vessel altered course, 'use our drone vessels to find out the status of our autonomous interceptor drone and take back control.'

They all felt the Sea Hunter vessel altering course. They grabbed the support rails as the heavy seas knocked the vessel around. Finally, it steadied up on a new course. Alex got up and moved among the small operations team while Max sat watching and thinking from his command chair about their next move.

***

After a few hours of quiet contemplation, listening and watching silent displays and plunging through heavy seas the console displays lit up again.

'We have the interceptor drone.. Control acquired through approaching drone vessels,' said one of the duty crew.

'Use interceptor drone to confirm the exact location of the pirate sub and its drones,' said Max. 'Get those drone vessels into position as well. Lock-on the pirate sub and deploy ARC torpedoes.'

The duty crew set about carrying out Max's orders. It would still be some time before they were in range themselves. Between being knocked around by the huge seas and preparing to engage pirates, everyone was busy.

'When interceptor is in range, try and get a visual on this Skimmer,' said Alex walking over to one of the displays.

The interceptor drone had a camera system onboard. They waited to see if anything came into view. Max watched on as did the others. The interceptor drone was approaching the location of the Skimmer.

'There's a delay, sir,' said one of the operations crew. 'Because we are getting the feed via a grid buoy and a drone vessel.'

'Let's see,' said Alex as they waited for a visual on the Skimmer.

'Interceptor drone has a lock on the pirate sub,' said one of the operations team.

'Deploy ARC torpedo,' said Max.

Alex watched as the interceptor drone display was used to lock a target and deploy one of its ARC torpedoes.

A pause followed.

Everyone waited in anticipation.

'Pirate sub is taking evasive action,' said one of the operations team.

'It's certainly not going to fire on the Skimmer,' said Max. 'Not with its own drone attempting to lock on and board it.'

'It will distract them from the Skimmer,' said Alex.

'Exactly,' said Max. 'Carry on.'

'There!' announced one of the operations team.

The Skimmer finally came into view via the interceptor drone camera feed.

The ocean was dim and dark, but the Skimmer was well lit. They could see the glow of its lights. Around it were other lights, presumably from the two pirate drones, the Xtracts and the pirate sub.

They watched as the interceptor drone closed on the chaotic display of lights moving about in the ocean a hundred meters below the supercell that raged above.

'Locate the pirate drone and use interceptor drone ARC torpedoes to disable it,' said Max. 'How's our connection with the drone vessels and grid buoy?'

'Looks like those pirate drones have already had a good go at them,' said one of the operations team.

'So far so good,' replied another. 'We've lost comms with the grid buoy we were using and have switched to another.'

'Right, let's do this before we lose the grid buoy link again,' said Max grabbing a rail as the Sea Hunter vessel heaved, battered by the enormous waves around it.

'Look at this,' said one of the operations team as he monitored the camera feed. 'The Skimmer is yawing side to side and the pirate drone is synced and attached to the topside hatch and airlock.'

'The pirate drone is too close to the Skimmer for the interceptor's ARC torpedoes,' said Alex.

'Focus team,' said Max. 'Confirm the other pirate drone is, in fact, disabled and distract the pirate sub.'

'Interceptor drone has acquired a target,' said one of the operations team.

'What about the ARC torpedo already deployed?' asked Max.

'Missed, sir,' he replied.

'Deploy another ARC torpedo,' said Max.

'Confirmed,' he replied. 'ARC torpedo deployed by SAI.'

'Drone vessel torpedo is also closing pirate sub,' said one of the operations crew.

'Damn,' said Alex as he watched the console displays. 'They have deployed countermeasures.'

'Deploy another ARC torpedo from a drone vessel at the pirate sub,' said Max.

'Target acquired,' said the operations team member. 'ARC torpedo deployed.'

'Let's keep them distracted,' said Max. 'Each time they deploy countermeasures launch another torpedo at them.'

'Yes, sir,' replied the operations crew member.

'Move the interceptor drone into a defensive position around the Skimmer,' said Max.

'Yes, sir,' replied one of the operations crew.

'Pirate drone is trying to evade interceptor torpedo,' announced one of the operations crew. 'It's closing the interceptor drone.'

'Take evasive action,' said Max. 'They're trying to use the pirate drone to lead the torpedo back to it. We could lose the interceptor.'

'Damn it,' said Alex. 'It's going to be too late!'

They watched through the camera system as the pirate drone closed the interceptor with the torpedo close behind. The camera went blank.

A moment of silence followed.

'Confirm status of the interceptor,' said Max.

'Disabled,' was the reply.

'And the pirate drone?' asked Alex.

'Disabled as well,' he replied. 'There was a collision.'

'We'll come back for our interceptor,' said Max. 'Confirm status of pirate sub and Skimmer.'

'Taking evasive action and continuing to deploy countermeasures in response to ARC torpedoes,' said one of the operations crew.

'And the Skimmer?' asked Max.

'Last update before the interceptor was disabled indicated that the crewed pirate drone was attaching to the Skimmer hatch and airlock.'

'We are still a few hours out from their location,' said Alex as he looked over to Max.

'Worst case,' said Max. 'The Skimmer is boarded, they try to stop them, the crew are injured, watertight integrity is compromised, they are forced to surface, and may or may not have time to use the escape pods.'

'So, a rescue then,' said Alex.

'A bit of both,' said Max as he stretched his arms then grabbed the handrail and nearly fell out of his command seat as the vessel heaved in the huge seas.

'Shit,' he said, grabbing the arm of his command chair. 'Set a patrol polygon for the two approaching drone vessels,' said Max. 'Keep that pirate sub engaged and distracted. Prepare to deploy assets for a sub-surface or surface rescue. Let's go.'

'Yes, sir,' replied the operations crew.

The duty operations officer contacted the SAI console to explain what was going on and to make an announcement to the whole ship.

'Alex,' said Max. 'You stay here. I'll go and brief Cam in the meeting room myself about all this.'

'Right you are,' said Alex as he briefed the operations crew on what was needed.

'SAI,' said Max. 'Notify Cam to come to the meeting room for a briefing now.'

'Confirmed,' said SAI. 'Notify Cam to come to the meeting room for a briefing now.'

Max got up out of the command chair. He looked briefly around the operations. He couldn't help thinking that this was all leading to something. That something big was coming. He wasn't sure what it was, though.

'Damn sure we are going to be prepared for it,' he said out loud walking out of operations.

'Prepared for what?' asked Alex.

'Not sure actually,' said Max. 'Whatever is going on isn't going away anytime soon. Let's discuss it later.'

Alex nodded his head as Max left.

Max entered a meeting room.

Cam wasn't far behind.

They sat as best they could in the heavy seas and discussed options and went over what to do next.

Chapter 21

The pirate drone had docked with the Skimmer. Whoever was in the drone was about to enter the airlock and board. An alarm went off and the ship's lighting dimmed to red.

'This is crazy,' said Jonny. 'An interceptor drone outside letting off torpedoes as it chases a pirate sub. A bunch of our Xtracts hassling a pirate drone and the other one docked with us!'

'Unauthorised entry topside hatch and airlock,' announced SAI. 'Skimmer security compromised. Emergency lockdown procedure activated.'

'Shit, shit and shit!' said Ngarra.

'Let's get out of here!' yelled Chang over open comms from the Xtract bay.

The Skimmer was still in open comms. Chang and Stella could hear everything that was said.

'Look,' said Jesse pointing to the view outside through the camera system.

The Xtracts, or some of them anyway, had gathered around the drone that had attached to the airlock hatch. Motionless, they appeared to be calculating their options.

'The Xtracts are determining the threat to their power source,' said Connor excitedly over open comms. He had been monitoring everything from the information hub. 'The pirate drone is a threat to Xtracts being rewarded with power from the Skimmer for delivery of nodules,' he carried on. 'Like ants swarming a threat to the nest.'

'Can you take control and use the Xtracts against the attached pirate drone?' asked Ngarra.

'No way,' said Connor. 'I said once the red queen was inserted, we wouldn't be able to. I can alter the operating parameters, that's all. The only other thing I can do is shut it down completely. The primary directive is to compete for resources and protect the source. To optimise the delivery of nodules in return for power from the Skimmer. We are their food source so to speak, The Xtracts will compete with each other to optimise this relationship.'

'What is all this rubbish,' yelled Chang over open comms from the Xtract bay. 'Who cares? We are screwed, Connor. Get that through your thick head! We have to leave!'

'Shut it, everyone,' said Jesse over comms. 'Now,' she yelled. 'Listen! Connor, get here to the SAI console now. SAI, secure the information hub.'

'Coming,' said Connor.

'Confirmed,' said SAI. 'Secure information hub.'

Connor did what he was told, exited the information hub, and raced along the passage to the SAI console.

'SAI, cancel yaw movement,' said Ngarra.

'Confirmed,' said SAI. 'Cancel yaw movement.'

The Skimmer stopped moving around.

'Can we surface,' said Jonny, 'the supercell will rip that thing off the top of us.'

'Yes, brilliant idea,' said Jesse.

'SAI, secure console entry from passages,' said Jesse.

'Confirmed,' said SAI. 'Secure console entry from passages.'

'Greetings, boys and girls,' a voice hissed from behind the secured entrance to the SAI console.

'Sue,' yelled Jesse as they looked at the security camera footage, 'I should have known!'

Sue and another had exited the airlock and walked up the passage to the SAI console entrance. They hadn't even bothered attempting to enter the information hub.

'How long will that sealed bulkhead entrance keep them there?' asked Jonny.

'There is an override,' replied Jesse. 'Look, the person with her is starting to work on it.'

'Damn it, we have to surface now,' said Ngarra. 'They won't be expecting that and will leave.'

'Depends how desperate she is,' said Jesse.

'Pretty desperate,' said Jonny. 'She's boarded a sub during a supercell.'

'SAI, cancel open comms. Open comms link between Xtract bay and SAI console only.'

'Confirmed,' said SAI. 'Cancel open comms. Open link between Xtract bay and SAI console.'

'If you give us the Skimmer, we will let you go once we are safe,' said Sue as she pressed the comms link and smiled into the security camera.

'You can't let that happen,' exclaimed Connor. 'Never. Don't let her use Gilgamesh. She wants it for those mimic drone programs. If the red queen is accessed, who knows what will happen? It won't be good!'

'And if they have a Skimmer to do it with, a lot of what is to come will be compromised,' said Jesse.

'What do you mean by that?' asked Ngarra.

'The overdrive trials and project Cygnus,' she replied. 'It's all been brought forward because of exactly this scenario. Too many people know now. We have to move forward.'

'Forward with what?' asked Ngarra.

'The overdrive trials, of course,' replied Jesse with a smirk on her face.

'Come on guys,' said Jonny. 'We have to get out of here!' he said, looking at the camera monitoring Sue's attempts to bypass the secure bulkhead entrance.

'Right,' said Ngarra. 'We surface the Skimmer and, on the way, launch the escape pods. Jonny contacts the nearest Skimmer and explain the situation. We are coming in the escape pods.'

'Onto it,' said Jonny. He got SAI to confirm eel drone and grid buoy proximity and contacted Skimmers in the vicinity with a recorded message.

'SAI, activate escape pods, port and starboard,' said Ngarra.

'Confirmed,' said SAI. 'Escape pods activated.'

'SAI, surface Skimmer,' said Jesse.

'Denied,' said SAI. 'Safety breach, command override needed.'

'What about the streamer?' asked Jonny.

'Stella,' he said over the comms link. 'Is the streamer fully retracted?'

'No, it sheared when we were yawing from side to side. It's still partially attached and stuck.'

'That's a good thing,' said Ngarra. 'It will act as a sea anchor when surfaced. Some stability while we launch the escape pods.'

'SAI, command override,' said Jesse. 'Surface Skimmer.'

A dull scraping sound started. Then a pop and a dull thud. Everyone looked towards the bulkhead entrance. It was ajar.

'You lot aren't going anywhere,' said Sue angrily.

They were about to squeeze through the entrance.

'Umm guys,' said Jonny, with a pale look on his face. 'I think I've been shot.'

Jonny looked to his left at his shoulder. A red stain appeared.

'Damn it!' said Ngarra, running over to him.

'To the stairs now,' said Jesse.

Ngarra helped Jonny and they all raced to the top of the entrance to the stairs and out of the line of fire of the pistol that was being aimed at them.

It was too late, though.

Sue and her offsider were through.

They entered the SAI console.

At the same time, the Skimmer shuddered and lurched.

Sue and her offsider lost their footing and stumbled forward.

That was the chance they needed.

Helping Jonny they raced down the stairs to the rec area.

Ngarra got SAI to override the watertight protocol so the entrance to the rec area could be opened. He got SAI to seal and secure the bulkhead entrance.

Chang and Stella got SAI to open the watertight entrance to the Xtract bay below.

'Eighty metres below sea level and ascending,' said SAI. 'Escape pods activated.'

'Hurry up!' yelled Jesse as Chang and Stella raced up the stairs to the rec area.

'Once surfaced it is going to be hard,' said Ngarra. 'The seas are huge, and we will be knocked around.'

'Seventy metres below sea level and ascending,' said SAI.

The Skimmer would soon start to roll around due to the size of the swell at the surface and its reach below sea level.

'Give us what we want, and you will survive all this,' said Sue over comms.

Again, her offsider had bypassed the lockdown protocol securing all watertight entrances. They were about to pry open the entrance to the rec area.

'I'm not feeling too good,' said Jonny, holding his shoulder.

'Geez,' said Stella, realising Jonny what had happened. 'She shot you?'

In all the rush, Stella hadn't noticed. She ran and got a medkit and towel and pressed it to the wound. Taking her shirt off, she tied it tightly around the wound. She opened the medkit and tended to the wound.

'Any excuse to get undressed,' said Jonny wincing as she cleaned and applied a temporary dressing. She gave him a shot to numb the pain.

'In your dreams, boy,' she said smiling.

Stella finished and she and Chang got to either side of him to support his weight.

'Sixty metres below sea level and ascending,' said SAI.

There were several dull thuds from outside the Skimmer. The hull shuddered and the Skimmer slowed.

'SAI, report on the status of Xtracts,' said Ngarra.

'Xtracts are positioned topside of Skimmer,' said SAI. 'Ascent speed reduced.'

'Brilliant,' said Connor. 'They are protecting the Skimmer and not wanting it to surface.'

'Probably a good thing right now,' said Jesse. 'We need to get out of here now.'

'Gilgamesh has learnt and adapted fast,' said Connor.

'What about us, mate?' asked Jonny jokingly as they moved off to the escape pods.

'I don't think we have adapted. Look at the state of me.'

They all stumbled as the Skimmer started rolling around.

Being close to the surface the roll from the huge seas was building.

'Jonny, Stella and Chang, go!' said Jesse.

'Take the port escape pod, we'll take starboard. Might as well use both. And it means Sue is stuck here. Just need that pirate drone of theirs to be ripped off topside by the swell.'

'Who is stuck where?' asked Sue as both entered the rec area.

Standing between the crew as they tried to enter the escape pods, she pointed her pistol at Ngarra.

The Skimmer was rolling heavily in the swell now. Everyone struggled to hold on.

'Fifty metres below sea level and ascending,' said SAI.

Stella let go of Jonny and approached her from behind. She was angry and wasn't thinking straight.

'You bitch!' she yelled about to punch her.

Sue's arm swung back and across. The butt of the weapon caught Stella on the forehead. It was a glancing blow, but it split her skin and blood ran down her face.

Stella stumbled, and Connor ran to help.

They were all trying to keep their balance. It was difficult. The Skimmer was not far from the surface and continued to roll heavily.

'Get over here now!' yelled Sue. They all grabbed something as the Skimmer rolled again.

'Forty metres below sea level and ascending,' said SAI.

Sue waved the pistol around as she got them to all stand together. Jonny was struggling with his shoulder wound. The others were worried. *We need to get out of here,* thought Jesse. She remained calm; watching Sues every move and waiting for an opportunity.

'You stay here,' said Sue to her offsider, 'and watch this lot. Connor get here! Take me to the information hub now!'

She tossed him a device and pointed her weapon at him.

'What is it?' he asked.

'Shut it and go,' she hissed at him.

Connor looked blankly at Sue then at the others. He was starting to freak out. Stella motioned calmly to him to go and that everything would be fine. Connor's changing demeanour had distracted Sue, though. She wasn't quite sure how to take it.

During this Jonny had been seated at the table to one side of the group and just out of Sue's peripheral vision. She hadn't thought of him as a threat. Jonny had been clutching his shoulder and wincing at the pain.

The bandages and bloodied cloth and shirt made it clear to Sue that he was not looking too good. He was not a threat.

Connor nodded at Stella and turned reluctantly to walk up the stairs. The Skimmer rolled in the swell again and he stumbled sideways. Sue went to grab his hand and force him up the stairs. Her offsider was distracted by the stumble and looked over to see if she needed assistance.

'Thirty metres below sea level and ascending,' said SAI.

The seas were huge, and the Skimmer was near the surface. It suddenly pitched violently. Jonny saw his moment. It would hurt but he launched himself across the rec area in the direction of the roll of the Skimmer.

Jonny used the momentum he had gained and slammed straight into Sue's back, and sent her flying. She landed heavily and smacked her head against the deck. Jonny couldn't break his fall and landed on his back; the wind knocked out of him. He passed out with the pain in his shoulder.

Jesse, Ngarra and Chang were standing directly in front of Sue's offsider. In that moment, with his head turned towards Sue, they jumped on him. Disarming him, they all ended up on the deck. Chang grabbed his pistol. The Skimmer rolled heavily again. The crew and Sues offsider slid across the deck into the bulkhead on the other side.

Jesse jumped up. She went and grabbed the pistol that was knocked out of Sue's hand. Sue was dazed and trying to stand up again.

Ngarra and Chang rushed to help Stella, who was still sitting on the ground with blood dripping down her face. Then they helped Jonny, who had come round from fainting. They all got to their feet.

'Go,' said Jesse as she and Chang pointed both pistols at Sue and her offsider and motioned for them to move.

'Move,' said Jesse. Pointing to an entrance that was open to one of the escape pods.

Sue and her offsider didn't say a word.

'You lot use the other escape pod. Now!' said Jesse to her crew.

'What are you doing?' asked Ngarra.

'Change of plans,' said Jesse.

She knew the bigger picture. There was no way she was leaving Sue stranded on the Skimmer.

'SAI, disable port side escape pod controls,' said Jesse. 'Set automated recovery program.'

'Confirmed,' said SAI. 'Portside escape pod controls disabled. Automated recovery program enabled.'

When the escape pod launched, there would be no way to take control of it. A rescue beacon would activate, and the Sea Hunters would pick up the signal.

'You can't do this!' hissed Sue as she turned toward them.

'Oh yes we can,' said Jesse, keeping her distance. She could see Sue eyeing up the distance between them and working out if she could take her out.

'I don't think so,' said Jesse in response. 'Now get in that pod!'

'You'll pay for this!' she hissed at Jesse.

'If you don't get in that pod,' said Jesse as they backed into the airlock. 'I will punch it out from here and you will both drown in the airlock.'

Reluctantly, Sue and her offsider entered the escape pod and the airlock closed behind them.

'SAI, activate escape pod launch sequence.'

'Confirmed,' said SAI. 'Escape pod launch sequence activated.'

The Skimmer crew entered the airlock to the other escape pod. It would be a squeeze. They were not designed to take the whole crew.

'Jesse, the pod can't take the whole crew,' said Ngarra. 'It's not designed for that.'

'I know,' said Jesse. 'Chang, come with me before it's too late.'

'The pirate drone,' Stella exclaimed. 'You're crazy.'

'It will be too late if you don't hurry up,' she replied. 'It will get ripped off the topside hatch and airlock.'

'Escape pod launched,' announced SAI.

'Good riddance,' said Jonny as they entered the airlock to the other escape pod.

'Twenty metres below sea level and ascending,' said SAI.

'We'll be fine,' said Jesse. 'Now go, go now!'

The airlock closed and they entered the escape pod. Jesse and Chang didn't wait around to watch it be jettisoned from the Skimmer.

They raced up the stairs and through the compromised watertight bulkhead entrances that Sue and her offsider had opened.

Despite the Xtracts topside attempting to slow the Skimmers ascent, it was not far from surfacing. Any minute now, the pirate drone would be ripped from the topside hatch.

Steadying themselves as the Skimmer rolled around in the huge seas, they raced through the SAI console, down the passage to the airlock behind the information hub.

'We don't have much time,' said Jesse as they listened to the groaning sound above them. 'SAI, on detaching the pirate drone from the airlock, descend to one hundred metres and hold the position.'

'Confirmed,' said SAI.

'What about the Xtracts?' asked Chang.

'According to Connor they will look after themselves,' said Jesse. 'They will follow the Skimmer back down and dock on their clamps until told otherwise. At least, that's what Connor said before he left the information hub.'

Chang reached down and grabbed Jesse's hand. He pulled her up into the pirate drone.

'Seal the hatch!' yelled Jesse.

Just in time, Chang reached down and closed both the Skimmer hatch and the pirate drone hatch. The pirate drone was ripped from the Skimmer hull and tumbled off. They were thrown around as the huge seas took hold of them. The Skimmer started to descend back down to a hundred metres below sea level.

'Strap in,' yelled Jesse as they continued to be tossed around, 'these are old drones!'

Jesse ran through the start-up sequence and got power online. She wrestled with the controls and tried to stabilise the pirate drone.

'Got it,' she said as they righted and descended from the heavy roll from the swell above them.

They descended to a depth that was out of harm's way.

Moving off, they headed towards the nearest Skimmer.

Jesse hoped her crew had got away safely and were also heading towards a Skimmer.

Looking behind they watched as the Skimmer slowly descended to one hundred metres. The Xtracts had moved off to the side and followed it down. Circling, the interceptor drone was still monitoring the Skimmer. It didn't follow them.

Somewhere above and not far away now, the two hunter unit drone vessels were approaching. During everything that had happened, the supercell had passed further south. The seas were still huge, but conditions had eased enough for the drone vessels to turn up.

Chapter 22

Jonny winced in pain as the escape pod headed towards another Skimmer. It was a squeeze to get the four of them in. However, over the short trip, the pod could cope.

'Shit, it hurts,' said Jonny as he tried not to lose consciousness again.

'Being shot does that to you,' said Stella trying to comfort him.

The pressure bandage was now soaked in blood.

'Not much further,' said Ngarra.

Stella was sitting in the cockpit next to Ngarra. Jonny and Connor were behind them.

'What will happen to the other pod?' asked Connor.

'Sue won't be able to control it,' said Ngarra. 'The locator beacon is activated. It will eventually surface, and they will be picked up by the Sea Hunters.'

'Bit of a rough ride for them, then.' Stella laughed.

'You could say that,' said Ngarra.

'I hope that bitch suffers,' said Stella. 'Nasty woman.'

Jonny managed a smile and a short-lived laugh.

'Stop,' he said, wincing in pain. 'Even laughing hurts. What about Gilgamesh?'

Connor looked blankly at everyone. He had been withdrawn and quiet. Not knowing what to think. The comment brought him back to focus on what was going on around him.

'Our Skimmer is secure and holding position,' said Ngarra. 'The sea state is easing, and the Sea Hunters will be here. Between their ship, the two drone vessels and their interceptor drones, it's not going anywhere.'

'Did you see what the Xtracts did,' said Connor excitedly. 'Red queen works, they learnt to adapt to the situation. All my work on Gilgamesh. It'll rapidly evolve. Nature's solutions accelerated and applied to AI.'

Stella smiled at the others. Despite a cracking headache, the bleeding had stopped. With help, she had managed to wrap a pressure bandage around her head. *Connor had been working on his pet project for quite some time now,* she thought to herself. His obsession was like a parent and child.

With nothing else to do for a while, they listened to Connor talking about all his work. It was a welcome and familiar distraction from what had happened. Connor had a captured audience and to him, that meant more than what was going on around him.

'Escape pod, escape pod, this is Skimmer over.'

A voice came over comms.

'Skimmer, skimmer, this is Ngarra over,' he replied.

'We have you and a pirate drone inbound with your other crew inbound. What happened out there? We got the message. Why are you in an escape pod and why are the others in a pirate drone over?'

'Long story over,' replied Ngarra.

'Okay,' was the reply. 'Our moon pool is open. Dock with us and once through the airlock, we will pressurise, and you can get out. Then we will deal with the pirate drone over.'

'Got it,' said Ngarra. 'Have your medic ready. One of our team has been shot in the shoulder and the other has a laceration on her forehead.'

'What? Shot. No weapons are allowed onboard. What the hell happened to you guys over?'

'Like I said,' replied Ngarra. 'Long story over.'

'Okay, we have got you. Skimmer out,' they replied as Ngarra saw the Skimmer come into view.

'On final approach,' said Ngarra to his crew.

'Yeah, well hurry it up,' said Jonny. 'Think I'm going to pass out again.'

'Harden up, boy,' said Stella as she pointed at her bandaged head.

Jonny managed a smile and a wink but that was about it.

They were approaching the Skimmer, one hundred metres below the easing sea above, black below and the dim light of the photic zone around and above them. It was surreal. The crew had forgotten what it was like to approach a Skimmer moon pool.

'These pods have an automated docking sequence with Skimmer moon pools don't they?' asked Stella.

'Yes, and done,' said Ngarra as he activated the docking sequence.

The escape pod slowed.

Turning in a wide arc, it moved into position a short distance in front of the Skimmer. It then proceeded slowly underneath the Skimmer to the moon pool entrance near the stern.

'Forgot what this was like,' said Stella.

'Me too,' said Ngarra.

They watched as the hull of the Skimmer slipped by above them. Ahead was the dimly lit entrance. They watch it come into view. The escape pod paused and then started its ascent. It surfaced in the moon pool and a docking arm grabbed them. It lifted the escape pod up and out of the water, through the airlock and into the maintenance bay. The airlock closed behind them.

'Maintenance bay pressurised,' announced SAI.

'You can exit the escape pod,' said one of the crew over comms from the maintenance bay monitoring console. 'The pirate drone is inbound with the rest of your crew.'

Ngarra could see some of the crew of the Skimmer that had picked them up watching from the Xtract console. Ngarra and Stella helped Jonny. He wasn't in good shape and needed medical attention fast. Connor followed behind.

'Bring him with us,' said the Skimmer medic as she came through the maintenance bay entrance.

Another of the crew came in and helped Jonny and they left with the medic. Ngarra and Connor stayed behind.

'We need to contact Xed straight away,' said Ngarra. 'Our crew vitals will have spiked all over the place. They will be wondering what on earth is going on. They would have got the emergency signal activation and notification of the use of escape pods.'

'Come with me to the SAI console,' said their security and communications officer who had also come down to meet them.

'Right,' said Ngarra. 'I'll go. Connor, you go to the rec area and get tidied up and have something to eat. We will have a briefing shortly when Jesse and Chang get here in that pirate drone.'

Connor nodded and they left the maintenance bay through the watertight bulkhead entrance.

Their rescuers got the moon pool and airlock ready to receive the pirate drone.

Moving through the Xtract console monitoring area they headed up the stairs to the rec area.

'I'll get something to eat now,' said Connor as they entered the rec area.

'Okay,' said Ngarra as he followed their security and communications officer up the stairs to the SAI console.

Once in the SAI console, Ngarra wondered what on earth to say to Jonah and Rick about what had happened.

'SAI,' said their security and communications officer. 'Urgent message for Xed Academy crewing monitoring. Open message board.'

'Confirmed,' said SAI. 'Message board open. Eel drone and grid buoy proximity are sub-optimal. Recorded message only.'

Ngarra started to record a message.

'Jonah, Rick. We escaped the Skimmer using a pod and docked with this one. Jesse and Chang will arrive shortly in a pirate drone. Long story. Propulsion on our Skimmer is damaged from ramming. A pirate drone docked, and Sue's team boarded. Jonny was shot in the shoulder but will be okay. Stella has a laceration on her forehead. Secured weapons and forced Sue's team into another escape pod. Sent them away on a pre-programmed vector for Sea Hunter interception. Our Skimmer descended to one hundred metres and is holding position.'

They waited for a reply.

A short time later, Jonah's image appeared.

SAI played the message.

'Ngarra, thank god you are okay. Sea Hunters are not far off. Supercell has passed and the course to your location is now navigable. Hold your position and wait. You are to recover your Skimmer with assistance from Sea Hunters. Stabilise Jonny and all return to Harvester for the uplift of your crew. Bring Gilgamesh to us. Be careful, Harvester may be compromised, and much is at stake. Listen to Sea Hunters.'

Her image disappeared.

'Out of the frying pan and into the fire,' said the security and communications officer. 'What is Gilgamesh?'

'You'll find out soon enough,' said Ngarra. 'Not to mention we will now have one very grumpy Skimmer contractor given the damage we took. Things were not meant to move this fast.'

'What things?' asked the security and communications officer.

'The overdrive trials,' said Ngarra. 'We are all involved in completing those now. And Connor's tech has changed things. Whatever is going on with that Harvester has also resulted in a change of plans.'

'Gilgamesh, you mean,' said the security and communications officer.

'We have been briefed about all that,' said the Skimmer operator. 'We know change is afoot. Let's go to the rec area so you can brief everyone. Looks like the rest of your crew has arrived as well.'

At the SAI console, they watched outside as the pirate drone arrived. They walked to the rear of the SAI console, through the watertight bulkhead and down the stairs.

In the rec area, Ngarra chatted briefly with the others.

They waited for Jesse and Chang to come up from the maintenance bay below.

'Can't say I ever want to do that again,' said Chang as he and Jesse came up from below, behind one of the Skimmer crew.

'You and me both,' said Jesse.

'Thank god you guys are okay,' said Stella walking up to them and giving them a hug. Her head wound had been tended to and tidied up.

'Please,' said Chang. 'Get off me, woman.'

Everyone laughed. Even Jonny managed a chuckle. The bullet had exited his shoulder. It hadn't hit anything vital. The medic had treated the wound. It would get proper attention onboard the Sea Hunter vessel.

'What, no smart comment, Jonny boy?' asked Stella.

'You'll keep,' said Jonny wincing at the pain from the bullet wound in his shoulder that had been tended to.

Everyone stood together off to one side or sat at the table. Both crews had gathered to hear what was going on.

'Right, listen up everyone,' said Ngarra as they quietened down. 'Stella, how is Jonny?'

'Okay, mostly,' said Stella. 'Bullet went through and missed anything vital. A lot of blood loss, though, so he is feeling pretty weak.'

Jonny nodded and managed a smile.

'Okay,' said Ngarra as he looked at Jesse. 'We have to move quickly. The Sea Hunters are on their way here to the lockdown area for all Skimmers. The supercell has passed south of us. Sea state is easing enough for them to close us.

We are to recover our Skimmer and head to the Harvester for uplift to the Xed Academy. We must bring Gilgamesh with us.'

'Um that might be a problem,' said Connor. 'You can't just take it anymore. Gilgamesh and re queen is now synced with the Xtracts. The sphere would have to be shut down. You can't just take it.'

'Can we take the whole sphere then?' asked Jesse.

'What is Gilgamesh?' asked one of the other crew members.

'A revolution in Xtract mining tech, that's what it is,' said Connor excitedly.

He was about to tell them all about it when Jesse interrupted.

'Later, Connor,' she said. 'Is it possible to uplift the sphere? What about the Xtracts?'

'Without the sphere,' said Connor, 'it shouldn't matter now. The Xtracts would carry on mining. But it's the red queen sequence inserted into Gilgamesh that is the key. So, without Gilgamesh, the Xtracts would carry on mining autonomously but would stop evolving. It's an autonomous interface, a child that needs guidance. We can take Gilgamesh, replicate it, insert the sequence, and install the sphere to do the same on all Skimmers now. It's a distributed and decentralised neural network. Gilgamesh is like the central nerve ring that connects their learning. Like the organisms I studied and developed it from, a starfish, for example. Each Skimmer would have Gilgamesh. Like independent autonomous learning nodes. One for each Skimmer.'

'Perfect,' said Ngarra. 'The Sea Hunters will remove the sphere of Gilgamesh for uplift and return to the Xed Academy. We avoid the Harvester altogether. We use our own repair drones to fix the damaged blades on the rim drive and return to the Harvester minus Gilgamesh for uplift to the Xed Academy.'

'Wait,' said Jesse. 'I have been briefed and things have changed. No one is to speak of this. A crew change out will occur at the Harvester. After repairs are carried out the other crew will operate our Skimmer as if nothing has happened. We will then be posted back to it in due course. Our mission will be to install the technology, the sphere of Gilgamesh, on all Skimmers.'

'But someone knows what's on our Skimmer,' said Chang. 'They want it for themselves.'

'Well, now it's going to be on all Skimmers,' said Jesse.

'No one is having Gilgamesh,' exclaimed Connor. 'Besides,' he said, smiling. 'I made sure it always required a human interface and a prime directive regarding the parameters within which red queen operates.'

'What do you mean?' asked one of the other crew.

'It means that even with red queen we still have oversight,' said Jesse.

'Yes,' said Connor. 'More than I can say for that mimic drone project your sister is working on.'

'Speaking of that,' said Jesse. 'We have to be careful. Something isn't right on that Harvester.'

'We noticed that too,' said one of the Skimmer crew members.

'You can say that again,' said Jonny as he went to get up and get some food.

'You shouldn't be up and about,' said Stella as she helped him.

'Too much going on to sit around,' said Jonny wincing at his shoulder. 'And I need sustenance,' he said, managing to rub his stomach. 'Besides, I may not have signed up for this, but now, well, let's do something about it.'

'Back to your old self, boy,' said Stella, poking his stomach.

The others smiled.

'Seems we all want this,' said Chang.

Jesse nodded. Adversity brings people together, she thought. With much to come, that was probably a good thing. Her crew and their Skimmer were about to embark on something very different to running mining operations. A greater purpose. There was more to it than her crew knew about. She caught the other Skimmer security communications and security officer's eye. He nodded at her in agreement. They had been prepared for this at the Xed Academy.

'Right,' said Ngarra to his crew. 'We have some time before the Sea Hunters arrive. All Skimmers are still in lockdown. Get some rest.'

The operator of the Skimmer they were on and their security and communications officer nodded their heads in agreement. They both stayed and talked with Ngarra and Jesse about what was going on.

Stella walked forward around the narrow esplanade on either side of the bulkhead behind which the overdrive was located. Opening into the forward viewing area she walked across and looked out into the dull and dark blue-green void above and the blackness below. The outer hull shields were retracted. She wondered what was coming. That's what it felt like. She longed for the beaches back at the Xed Academy and the innocence they had. That was gone now. But they would go back for a time. That was something she held onto. Her head hurt from the laceration, and she had a headache.

***

In the depths of the ocean, the escape pod carrying Sue and her offsider continued. With having no control over any of its systems, all they could do was wait to be picked up.

'Here they come,' said Sue as she looked out of the viewing port.

From out of the depths below, a huge black shadow rose. It dwarfed them; coming alongside and then moving slowly over the top of them.

'About time,' said Sue. 'I have much to discuss.'

She sat back with her offsider and they waited.

They felt several dull vibrations and some shaking as their escape pod was secured and taken inside. A short time later, the pod was opened, and Sue and her offsider stepped out.

Chapter 23

Sometime later and with easing seas the Skimmer that had recovered Ngarra's crew surfaced. Max and Alex were at the Hunter vessel SAI console and could see it in the distance. The sea state had reduced to a slow heaving swell.

'Did you brief them on how this is going to go?' asked Max.

'Yes, both our crew and the Skimmers',' said Alex. 'Cam is taking a boarding party in the sea boat. Ngarra's crew will be uplifted from the Skimmer they are on and Jonny and Stella will be tended to. Once we get to Ngarra's Skimmer, Cam's team will secure Gilgamesh. A patrol drone will hook up to it and fly it across to our drone deck.'

'Sounds like a plan,' said Max, nodding his head and stretching his arms. 'Not much sleep over the last few days. Starting to feel it. I must be getting old.'

'Sir, on final approach,' said the duty officer.

'Right,' said Alex. 'Deploy a sea boat and standby to launch a patrol drone.'

The Hunter vessel slowed and took up position patrolling a perimeter around the surfaced Skimmer.

They watched from the SAI console as the sea boat left the well deck aft and headed towards the Skimmer.

The two drone vessels were still in the vicinity of Ngarra's submerged Skimmer which was some distance away from their current position.

***

Cam's boarding party approached the Skimmer wing starboard side. Coming alongside Cam and his boarding party grabbed the rungs and climbed up the side. Walking across the Skimmer wing and between nodule trays, they reach the Xtract recess. A gangway was lowered, and they walked up to the entrance to the rec area. Some of the Skimmer crew and Ngarra and Jesse were waiting for them.

'You have no idea how glad we are to see you,' said Ngarra.

'Where's Jonny?' asked Cam.

'Here,' he said, moving slowly forward with some help from Stella.

'Right, let's go then,' replied Cam. 'Get him to the sea boat along with the rest of you. Everything else all right here?' he asked the Skimmer crew.

'Fine,' said the Skimmer security and communications officer. 'Glad we could help with this and that it wasn't us.'

Cam and his team left.

Walking back down the gangway they followed the others across the Skimmer wing and back to the sea boat. They managed to get Jonny into it. The slow-rolling swell was not too hard to negotiate as they boarded the sea boat.

'Why do you have to be such a big boy?' asked Stella as she and the others helped him in.

'Because someone has to keep saving all your arses,' said Jonny as he sat down and winced at the pain in his shoulder.

The others sat down and gripped the handrails. The sea boat took off and made its way to the circling Sea Hunter vessel.

The ocean was still heaving, but long and slow, up and down as the swell rolled through. It was gentle enough, like riding through undulating hills, all the way up and all the way down.

Being low to the water in the swell, the Hunter vessel passed in and out of view until it loomed large in front of them.

Coming astern the Hunter vessel had straightened upon its course heading to the location of Ngarra's Skimmer. Opposite the well deck and holding position, they got the signal to approach.

Cam drove the sea boat into the well deck and straight onto the shallow ramp it had been launched from. It was secured in place and lifted out of the water.

The controller checked in with the SAI console on the bridge. The Sea Hunter vessel then sped up and headed towards the location of Ngarra's Skimmer.

A medic and a few crew members approached the sea boat.

'Let's get you fixed up,' said the medic as they helped Jonny out.

'He's lost a fair bit of blood,' said Stella. 'The bullet went straight through. Nothing vital hit.'

'Right,' said the medic as they left with him, 'and you can come too so we can check out that head of yours.'

'Okay,' said Stella, shrugging her shoulders.

'Let's get the rest of you tidied up and to the mess for some food and rest,' said Cam. 'Alex and Max can debrief you over a meal before getting to your Skimmer. There is enough time. They want a full account of what happened. A full report has to be submitted to "the Authority" on all this.'

Ngarra, Chang, Jesse and Connor followed Cam to the rear of the well deck and up the stairs.

Past operations, they arrived in the mess and helped themselves to some food and drink.

A short time later, Alex and Max entered the mess. They all moved off to a meeting room for a debrief.

'How's Jonny and Stella?' asked Ngarra as they all sat down.

'They will be fine,' said Alex. 'Now, when you get back to the Harvester, nothing is to be mentioned of any of this. Complete the crew change out and return to the Xed Academy.'

'What about Gilgamesh?' asked Connor.

'How will you get Gilgamesh back to the Xed Academy?'

'Let us take care of that,' replied Max.

Jesse looked at Ngarra. A look of concern. She needed to talk to Jonah about all this. Last time, they were told not to trust the Sea Hunters or Rick for that matter. The situation had changed, but by how much.

'Why don't we use the overdrive to go back to Xed on the Skimmer?' asked Chang.

'It's still a contractor Skimmer,' said Max as he sat back in his chair and looked at each one of them. 'You can't just take it.'

'But what about the overdrive trials?' asked Chang.

'Done during mining operations,' said Max. 'At least, that is what Rick told us to expect from now on.'

'We need to hear this from Jonah,' said Jesse.

Alex looked at Max and he nodded.

'Fine,' said Max. 'Let's contact her from operations. We will be at your Skimmer soon.'

Jesse and Ngarra got up and followed Max and Alex through the mess and into operations.

'One of us should stay with Gilgamesh,' said Ngarra quietly as they walked behind Max and Alex.

'Definitely,' replied Jesse.

'Right,' said Max as they entered the comms room in operations. 'SAI, contact Xed crew monitoring and communications. Request Jonah.'

'Confirmed,' said SAI. 'Contact Xed and request Jonah.'

They waited.

A silent pause pierced the air.

Ngarra and Jesse looked at each other and then at Max and Alex. Max ignored them.

Then Jonah's image appeared on the message board.

'Max, glad to hear from you,' she said. 'How is my crew after their ordeal?'

'Jonny is recovering well. Bullet went clean through his shoulder. He will be fine. Stella has stitches and a headache. Your crew will be returning to Xed on the next crew change from the Harvester. We will remove Gilgamesh and organise its return to Xed.'

'I'm not going anywhere without Gilgamesh,' blurted Connor.

He had walked behind them, curious about what they might say about Gilgamesh. He had been quiet for much of their ordeal. Sensory overload had made it hard for him to communicate. He had focussed on Gilgamesh the whole time. It was something to hold on to while chaos surrounded him. He liked routine and nothing about any of what was happening appeared routine.

'We would like someone to accompany Gilgamesh,' said Jesse as she looked at Connor and nodded. 'It's only right that we shouldn't let it out of our sight.'

'I'm sure it is in good hands,' said Jonah. 'Rick has organised all this. We need it back here. You lot are going to run the rollout across all Skimmers during overdrive trials.'

'I must insist,' said Jesse looking at Jonah with an intense and unusual gaze, 'that one of our crew accompany Gilgamesh.'

A pause followed and Jonah also looked at Jesse intensely. Ngarra watched them. He was certain they were silently communicating something between them. *Women*, he thought to himself.

'Okay,' said Jonah. 'Jesse, you and Connor stay with Gilgamesh and Max and Alex will organise uplift and your return. The rest of you take the Skimmer to the Harvester and as usual swap out with your replacement crew and return to Xed.'

'How will they get Gilgamesh back to Xed?' asked Chang.

'Leave that to us,' said Alex. 'We will meet with another asset out here and they will return Connor, Jesse and Gilgamesh to Xed.'

'Right,' said Jonah. 'I will brief Rick. Got to go. See you all soon then.'

Jonah's image disappeared.

'Approaching Skimmer location,' announced the SAI console duty officer over comms. 'Drone vessels are patrolling a perimeter and the interceptor is circling below.'

'Right,' said Alex over comms to the SAI console duty officer. 'Get SAI to recover both the interceptors.'

'Yes, sir,' he replied.

In operations, the crew heard the instruction and got ready.

'Now,' said Alex. 'Let's get you lot to the well deck. Ever been in a breaching pod?'

They shook their heads.

'Given the damage to the topside hatch we will use one and enter the Skimmer using the moon pool,' said Alex. 'Can you communicate with your SAI and open the moon pool?'

'Yes,' said Ngarra. 'The Skimmer can be accessed externally by the crew if no one is onboard.'

'Great,' said Alex. 'We'll take Ngarra and Chang. You need to surface the Skimmer. Given Jonny and Stella's condition, they will join you by sea boat from here. We will then extract Gilgamesh, using the main entrance, and bring Gilgamesh out onto the Skimmer wing. Our patrol drone will use a cable and winch and lift it off.'

Everyone agreed on the plan. The sea state had calmed considerably. It was safe to conduct an extraction from the Skimmer.

Returning to the others a quick discussion amongst the Skimmer crew followed.

They said goodbye to Jesse and Connor.

'Catch up back at Xed,' said Jesse as she and Connor watched them go.

'You bet,' said Stella. 'I have a date at the beach.'

The others smiled and headed down to the drone bay well deck.

'Will you be right with that arm of yours?' asked Chang as they walked off. 'Not the tough guy now, are we?'

'Says who?' asked Jonny wincing. He made a warrior face at Chang. He was startled and jumped back.

'Gets you every time,' said Jonny laughing and then wincing at the pain in his shoulder.

At least, the crew still has some humour in all this, Ngarra thought to himself as they made their way to the well deck drone bay.

Cam was there with another crew member watching. They were watching the technicians check over the breaching pod. It would be connected to an interceptor drone once they boarded it.

They could squash four people into an interceptor drone breaching pod.

At the Skimmer, the robotic arm would lift the breaching pod out of the moon pool and into the airlock. Once in the Xtract maintenance bay and while suspended from the robotic arm they could exit the bottom of the breaching pod. It was designed to lock onto the Skimmer topside hatch so the only way in and out was from underneath it.

'Cam,' said Alex. 'Once surfaced, get Gilgamesh onto the Skimmer wing for uplift. Get a patrol drone operator crew together and task them for it.'

Cam nodded his head and spoke to the bay controller. He then contacted the drone deck and arranged for a crew to prepare for the uplift of the sphere of Gilgamesh.

'Done,' said Cam as he walked over to the beaching pod and climbed into the front. He waved Ngarra and Chang over and they climbed in as well.

A couple of technicians closed the capsule and directed the interceptor overhead to connect with the breaching pod.

Alex, Jonny, and Stella watched as the breaching pod was secured in place. A robotic arm lifted the interceptor drone up and along. The bay door to the well deck was open.

The interceptor was slowly lowered into the water. The long, slow swell was a welcome respite from the supercell that had passed through.

The robotic arm released the docking clamp and the interceptor briefly settled in the well deck water. It then submerged as it moved out behind the Hunter vessel and disappeared.

Chapter 24

The interceptor drone approached the Skimmer. Ngarra and Chang watched one of the other interceptor drones that had been monitoring their Skimmer leave and return to the Hunter vessel.

'On final approach,' said Cam. 'Ngarra, get on comms with your Skimmer SAI and get us approval to board using the moon pool.'

'Right, let's do this,' said Ngarra.

He communicated with the Skimmer SAI and went through security protocols to access the Skimmer externally, using the moon pool when no crew were onboard.

He gave Cam a nod that it was all done.

'Switching to automated docking sequence,' said Cam.

The Skimmer was in sleep mode. Xtracts had docked and it was running on minimum power.

No sign that Gilgamesh was active either, Ngarra thought to himself. *But the Xtracts were not mining so why would it be?*

On receiving instruction from Ngarra and sensing activation of the automated docking sequence by the interceptor, the Skimmer woke from its slumber.

Rows of lights came on and the interceptor moved underneath the Skimmer. The topside breaching pod entry hatch had been damaged when the pirate drone had been sheared off. It couldn't be accessed. The damaged blades on the rim drive were also visible.

Slowly, it was positioned under the moon pool and then rose slowly into it. Surfacing, they watched as the robotic arm hooked onto them and lifted them up and out and through the warlock, which closed behind them.

Once pressurised, the other side opened, and they were moved into the maintenance bay. A soft bump was felt and then nothing.

'Automated docking sequence completed,' said Cam. 'Watertight integrity confirmed, airlock secure. Open hatch.'

Ngarra and Chang watched as Cam opened the hatch and climbed out onto the maintenance bay deck.

'Over to you,' said Cam as he waved them to come out.

Ngarra and Chang climbed out of the breaching pod.

'Feels like home,' said Ngarra as they walked through the watertight bulkhead entrance into the maintenance bay console and then up the stairs to the rec area. They passed the damage done by Sue.

They made their way to the SAI console.

'SAI, confirm Skimmer status,' said Ngarra as they walked in.

SAI displayed in a hologram the Skimmers propulsion and life support systems.

'Confirmed,' said SAI. 'Life support systems nominal, starboard propulsion offline, rim drive blades damaged, overdrive offline, Xtracts recovered, streamer sheared.'

'SAI, activate repair drone. Secure sheared streamer.'

'Confirmed,' said SAI. 'Activate repair drone and secure sheared streamer.'

A repair drone was launched from the maintenance bay, through the airlock and into the moon pool by SAI.

Ngarra went through more checks with Chang while Cam watched on.

'We'll have to get back to the Harvester on one rim drive,' said Chang. 'Unless we use the overdrive.'

Ngarra nodded and checked the status of the powertrain to the rim drive.

'Once we get back to Xed,' said Chang. 'You realise there will not be much downtime. They will want us to get back out here to roll out Gilgamesh for them and participate in these overdrive trials.'

'I know,' said Ngarra. 'So much for mining. Whatever the deal is between Skimmer contractors, Xed, the technology and trialling these overdrives it's all about to get very complicated.'

'What do you mean?' asked Chang.

'Well, obviously Rick has an agenda,' said Ngarra. 'Which has changed now that Gilgamesh is ready.'

Ngarra watched to see how Cam would react to his comment but he didn't flinch. He just stood silently watching.

'Maybe,' said Chang, 'but whether owned or leased these Skimmers, their servicing, trialling, and any upgrades trumps, everything. It's the company that designed them that has real control. They built them and made a deal with contractors over installing or retrofitting the overdrive.'

'But Gilgamesh is now a bargaining chip,' said Ngarra.

Cam appeared to watch on silently. *He's taking all this* onboard, thought Ngarra.

'Right, let's surface,' said Cam as he interrupted their conversation.

'That we will,' said Ngarra. 'SAI, surface drone.'

'Require override of mining protocols,' said SAI.

'SAI, override mining protocols and surface Skimmer,' said Ngarra.

'Confirmed,' said SAI. 'Surface conditions within operating parameters. Surfacing Skimmer.'

The marine life that had surrounded the Skimmer moved away.

The repair drone had secured the streamer and returned to the moon pool and airlock and was back in the maintenance bay.

The Skimmer slowly ascended to the surface.

Breaking the surface, they watched as the ocean rolled off and the SAI console.

The outer hull shields were retracted. As far as the horizon stretched, a blue ocean could be seen that was limitless and entrancing. A large slow swell rolled gently through; remnants of the supercell that had passed through. For a moment, they all forgot what they were doing and stared into the distance.

'Right,' said Ngarra as he snapped out of it.

'Hey, I was just getting used to the view,' said Chang.

'Let's get Gilgamesh to the Skimmer wing ready for my crew to uplift,' said Cam.

'Yes, let's go,' said Ngarra. 'We need to remove Gilgamesh from the information hub. That sphere will take all three of us to negotiate through and down to the rec area for uplift. Come with me. Chang get SAI to disarm the main entrance to the Skimmer. I'll contact the Sea Hunters and tell them we are ready.'

'Good,' said Cam.

He waited while Ngarra contacted the Sea Hunter vessel to confirm they had surfaced and were preparing for the uplift of Gilgamesh.

Once done, they left the SAI console and walked down the port side passage to the information hub.

Entering, Gilgamesh was positioned in the centre of the hub. It had been transformed from a hologram that simulated various scenarios for Connor's work to a semi-solid sphere containing a giant mesh. Like a neural network consisting of part hardware and part software.

'It has its own power source now,' said Chang as he walked around one side. 'Connor installed it, a micro-reactor. We lift it from here.'

Chang pointed out to Ngarra how to lift it.

'Okay, got it,' said Ngarra.

They removed it and walked out into the passageway, back to the SAI console, down the stairs and into the rec area.

'This isn't light, is it?' asked Ngarra as they negotiated the stairs.

'Could be worse,' said Chang. 'At least, it is small enough to remove.'

SAI had disarmed the main entrance.

They entered the rec area and moved Gilgamesh over to the entrance, Ngarra opened it and they looked out.

In the distance, they could see the Sea Hunter vessel approaching.

A patrol drone had taken off and was making its way over. As it approached, they could see a winch and strop to was extended below it. A sea boat could also be seen leaving the Hunter vessel. It raced towards them at speed.

'Looks like we have some help coming,' said Ngarra.

He could see the sea boat was full.

'Will make it easier to get Gilgamesh onto the Skimmer wing,' said Cam.

'So, after this, we return to the Harvester in time for a crew change and return to Xed,' said Chang.

'That we do,' said Ngarra.

The sea boat approached and came alongside the Skimmer wing. Two crew got out and walked across the wing, past the nodule trays to the edge of the recess along which the Xtracts were docked.

Jonny and Stella followed behind.

'Glad to see you two,' said Ngarra as he looked down at them.

'Likewise,' said Jonny, holding his shoulder.

A gangway was extended.

'Okay,' said one of the sea boat crew walking up the gangway. 'Bring it down.'

Jonny and Stella walked up the gangway and inside out of the way. They watched on. Two crew members remained in the sea boat. The other two helped get Gilgamesh into position on the Skimmer wing.

The patrol drone flew in low. A large but gentle swell rolled through. They had to watch their balance.

It hovered and lowered the winch and strop to the Skimmer wing. Ngarra and Chang helped get the sphere of Gilgamesh in position and then stepped back. The two Sea Hunter crew members attached the strop and cradle around it. Once secure, they gave the thumbs up and the patrol drone lifted it off the Skimmer wing. It paused briefly, then turned and rose slowly, heading back to the Sea Hunter vessel.

'That's that then,' said Cam, turning to the Skimmer crew. 'We will be on our way.'

Cam shook hands with them and both he and his two crew members walked back down the gangway and across the Skimmer wing to the waiting sea boat and left.

'Let's get out of here,' said Chang as they walked back into the rec area.

The gangway retracted behind them and the main entrance closed.

'SAI, arm main entrance,' said Ngarra.

'Confirmed,' said SAI. 'Main entrance armed.'

'Propulsion is offline,' said Chang. 'We only have starboard to work with.'

'Chang and Stella, you go to the Xtract bay as usual,' said Ngarra. 'Check those Xtracts. We will have a leisurely cruise back to the Harvester then raher than use the overdrive. And take it easy with that head of yours.'

'I'll manage,' said Stella. 'Chang will keep an eye on me.'

Ngarra and Jonny walked up the stairs to the SAI console.

'SAI, prepare for departure to Harvester on starboard propulsion. Descend to one hundred metres.'

'Confirmed,' said SAI. 'Starboard propulsion online, watertight bulkheads secure. Portside propulsion offline.'

The outer hull shields closed, and the camera system activated. Jonny put his interface lenses on wincing at the pain in his shoulder from being shot.

He popped another pain killer.

'We'll be there soon enough,' said Ngarra. 'We can get that wound checked again.'

Jonny nodded his head.

Ngarra zoomed in on the navigation hologram at the SAI console. Then he sent a recorded message to Xed outlining the situation.

The Skimmer slipped beneath the rolling swell and slowly descended.

A Skimmer crew change had been arranged. The lockdown for the supercell has passed. All current Skimmer crew were to return to the Harvester after their mining run.

They timed their slow run back to coincide with the crew change.

***

At the Harvester, before the next crew took over Ngarra's Skimmer, repair drones would fix the damaged rim drive propulsion blades and check over the streamer. With Gilgamesh removed, there was no danger that during servicing by Harvester technicians, the technology would be compromised.

In the moon pool, Ngarra's crew made final arrangements to leave the Skimmer.

'Can't wait to get out of here for a while,' said Chang as he came into the SAI console. 'Any chance I can catch up with my sister before we leave?'

'Not this time,' said Ngarra. 'We have to be cautious until we are debriefed back at the Xed Academy. We can't risk any exposure or inquiry about Gilgamesh now, nor the plan to bring forward the overdrive trials.'

'I worry about my sister though,' said Chang. 'And that Sue is still out there somewhere.'

'Jonah will contact your father about all this,' said Jesse.

'What's my father going to do? He's not out here dealing with all this. If something is wrong out here, she is by herself.'

'Come on, mate,' said Jonny. 'I'm sure Ying Yue can look after herself. Judging by what we've seen.'

'I'm not your mate,' said Chang as his frustration surfaced again and got the better of him.

Jonny shrugged his shoulders.

'Once we get back out here with Gilgamesh, we can catch up with your sister,' said Stella as she walked into the SAI console and heard what was going on.

'I guess so,' said Chang.

'Anyway,' said Ngarra, changing the subject. 'Get your stuff together, folks and meet in the rec area. We have a transport drone to catch.'

A Harvester security officer appeared on the message board. He outlined the timing of crew changes and departure. They stopped talking and listened.

'Is it just me or does the blank stare and monotone voice of this guy seem off?' asked Jonny.

'No more than usual for security here,' said Ngarra. 'Communication is always bland.'

'Doesn't it look like fear though?' asked Jonny.

'Fear of what is the question,' said Stella.

'Let's not hang around to find out,' said Jonny.

He left the SAI console and the others followed.

'How long will it take to repair propulsion?' asked Chang as they walked down the stairs and into the rec area.

'The damage is structural,' said Ngarra. 'Can't say for sure but swapping out blades won't take that long.'

The crew went and got the few belongings they had, and a short time later, returned to the rec area. Exiting the Skimmer and walking down the gangway, they passed two technicians waiting to coordinate repairs.

'See,' whispered Chang as they passed. 'They don't even acknowledge our presence. And they keep looking around as if being watched.'

'They are always being watched,' said Ngarra. 'Nothing unusual about that. But by their expressions, I would say something has changed around here.'

'Do you think this mimic drone program has something to do with it?' asked Chang as they walked along the gangway to the nearest lift to the drone deck.

'Not here,' whispered Ngarra. 'Not here. Not until we are back at Xed.'

Chang shrugged his shoulders and nodded. *What's the big deal?* he thought to himself.

The lift stopped at the drone bay and they walked across to another lift that would take them up to the drone deck. A security officer met them and escorted them the rest of the way. Ngarra motioned for them all to keep quiet. Other crew had gathered in the drone bay and were making their way topside as well.

Once on the drone deck not far away, they could see the hex tower. Along the drone deck were three transport drones waiting to depart. Ngarra's crew were directed to one of them along with the other crew.

As the transport drones glistened in the sun, Ngarra, Stella, Chang and Jonny, walked up the stern ramp of one and sat down, strapping in. A few of the other Skimmer crew recognised them and got talking about the supercell and piracy and what happened.

The stern ramp closed, and the transport drone powered up. The docking clamp rose and released them. For a moment, they hovered, then tilting forward the transport drone moved out over the side of the Harvester. It gained speed and raced ahead low over the water. Banking it then rose and headed off towards Xed. Ngarra's crew relaxed. For the time being, their thoughts turned toward home.

Milton Keynes UK
Ingram Content Group UK Ltd.
UKHW022028081223
434043UK00008B/400